"Is your plan to drive me crazy _____ **et my clothes off?"**

Tyler lifted his head and grinned.

"Don't look so pleased with yourself," Lanie teased. "I'm waiting to see how the rest of this goes before I offer a critique."

"How am I doing so far?"

"Still reserving judgment."

"Tough sell."

His mouth covered hers again, his tongue parting her lips and searching her mouth. The touch of his hands on her skin sent a wave of lust through her body.

"Patience is a virtue," she said breathlessly.

His hands skimmed up her sides. He slowly pushed the blouse off her shoulders, letting the fabric fall down her arms to the floor. He lifted his gaze to hers, his mouth twisting into a seductive smile.

"I have to warn you, Lanie. I'm not feeling very virtuous."

UNTIL YOU

ALSO BY DENISE GROVER SWANK

The Bachelor Brotherhood Series

Only You

The Wedding Pact Series

The Substitute
The Player
The Gambler

UNTIL YOU

DENISE GROVER SWANK

WITHDRAWN

FOREVER

NEW YORK   BOSTON

Copyright © 2017 by Denise Grover Swank
Preview of *Always You* copyright © 2017 by Denise Grover Swank
Cover design by Elizabeth Turner
Cover photograph © Tom Merton/Getty Images
Cover copyright © 2017 by Hachette Book Group, Inc.

Forever
Hachette Book Group
1290 Avenue of the Americas, New York, NY 10104
forever-romance.com
twitter.com/foreverromance

First Edition: May 2017

Forever is an imprint of Grand Central Publishing. The Forever name and logo are trademarks of Hachette Book Group, Inc.

The publisher is not responsible for websites (or their content) that are not owned by the publisher.

The Hachette Speakers Bureau provides a wide range of authors for speaking events. To find out more, go to www.hachettespeakersbureau.com or call (866) 376-6591.

ISBNs: 978-1-4555-3980-2 (mass market), 978-1-4555-3979-6 (ebook)

Printed in the United States of America

OPM

10 9 8 7 6 5 4 3 2 1

ACKNOWLEDGMENTS

My name may be on the cover, but it takes a village to make a book come to life.

Many thanks to Amy Pierpont, and her infinite patience with this book. Some books are easier than others, and Tyler and Lanie were slow to share their story with me. Many thanks to Amy for helping me coax it out of them.

At this point in my writing career, I'm so thankful for my friend Angela Polidoro. She's always there when I need writing or business advice. I'm also thankful for my friend Shannon Mayer. We still haven't met in person, but we've spent countless hours on the phone and in Facebook message chats talking about kids, books, politics, business, and friendship. We may live in different countries, but we're only a phone call away.

Thank you to my children and their continued patience with Mommy and her crazy job, although I think they sometimes secretly love when I'm buried in my laptop and headphones—they've learned how to use my distraction for their own purposes.

And finally—and *always*—thank you to my readers, who chose to read me out of the millions of books available. That is never lost on me.

UNTIL YOU

Chapter One

"Tyler Norris...This is the *last* place I ever expected to see you." The blonde was eyeing him like he was the last margarita on ladies' night at La Fuente Bar and Grill.

Tyler leaned back in his patio chair and sipped his beer, hiding his annoyance with a smirk. This was the fourth woman to approach him tonight, and while he was used to women hitting on him, this seemed to be a bit much given that he was a single man at a *couple's* wedding shower.

"How'd you get roped into it?" she asked, her right hand on her hip.

Theresa Fink. He hadn't seen her since high school, but the look in her eyes told him she was *very* happy to see him. She lifted the wineglass in her left hand, spotlighting her bare left ring finger, even going so far as to slightly wiggle it to catch his attention.

She continued studying him with lust-filled eyes, apparently expecting an answer. He finally shrugged his nonchalance. "Turns out being groomsman means the bride can strong-arm you into anything she wants." That wasn't entirely true—he had a soft spot when it came to Brittany—but no need to tell Theresa that.

Her eyes lit up. "Maybe she can spill some of her secrets. Your legend precedes you, Tyler Norris."

Chuckling, he took a drag of his beer. "And which legend is that? I hear there are many." He winked. "And the ones about my size and endurance are *all* true."

Theresa flushed, pressing her hand against her chest and fluttering her eyelashes.

Jesus. Why did he tell her that? Old habits were still hard to break, but now she looked like a barracuda ready to gnaw off his leg. Or more specifically, another body part in very close proximity.

"Tyler," a deep voice said behind him. "Holly needs your help with the ice."

Tyler tried not to look relieved when he jumped to his feet and turned to face Kevin Vandemeer. "Yeah. Be more than happy to."

Disappointment washed over Theresa's face, but he ignored her as she called after him, "Want to get drinks later?"

Tyler walked through the suburban backyard, feeling like he was about to break out into hives just being here, let alone sitting outside in the hot and humid Missouri August evening for the last hour. He tugged at his collar, regretting his decision to wear a tie.

"Thanks for the save," he said as he followed Kevin to the back deck, then stopped to grab another beer from a bucket of ice water.

"The save comes at a price," Kevin said with a chuckle. "You're refilling the drink tubs with ice."

"Me?" Tyler asked, standing upright and turning to face

his friend. "Shouldn't that be your job since *your wife* is in charge of the party?"

Kevin's wife. Damn, that was hard to spit out. Not that he had anything against Holly, he actually liked her, and if Tyler was honest, she was a good fit for his friend. But of his two best friends, Kevin had been more like Tyler when it came to women. Lots of girlfriends that never lasted. So when Kevin had moved back home two months ago after his last tour in Afghanistan, the three friends had commiserated on their extremely unlucky love life and decided to give up on marriage, imposing a ban on women and forming the Bachelor Brotherhood.

Kevin Vandemeer had lasted one fucking day.

"My *wife*," Kevin said in a warning tone, "was the one to suggest I save your ass, you dickweed. So get out to the garage and grab a couple of bags of ice out of the freezer or I'll tell Theresa Fink that you want to leave the shower and go out for a candlelight dinner. Just the two of you."

"You suck, Vandemeer," Tyler grumbled.

Kevin's answer was a shit-eating grin.

Tyler would have loved to kick his friend's ass right then and there, but Brittany would have killed him. And while he considered doing it anyway, instead he went into the dark garage, deciding this wasn't such a heinous task after all. It had to be ten degrees cooler in the two-car garage, and he was alone. Maybe he could hide in here for ten minutes or so, then tell Britt a work emergency had come up and he needed to go.

She'd see right through it and call his assistant to verify. And since her fiancé worked at his law firm, she definitely had the number.

Shit. He was stuck.

Tyler had been at Randy's house enough times to know

the garage refrigerator was stocked with beer, some of which were Randy's precious import beers. Tyler opened the door and grinned. Jackpot. He grabbed a Stella and popped off the top using the opener attached to the wall, then took a long drag, letting the cold beer coat his dry mouth.

"I see you found Randy's stash," a woman said in the darkness.

Caught off guard, he choked, spitting beer down his shirt. He spun around and found her sitting on Randy's workbench with her own bottle. Unlike every other guest at the shower, with the exception of him, she was still dressed in business attire—a sleeveless, light gray dress that ended just above her knees. Her legs were crossed, and she bounced one black, three-inch pump as she watched him, lowering the bottle from her mouth. She wore her long, dark hair down, and he couldn't help but notice the strands that lay over her shoulder, brushing the tops of her breasts. He forced his gaze to rise to her face.

"Didn't mean to startle you," she said, her dark eyes dancing with amusement.

She was gorgeous, and damned if he wasn't intrigued. "I didn't see you over there."

She grinned. "Obviously."

He moved toward her, unable to stop himself. "Looks like we both have the same idea."

She laughed. "If your idea is hiding from Brittany and drinking Randy's import beer, then we do."

He gestured to the empty spot on the workbench next to her, and she lifted her shoulder into a half-shrug invitation. Tyler hopped up on the bench and perched next to her, leaving a few inches between them. "So what's a nice girl like you doing in a musty garage like this?"

She laughed again, uncrossing her long legs and turning

toward him, her eyes full of mischief. "I bet you use that line on all the girls."

"Only the ones I find in musty garages." Up close like this, he could see that her dark eyes were a milk chocolate brown and framed by long, sexy eyelashes. She lifted her beer and took a sip, and he suddenly found himself jealous of the bottle in her hand.

"I know why you're hiding," she said as she set the beer next to her on the bench.

He smirked. "Okay, tell me why I'm hiding."

"Brittany. She's playing matchmaker again." His eyes widened and she gave him a knowing smile. "It wasn't that hard to figure out. For the last hour, she's been sending women to you like they're going through the turnstile at a ride in Disneyland, and you keep sending them away." She flicked her fingers to demonstrate.

He lifted his eyebrows as he studied her face, then teased, "You've been watching me? I haven't seen you before now."

She cocked her head to the side, rolling her eyes. "Amateur. I've spent most of my time hiding. You obviously haven't known Brittany for long."

"About a year." While they'd gone to high school together, they hadn't been friends. He'd gotten to know her through Randy.

She laughed again. "I have about thirty years on you."

Thirty years? Had she gone to school with them?

She gestured to his beer. "Since you have exceptional taste in beer *and* hiding spots, I'll be generous and give you a few pointers."

"Should I be taking notes?" he teased. While she was flirty, she wasn't coming on to him, and it only intrigued him more.

She shrugged. "It wouldn't hurt, but I suspect we'll be

seeing each other again in a month, so I can give you a refresher course at the wedding."

Finally. Something to actually look forward to at the wedding.

"First," she said in a conspiratorial tone,"Britt comes across as this sweet and unassuming woman, but don't let that fool you."

"No?"

"*No*," she said, pointing her finger at him. "She uses her charm to get you to do what she wants." She stabbed his chest to make her point. "Look at poor Randy."

Tyler was loyal to the people who stood by him, and he was about to defend Britt until he saw she was teasing. There was no doubt that Randy had been ensnared by Brittany, but it was just as obvious the adoration went both ways.

"You have to be firm." She brought her hand down sideways onto her open palm, like a karate chop. "If you show the slightest sign of waffling, she'll pounce."

"So," he said slowly, "you're saying I haven't been firm enough? That I can't hold my own?" He gave her an arrogant grin. "Because I have a nickname that disputes that."

"Oh, really?" she asked, her face lighting up in mock surprise. "Are we talking about cute nicknames that your *guy* friends have given you? Like The Terminator? Or Maverick?"

He shook his head and laughed, trying to think of the last time he'd enjoyed a woman's company so much. "Sounds like somebody's been binge-watching eighties movies on Netflix."

"Busted." She laughed, leaning her head to the side and exposing her long neck.

A wave of lust washed through him, and he struggled to control it. It was obvious she wasn't an easy conquest. Oddly enough, he considered playing the long game with her.

What the fuck was wrong with him? He wasn't supposed to be playing the game at all.

She shook her head, her grin tugging at the corners of her full lips. "So what's this awesome nickname of yours? I take it my suggestions came from the wrong decade."

He gave her a long look, now reluctant to share. "The Closer."

Her eyes widened in amusement. "Because you're so good with *the ladies*?" She waggled her eyebrows.

He laughed, feeling like an idiot. "And because I can close a case before it goes to trial."

"Uh-huh. *Sure*." She hopped off the bench and wobbled a little on her heels, cluing him in that she'd had more than the one beer tonight. "Well, *Mr. Closer*, Brittany Stewart is much more subtle than that." She pushed his legs open and stood between them, grabbing a handful of his tie and pulling his face inches from hers. "She sees you as a challenge. She thinks everyone in the whole wide world needs to be in love, and she won't rest until it happens. And *you* are the perfect challenge." She dropped his tie and spread her hands out. "Big bad womanizer who can't bring himself to let his guard down and let a woman in, much less love her. Why Britt just can't resist." She laughed and grabbed his tie again, slowly leaning closer. "The more you resist her efforts, the more determined she becomes."

Her breath fanned his face, and it took everything within him to keep his hands to himself, because instinct told him that if he made a move, she'd give him a brush-off so epic, an 8.0 earthquake would pale in comparison.

And he definitely did *not* want her to give him a brush-off.

"And how do you know all this?" he asked, proud that he sounded so in control.

Her lips hovered inches over his, and she whispered, "I've been her number one project for the last ten years. Lucky for me, it looks like I've just been usurped." She dropped her hold on his tie, then smoothed it down his chest, her fingertips trailing to his abdomen in small sweeps.

A fresh jolt of lust rushed through his blood, and he gripped the sides of the bench, hoping she didn't see how much she affected him when her eyes lifted to his.

"So why didn't she try to fix me up with you?" he asked, his voice husky despite his intentions.

Her smile became sardonic. "Because she's figured out that I'm a lost cause." Then she turned and walked back into the kitchen, her tight dress perfectly hugging her rounded ass.

As he took the last drag of his beer and tossed the bottle into the recycling bin, he realized that never in his thirty-three years had he been so turned on by a woman.

And he didn't even know her name.

Chapter Two

Lanie Rogers left Mr. Tall, Dark, and Handsome in the garage and headed to the backyard in search of her cousin. The heat hit her as she walked out the back door, and beads of perspiration instantly popped out on her forehead. She might have been born and raised in the Midwest, but fourteen years away had made the summer humidity unbearable—reason number two for hiding in the garage.

She was overdressed, but her conference call with the West Coast office had run long, which meant she hadn't had time to change. She should have taken comfort that the sexy guy in the garage was even more overdressed than she was, but it only made her think of running her fingertips down his tie...and lower.

Good Lord. What had she been thinking? Even the two beers she'd downed in thirty minutes didn't explain it. She could chalk it up to stress. And going nearly a year without a relationship.

And the fact that he was so sexy.

She shook her head. No. She couldn't go there. She had enough trouble at work. She didn't need the complication of a man. Especially when she was moving on to Phoenix in a month.

"Does that head-shake mean you *won't* go to lunch with me this week?" a voice asked to her right.

Lanie blinked and realized Brittany was studying her. Her long hair was pulled up in a ponytail, and she was wearing a yellow sleeveless dress that looked great with her tan skin and dark brown hair. "Sorry. I was thinking about...work."

Brittany gave her a smirk. "You promised no work tonight. Your secret store isn't going anywhere."

Lanie's eyes widened, and she glanced around to see if anyone had heard her. "Britt, you can't talk about it. It's classified." As soon as the word left her mouth, she regretted it.

That damn beer.

"Classified," Brittany scoffed. "You make it sound like you're working with the nuclear warhead codes."

After her conference call two hours ago, Lanie would have preferred the detonation codes. She made sure no one was nearby, then lowered her voice. "Okay, wrong word choice, but you get the point. Joke all you want, but if this leaks, I'm as good as fired."

Her cousin looked dubious. "You're kidding."

"And why do you think we make all the people in the know sign NDAs?"

"Surely word's leaked out before the opening of one of *those* stores." When she saw Lanie's warning look, she rolled her eyes. "Calm down. I never even said the name."

Margo Benson Boutique.

Margo Benson designs were sophisticated yet affordable, and there were only fifteen stores in the entire world. Before one opened, secrecy was the absolute name of the game, and Lanie's job depended on it.

"You can't even *hint* at it." Lanie's stomach knotted with anxiety. Britt didn't need to name the store. The term *secret opening* was clue enough to cause speculation. Up until today, Lanie had been sure her ruse was working. It had taken a few strings to get everything lined up, but the community seemed to have accepted that the retail space in the nearly century-old outdoor shopping plaza where the boutique was opening was undergoing a structural update.

But during her earlier conference call from her new West Coast VP, Lanie had found out rumors were floating around that a Margo Benson was going into the Country Club Plaza. A *Kansas City Star* reporter had called corporate in LA asking for confirmation, but the public relations manager had given her the brush-off, saying there were larger metropolitan areas higher on the potential location list.

The crisis seemed temporarily averted, but the VP had made her displeasure clear and placed the blame on Lanie. Not that Lanie was surprised. Eve Gaines had made it clear from day one that she planned to come in and put her mark on everything. Which included fixing things that didn't need to be fixed. It was nothing new. Lanie had been through it several times before, but it didn't make it any less annoying now.

"Eve," Lanie had said, trying to keep her cool, "I realize this is your first Margo Benson opening, but this is my twelfth. The secret openings were easy to pull off the first four or five times, but people are watching now. It's next to impossible to keep them under wraps."

"Are you saying you can't do the job?" her boss had asked in a sharp tone.

"I'm saying that I'm having to become more creative. We

paid the management of the Plaza a handsome fee to support our cover story."

"Well, someone knows that Montgomery Enterprises is opening a store in Kansas City," Eve countered.

"They don't *know*," Lanie countered. "They only speculated. For all we know, it was a cold call hoping to strike gold. The same thing happened in Seattle. But I'll talk to the handful of people who *do* know tomorrow and remind them of the importance of minding their NDAs."

"And remind them that negating those NDAs comes at a steep price."

Literally.

The first two Margo Benson locations had surprise grand openings, and since the brand was so popular, corporate discovered that each new opening was met with greater fanfare than the last. Every city wanted a Margo Benson Boutique, so when the tarps covering the storefront were pulled away on opening day, it was a media phenomenon. The store received publicity they couldn't buy even if they tried. But keeping the press off the scent and the openings secret had been a nightmare at the last two stores.

What if she couldn't pull this one off?

Britt tugged on Lanie's wrist. "Come on. I'll introduce you to the other bridesmaids before I open my gifts. I promise to maintain your cover story." She winked. "You're a retail time management consultant and offer suggestions on increasing productivity."

Lanie grinned back and shook her head, sending a shooting pain through her skull. She touched her temple in an effort to ease the beginning of a headache. "I love you, Britt, but you know there's not a domestic bone in my body, so I'm going to beg off watching you open gifts. Toasters and juicers give me the hives."

Britt wrinkled her nose. "A juicer? Like I'd ever use a juicer."

Lanie paused, then pointed to the present table. "See that white rectangular box with the white bow? Just hide it under the table, and I'll bring you the receipt when we meet for lunch."

"A juicer?" Britt asked with a laugh. "Do you even know me at all?"

The question was asked in jest, but Lanie turned serious. She and Britt hadn't gone to the same schools when they were kids, but they'd lived five miles apart and had been best friends until Lanie had headed to the East Coast for college. She'd tried to keep in touch, but her job had gotten in the way. Just like it had gotten in the way of relationships with her past boyfriends and cultivating friendships. As she stared at her cousin and looked around at the backyard full of people who clearly loved Brittany and Randy, Lanie suddenly wondered what she'd sacrificed for the sake of Margo Benson.

Worry filled Britt's eyes. "Are you okay?"

Lanie waved her off. "Just my headache."

"Okay, I'll give you a reprieve this time. You go home, and I'll fill you in about all my presents when we meet for lunch."

"Thanks."

"Brio at noon on Thursday," Britt said. "It's close to… where you're working, so you'll be less likely to back out at the last minute."

Lanie didn't deny it. She'd already cancelled a lunch and a happy hour with her cousin. She vowed to make it this time.

Britt kissed Lanie on the cheek. "You work too hard. Life's short, Lanie. Don't waste it."

Lanie watched her cousin walk over to Randy, snagging his hand and pulling him toward the present table. Adoration filled his eyes as he gazed down at his bride-to-be.

Lanie had sacrificed this. And until this afternoon, it had been worth the price.

Now she wasn't so sure.

Chapter Three

On Wednesday morning, Tyler was supposed to be preparing for a deposition, but his mind kept wandering *again* to the mystery woman in the garage. He'd seen her talking to Brittany when he'd brought out the ice to Holly. She'd left soon after, and he'd never found out who she was—not that he'd tried very hard. He hadn't dared asked Britt, and the few people he'd questioned had no idea.

It hadn't stopped him from thinking about her. In his bed. And in his shower. And even on his kitchen counter.

And it bothered the shit out of him.

Of course he'd had his share of daydreams and fantasies, but he'd never had so many of just one woman. Tyler was an equal-opportunity fantasizer. But then, he'd never gone five months without sex either. Maybe the two were related.

"Hey, Tyler." Victor Minecroft, one of the associates at Goldman, Taylor, Hughes, and Evans, stood in his doorway. "What can you tell me about your case a few years ago, the one about the real estate contract."

Tyler gave him a sardonic grin. "That narrows it down to about twenty."

"The one with the noncompete lease." When Tyler continued staring at him, Victor added, "The case with the hot blonde."

"Oh." Tyler nodded with a grin. "That one."

"You totally screwed her, didn't you?"

Leaning back in his chair, Tyler picked up his pen and clicked the top. "I would never hook up with a client." Then he grinned. "But after I won, we might have had a celebratory evening."

"You're the man, Norris."

He used to be that man. He'd slept with a lot of women, never forming any deep attachments. And that's exactly how he'd preferred it. Then last spring, he'd decided he was thirty-three and it was time to settle down. So he'd found a woman who had seemed normal, if not boring. He'd been so wrong.

As though Victor could read his mind, he asked, "Hey, what ever happened with your crazy ex?"

Tyler tried to hide his unease, shifting in his seat. "Which one?"

"You know, the one who tied you to your bed naked." Tyler didn't respond, but Victor didn't seem to get the hint. "Didn't she have a shrine with your pictures and your underwear in her apartment?" He chuckled. "I heard she hung a few condoms around it, too."

Everything but the condoms was true, but Tyler didn't care to get into the specifics. He narrowed his eyes. "Do you have a point?"

Victor had never been a very perceptive guy. God only knew how he'd gotten this far in their competitive, four-partner, twenty-associate law firm. Tyler was sure it had something to do with the fact that his uncle was a founding partner. But Victor seemed to finally understand this was unwelcome territory. "Was she convicted?"

"Probation... and a restraining order."

"That's all?"

Tyler had been the one to push for probation and a psych evaluation. He was certain she wouldn't have hurt him. She was just looking for someone to love her. He just hadn't been that person. He was pretty sure he was incapable of loving anyone. He was too damn selfish.

Tyler cleared his throat. "Back to the Carothers case. What exactly are you looking for?"

"What precedent did you use to get the tenant kicked out?"

"Higgens versus Clark."

"Thanks," Victor said as he turned to leave.

"Is it a commercial space?"

Victor glanced over his shoulder. "Yeah. A retail store on the Plaza."

Tyler was about to ask him for more details—while he'd used the precedent, the Carothers case had been tricky, so he'd used it in an unorthodox way—but his cell phone rang with a number he didn't recognize. And Victor was already halfway down the hall.

"Tyler Norris."

"Tyler, this is Principal Carter at Blue Springs High School. I'm not sure if you remember me."

Tyler released a chuckle. "Mr. Carter, you're pretty hard to forget, considering how much time I spent in your office."

The older man laughed. "I was a brand-new assistant principal your freshman year. You gave me plenty of disciplinary experience to help bump me up to principal."

Tyler grinned. "I'm sure I deserved every punishment you doled out."

"Maybe so, but you've turned into a man your father should be proud of."

Ah...there was another touchy subject. "I suspect you didn't call about my previous bad behavior."

"You're right. I'm calling about your brother Eric."

"Is he okay?" Common sense told Tyler he was, otherwise the principal would have led with that, but he couldn't imagine why Mr. Carter was calling him.

"He's physically fine, but he's in some trouble."

Tyler rubbed his temple. "Uh...no offense, Mr. Carter, but why are you calling *me*?"

"I can't get ahold of your father. In fact, I've tried to reach your father for the past two weeks, and he hasn't returned any of my phone calls. Since you're listed as Eric's emergency contact, I'm now contacting you."

Tyler's father had devoted most of his time to his auto repair shop and hadn't been the most attentive parent, even after their mother left when Tyler was sixteen, but he'd always responded to the schools. And Tyler had raised plenty of hell in high school to prove that to be true. "What's Eric done?"

"We're only two weeks into the school year, and Eric's already falling behind in several of his classes. His teachers say he's apathetic, not turning in assignments and skipping classes."

Tyler resisted the urge to say, *That's all?* Hell, he'd done much worse during his time at Blue Springs High School. "No offense, Mr. Carter, but isn't that typical teenage boy behavior?"

"Not for Eric. Until the beginning of the school year, he was the model student. Turned in his work on time.

Respectful of his teachers. Straight-A student and decent basketball player, given the fact that he was just a sophomore last year. But his teachers see a change in his attitude. He hasn't turned in a single assignment."

"No offense," Tyler said, "but why are you calling me instead of our brother Alex? Given my high school history, I'm not actually the best role model for Eric."

"Which is exactly why I'm calling you. I thought you might be able to get through to him, since you went through the same thing yourself. Maybe you can give him some insight to pull him out of this."

Tyler's relationship with his younger brother was far from close. He'd seen him twice over the entire summer and both times had been when Alex coerced them to meet for dinner at Olive Garden.

"With all due respect, Mr. Carter," Tyler said, "you and my two best friends were what pulled my head out of my—" He cut off the curse, remembering who he was talking to, but it didn't make the statement any less true. When Mr. Carter had threatened expulsion after a senior prank gone wrong, Kevin and Matt took him to the secluded camping spot Kevin's father had taken him to on their monthly camping trips and threatened to beat the shit out of him until he admitted he was screwing up his life. The sad truth was that Tyler hardly knew anything about his kid brother's life. Did Eric have friends who would have his back like that?

"Eric's a bright young man and reminds me a lot of you," Mr. Carter said. "You seem to be doing well for yourself. You harnessed your powers for good instead of evil."

Tyler laughed. "I just applied my deviousness to my career. My clients tend to appreciate it, although their opponents not so much."

"Let's hope you can convince your brother to do the same."

Tyler hung up, not overly concerned. Principal Carter had been right. Tyler had been a much worse fuck-up in high school, and he'd turned out pretty well. Eric was a smart boy. He was just testing his boundaries.

Still, it wouldn't hurt to talk to his brother. He set an alarm on his phone to call Eric when he got out of school, but Eric beat him to it.

"I hear Mr. Carter called you," Eric said, sounding pissed.

Nothing like cutting to the chase. "You heard right."

"So are you gonna lecture me?"

Tyler released a sigh. "Look, I'm not your dad, but I will say this…It's okay to screw off every once in a while, but Jesus, moderation, dude. You can't blow off *everything*."

"Yeah, okay…"

"So…is it a girl?"

"What?"

"You're trying to impress a girl, right?"

Eric was silent for several seconds until he finally said hesitantly, "Yeah…right."

Tyler grinned. Maybe Eric was more like him than he thought. "Look, I know this bad-boy routine is new for you, but you have to figure out what you can get away with and what you can't. You have to make *some* effort at school, okay?"

"Yeah. Thanks." His brother was silent for several seconds. "Alex is coming over to watch the MU football game on Saturday. Want to come over?"

"I've got plans," Tyler said as his assistant walked into his office and handed him a file. "Maybe some other time."

"Yeah. Right," Eric grunted before he hung up.

Tyler often turned down Norris brother events, but he had

a real excuse this time. Brittany had some wedding activity planned.

He'd love nothing more than to tell Brittany no, but she and Randy had been there for Tyler after his crazy stalker incident, and he felt like he owed her.

Tyler set his phone on his desk as Victor popped his head in the doorway. "Thanks again for the case reference. We filed an injunction this afternoon, and the papers should be served tomorrow morning. I owe you. If you need something, just tell me what it is."

Tyler waved his hand as he turned to his computer screen. "Thanks. I'll file that away for future use." Victor's Royals season tickets came to mind.

If only he could get his phone call with his brother out of his head. Tyler had screwed around in high school and turned out just fine. Eric would too, right?

Chapter Four

Thursday afternoon, Lanie stood impatiently at a street corner as she waited for the light to change. A quick glance at her phone confirmed that it was 2:03, one minute later than the last time she'd checked.

The pedestrian walk signal popped on, and she ran across the pavement, an impressive feat given her three-inch heels. She glanced up at the entrance of Brio and saw her cousin standing in the open doorway.

Brittany quirked an eyebrow. "You're late. Even after you postponed our lunch for two hours."

Lanie held her hands out at her sides. "I'm sorry. This morning's been crazy."

"And apparently your afternoon, too." Brittany gave her a mocking glare, then laughed. "I'm just glad you showed up at all."

Feeling terrible, Lanie followed Britt inside. The hostess led them to their table. When they were settled, Lanie said, "So...tell me all about your gifts from the shower."

Britt laughed. "You should have stayed. You might have actually enjoyed a few of them." She picked up her water glass. "It was a *couple's* shower, and some of the gifts fit the theme."

"Oh," Lanie teased. "Did you get a few naughty things?"

"A copy of the Kama Sutra."

"Tame."

"His-and-hers dildos."

That got her attention. "When you say his-and-hers... how can you tell? Maybe they just gave you a variety... of sex toys," Lanie suggested with a grin as she picked up her water and took a sip.

"Because they were pink and blue... and engraved with our *names*."

Lanie sputtered water onto the table and started coughing. "I'm sorry, did you say they were *engraved* with your *names*? Who gave you that?"

"Celesta. She's one of my bridesmaids. I need to apologize for her in advance... but she's Randy's cousin, and his mother insisted we include her in the wedding."

"Okay." If Celesta was gifting his-and-hers dildos, she might not be so bad. "I'm trying to imagine the engraving. How does that work?"

Britt laughed with a shrug, her face turning pink. "Well, more like stamped. I guess you can't engrave latex, but then I guess they're not latex, are they? Not with latex allergies and all." Britt's eyes widened. "How do you suppose those allergies work? Like with latex condoms, do you think their... you know... their penises get red and itchy?"

Lanie laughed as she flagged down a passing waitress. "You're thirty-two years old. If we're going to have the sex talk, then we need appropriate drinks." She turned to the waitress. "We'll take two Pink Pantie Pull-downs."

"*What?*" Brittany gasped, leaning forward.

Putting her hand on the waitress's arm to hold her back, Lanie asked, "Does the bartender know how to make them?"

The waitress laughed. "With a name like that, I'll be more than happy to look it up for him if he doesn't."

"I don't need to have the sex talk," Britt said, but her cheeks were still pink. "My sex life with Randy is just fine."

"And about to get even finer with your his-and-hers dildos. Tell me, how did Randy take his personalized gift?" Lanie asked, while she used her napkin to wipe the water off the table.

"Well…his response was similar to yours, only it was in front of all the shower guests, and he spit out beer instead of water. When he stopped choking, he said he was glad that his was the smaller one." Both women laughed, then Britt gave her a serious look. "So, tell me about *your* love life."

"Changing the subject, huh? Sorry to disappoint, but my love life is exactly the same as when you asked two weeks ago. Nonexistent."

"I just find that so hard to believe." Britt gave her a soft smile. "With your looks and your *almost* charming personality—"

"Very funny."

"I would think you'd have men falling over themselves to go out with you."

"And we both know that has nothing to do with my lack of *male companionship*." She shrugged. "It's hard to meet guys when I'm hiding behind a building covered in tarp."

"You could try Tinder or one of those new dating apps."

"I have, but right now I don't have time for a real relationship." Plus, her job involved so much secrecy…it was hard to get close to a man when her job was the sum of her existence, and her NDA kept her from discussing it. It had all led to a string of meaningless relationships that had left her feeling emptier with every breakup. Not that she'd been looking for something meaningful. The thought of a serious relationship made her want to break out in hives.

Brittany studied her face. "Don't you get lonely?"

The question chafed, but she brushed it off with a snort. "I'm here with you. Of course I'm not lonely."

"You've seen me three times in the two months you've been here, and you only have one month left. Both of our schedules are about to become insane, which means we'll spend even less time together." She paused, and tears filled her eyes. "Who's your person? The one you call when you have a shitty day? Once upon a time, it used to be me."

The question was a double-edged sword, not only reminding Lanie how alone she actually was, but that she'd lost her cousin along the way too.

She opened her mouth to answer, still unsure what to say, when the waitress appeared with their drinks. She set two tall glasses in front of them, each topped with a lemon slice. "We didn't have pink lemonade, so the bartender used regular lemonade. And he included tequila along with the vodka."

"Tequila and vodka?" Britt asked.

"And beer," the waitress said.

"Perfect," Lanie said, picking up her glass and taking a sip.

After the waitress took the two women's orders, Britt picked up her glass and took a tentative sip. "This isn't so bad."

"But it's strong as hell, so be careful."

Britt took another healthy drink.

"Now that we have our fortitude, we can have *the talk*."

Lanie folded her hands on the table and tried to look serious. "Now, when a man loves a woman..."

"Stop." Bitt laughed. "I know about sex. We both know I lost my virginity my freshman year of college."

Lanie gave her a naughty grin. "And with your matching dildos, it sounds like you'll have even more experience than me."

"Not matching. Randy's is several inches shorter and much narrower." Britt took another sip, then added, "But he's got no reason to be jealous of mine. His *manhood* is much broader than my dildo."

Lanie held up both hands in surrender. "Whoa! TMI. The next time I see Randy, I don't want to be thinking about his *manhood*."

"He definitely knows how to use it." Britt gave a little shimmy. "He's got this move where he—"

"That's enough!"

"Which one of us needs the drink now?" her cousin asked with a wink.

Lanie picked up her glass and took a sip. "You win."

Britt turned serious. "Who's your person, Lane? I'm not that easily distracted."

She hesitated. "My assistant. Stephanie."

"Your employee?"

"She's not *my* employee. She works for the same company. We travel together. We spend a lot of time together. We're friends."

"That's sad."

"How is that sad?"

"All you have is work. Once that goes away, will you still be friends?"

The hair on the back of Lanie's neck stood on end. "Who said my work is going away?"

"I'm not saying it is. But don't you want more? Friends outside of work? A boyfriend—a husband?"

Lanie shot her a wry grin. "I doubt my future husband will appreciate me having a boyfriend."

"You know what I mean. Don't you want to settle down and have a family of your own?"

"That was always your dream, not mine, Britt." She'd seen how marriage worked, with her parents' constant bickering and resentment. No thanks.

"Okay," Britt conceded. "I'll cop to that. But there are all kinds of families. It doesn't necessarily mean kids and a minivan. I can't see you driving one of those. But don't let your own experiences sway you. I love my parents and I want to have what they had. Just because your parents didn't get along doesn't mean—"

"Britt, stop. Please don't psychoanalyze me like I'm one of your marketing research studies. You want me to leave my work checked at the door, but that means you have to, too." She picked up her phone. "See? I haven't looked at it once."

But then she noticed she had six missed calls from Stephanie. All within fifteen minutes. "Shit."

"What?"

Lanie was already calling her assistant back when she saw the young woman hurrying across the restaurant toward them. Lanie's heart beat against her chest. In the five years she'd worked with Steph, she'd never seen her look so panicked.

Lanie stood just as Stephanie reached their table. "What? What happened?"

Stephanie took several deep lungfuls of air, trying to catch her breath. "Oh my God, that yoga teacher is full of shit. She claimed I'd be able to run a ten-minute mile if I increased my core strength."

"A ten-minute mile's not that great. You need a new yoga

place," Britt said, finishing off her glass. "I want another one of these." She looked up at Steph. "You should totally go to my studio in Blue Springs. There's this grandma that teaches some of my classes, and you should see the things she can do with her ass."

Lanie's eyes flew open. "Okay! No more drinks for you. I think I'm scarred for life now. Can we focus?" She turned to her assistant. "What happened?"

"We got served."

Lanie shook her head. "What does that mean?"

"This." Stephanie handed her the tri-folded set of papers that Lanie had just noticed in her hand.

Lanie opened the papers and quickly scanned their contents.

"The man who brought it said we have to shut down all work. It looks like it says we can't open at all."

"No," Lanie said, still looking over the papers. "It's a temporary injunction. It says we violated a term of the lease, only it's not the leasing agency who's suing. It's some corporation." She looked up at Stephanie. "I bet it's that art store around the corner. They got all pissy because they think we're going to sell art supplies."

Britt shook her head in confusion. "Why would they think you're an art supply store?"

"Because the working name for the store is Broad Strokes." She pushed out a sigh. "I need to call corporate right away." She glanced back at her cousin. "Oh, crap. I can't leave you here like this."

"Like what?" Britt asked, taking a drink from Lanie's half-empty glass. "Alone? It's not like this is the first time you've skipped out on me."

Lanie sat down beside her. "Britt, they're shutting down my store. I have to deal with this."

"Because your job is your life, Lanie, but jobs are cold, fickle bitches. It will bite you in the ass in the end."

"Which will look really good if you go to your cousin's yoga class," Steph said.

Lanie shot her a glare. "Not helping." Her stomach was twisted into knots. She knew she was about to find out how much of a cold bitch her new VP actually was. "Randy's office is close to here, right? How about we walk you there?"

Britt gave her a belligerent look. "I haven't gotten my Italian Wedding Soup yet. I'm pretty sure it's bad luck to skip out on wedding soup when you're getting married."

"Then we'll get it to go."

"No!" Britt pointed her finger at Lanie. "I'm finishing my lunch."

"I can't just leave you here."

"Why not? You've never worried about me before. I've worried about you since you started this vagabond life."

"Vagabond?" Lanie laughed, trying to lighten the mood. But Britt shot her a glare, and Lanie felt like the world's biggest bitch. "Britt, of course I care about you."

"When was the last time you called me?" Lanie started to speak, but Britt pointed her finger at her again. "And calling to say you were going to be late to lunch—and my shower—doesn't count."

God, she really was a bitch. "Britt, I'm sorry."

Tears filled Britt's eyes. "I made my peace with it a long time ago. But you being here is reopening old wounds. I miss you, Lanie."

Lanie's phone began to ring in her hand.

"Go deal with your current crisis."

Lanie's stomach twisted even more. What was the right thing to do here? The opening was already running behind schedule. She couldn't afford to lose any more time. But she'd let Brittany down too many times to count.

She thrust the papers at Stephanie. "Take these back to the office. Scan them and send them to Eve, then call her and ask her if they have legal covered or if we need to take care of it. Then call those employee interviews we have set up for next week and see if we can conduct them tomorrow. Tell Eve we're making the most of the shutdown."

"You want *me* to talk to Eve?"

"You know everything that I know about the job site, so why not?"

"She'll want to talk to *you*."

"Tell her I'm not available."

"But she'll be pissed."

Lanie took a breath. "I don't care." But then she realized she was throwing her assistant under the bus. Every boss Lanie'd had before Eve had done the same to Lanie in one way or the other, but she'd be damned if she did the same to Stephanie. "On second thought, I'll do it."

Stephanie's eyes narrowed. "Do you think I can't handle it?"

"No. Not at all. But just because you can handle it doesn't mean I should throw you to the wolves."

Pride filled Stephanie's eyes. "Then I'm doing it. You're the one who always catches all the crap. I'll take point on this one." She paused. "But we need to figure out what to do about the interviews. We have confidential information all over our office, and we don't get the space we set up for interviews until next week."

"Then we'll have them at Starbucks."

"*Are you crazy?*"

"We'll use the working project name for the store name, but still tell them it's a clothing store. Then we'll have the ones who make it to the next step of the process sign NDAs when we interview them in the store space, because we *will* be open by tomorrow afternoon."

Stephanie gulped, then nodded. "Okay."

"I'll be back within an hour."

"Okay."

Stephanie hurried off, and Lanie turned to find her cousin gawking at her.

"What have you done?" Brittany asked.

"Getting my priorities straight." She sat down and hid her shaking hands in her lap. "Where's our food? We're sitting in an empty restaurant. Surely it shouldn't take this long."

"Lanie. Go. I was being a self-centered bitch."

"No." She took a breath to steady her nerves. "Stephanie can take care of it. It's good experience for her." Lanie wasn't about to sabotage her career, but between this latest delay and Eve's obvious displeasure with the last few openings, Lanie wasn't confident she was going to have a career at Margo Benson much longer. But maybe changing things up professionally wouldn't be a bad idea.

"You should talk to Randy. He can give you advice about the injunction."

Lanie gave a tiny shake of her head. "I'm sure corporate will have their own lawyers all over it."

"Then talk to him about your own options. You know... just in case." When Lanie hesitated, Britt added, "It can't hurt."

Then, before Lanie could protest, her cousin grabbed her phone out of her purse and called her fiancé, explaining the situation. Brittany glanced over at Lanie. "Can you go see him first thing tomorrow morning? His first client is at nine, but if you get there by eight thirty, he can see you."

Lanie agreed, but she knew she wasn't meeting him to find out what she could do about the injunction. Yesterday she thought she'd been happy with her job, and now she was strongly considering leaving.

Those Pink Pantie Pull-downs must be stronger than she'd remembered...

Chapter Five

Tyler stood in line at the coffee shop on the first floor of his office building. He had several depositions this morning and early afternoon, and then a consultation, before he met some of the single associates for drinks. He was going to need caffeine to make it through this day.

His phone vibrated in his pocket, and he groaned when he took it out and saw his father's name on the screen.

"Why are you talking to Eric's principal?" his father demanded without preamble.

He'd been expecting this call. "Mr. Carter said he'd tried to get ahold of you for two weeks, and you never called him back."

"I've been busy at the garage, but that doesn't give you the right to interfere. Besides, since when do you care? Ever since you became that big fancy lawyer, you think you're too good for us."

"Dad, that's not true."

The man in front of Tyler finished his order and stepped to the side.

"Can I take your order?" the girl at the counter asked, looking annoyed at the phone pressed to his ear.

He lowered it and said, "Grande Americano."

As she rang it up, he brought the phone back to his ear, not surprised that his father was still going through a litany of things Tyler had missed.

". . . you can't even come over to watch a damn football game."

"Dad," Tyler said with a sigh as he swiped his card in the machine, then stuffed it back in his wallet. "It's common knowledge that I'm a bitter disappointment. No need to recite the list all over again. What do you want?"

The girl behind the counter handed him his coffee.

"Stay out of our business. We don't need you."

"I never asked to get involved in the first place," he barked, ending the call before his father could respond. Turning around, he plowed into a woman standing directly behind him.

The lid to his coffee cup popped off, and the liquid spilled down the front of her blouse. She gasped in shock.

"Jesus!" He'd just dumped half a cup of burning hot coffee all over the woman's chest.

He quickly set the cup and his phone on the counter, then grabbed a handful of napkins from a dispenser next to the register. When he pressed them against her chest, he realized the silky fabric had plastered itself to her breasts, increasing the probability of a damaging burn.

With that thought in mind, he grabbed the gap between buttons below her breasts and ripped the blouse open. The little pearl buttons flew everywhere, bouncing on the wood floor, and the woman's eyes flew open in a panic as he pulled the shirt open, exposing her to the now lengthy line behind them.

He stared at her chest, trying to assess the damage. Why wasn't her skin red?

"You're the guy who stole one of Randy's beers," she said in shock as she took a step backward and pulled her shirt back into place. "Musty garage pickup-line guy."

Several thoughts went through his head as his gaze lifted to her face. One, she wasn't burned, thank God. Two, she was the woman he'd met in Randy's garage. Three, while he'd had the best of intentions, he could very well be facing sexual assault charges. Four, he'd fantasized about her the last two days, about spreading her legs apart on the damn work table and taking her right there, but seeing the swell of her breasts in her lacy, pale blue bra proved she was even more gorgeous under her clothes than he'd imagined. And five, while he'd thought of her as the gorgeous woman he'd met in the garage, she remembered him as musty garage pickup-line guy.

Musty. Garage. Guy.

What the actual fuck? How the mighty had fallen.

He shook his head. "Uh...the name's *Tyler*. And I didn't really steal it." Great, Norris. Way to sound lame.

A grin cracked her lips. "I'm used to guys wanting to get to second base, but they usually *buy* me the coffee first."

"I..." *Jesus.* What was wrong with him? He was never tongue-tied with women, but with her..."I thought you were burned. How are you not burned?"

Gripping her shirt closed with one hand, she glanced at his open coffee cup and stuck her finger into the remaining liquid, then licked it. "It's not hot. All you're missing is the ice if you're going for an iced coffee."

"Uh...no." He needed to get his shit together. And quick.

He was acting like an inexperienced moron. But her scent filled his nose as she stood next to him, an exotic blend of citrus and floral, distracting him even more.

"Then you should demand a refund." She didn't look angry; if anything, she looked amused. She nodded toward the stunned cashier. "You should either give him a refund or make a new whatever he had." She turned to Tyler. "Americano?"

"Uh... yeah."

She winked. "I know my coffee." Then she lowered her voice. "It's Colombian. If you asked for the Kona, you got ripped off."

"I didn't specify." What the hell was happening? One minute he was ripping her shirt off in front of the entire coffee shop, and the next she was quizzing him on coffee blends.

The cashier stood behind the counter gaping at both of them, but then she gave a slight head shake and asked, "So which do you want?"

He barely heard her; he was too busy studying the brunette next to him, in complete shock that she hadn't reamed him up and down.

God, she was even more beautiful than he'd remembered her. Her hair was piled into some kind of elaborate knot on the back of her head, and she wore less makeup than she had a couple of nights ago, giving her a more natural look. But with the silky blouse, the skirt, and the sexy heels, her face didn't need to be made up to make her look classically beautiful.

"Which one?" the cashier repeated with more force.

"Which what?"

The sexy brunette rolled her eyes and chuckled as though he were an adorable three-year-old. "A new coffee or a refund?"

Good God. Get it together, Norris. "It's hard to demand a refund when you could have had second- to third-degree burns if she'd made it correctly." He picked up his cup and reached over the counter for a new lid. He snapped it on and lifted her gaze to hers. "I'll stick with this one."

"But I stuck my finger in it."

He gave her a look of nonchalance, but refrained from telling her that was part of the reason he was keeping it. He turned to the cashier, who was still staring at them both as though they had asked her to do backflips.

"I'll take a Grande Chai tea," the sexy brunette said to the cashier.

Tyler reached for his wallet. "I'll pay for whatever she's having."

"You don't have to do that," she said. She held her blouse closed with one hand while trying to reach into her purse.

"It seems the least I can do after I just ripped your shirt off in front of Martha and Greg back there." He gave his colleagues standing five places back in line a half wave. *God. Could this get worse?* He was never going to hear the end of this in the office.

Still gripping her shirt, she turned at the waist and gave a half wave of her own before she looked up at him. "Had I known I was going to have an audience, I would have worn my Agent Provocateur bra."

"The one you're wearing is really pretty," a boy who looked to be in his late teens said as he leaned forward, trying to peer over Lanie's shoulder for a better look. "You'd make a sexy secret agent. Just like on TV."

"Jesus," Tyler said to the boy as he shrugged out of his jacket. "Didn't your parents teach you about sexual harassment?"

"Hey, *old dude*," the kid protested. "You're the one who

ripped her shirt open. It was just like something you'd see in the movies. You must have experience. Can you teach me how to do that?"

Old dude?

The sexy brunette began to chuckle. "The boy has a good point."

"About which part?" Tyler dared to ask. Surely *she* didn't think he was old. They had to be around the same age.

"Your shirt-ripping skills, of course. Quite impressive. Every single button popped off."

"I'll be happy to pay to replace your shirt." His face began to burn as he held his suit jacket out to her. "Here. Take this."

"You can't replace it," she said, slipping her arms into the sleeves, then buttoning one of the higher buttons on his jacket. "It's...uh...vintage."

"Then can I reimburse you for it?"

"Don't worry about it." She glanced down at her chest. The damp cloth was plastered to her skin again, hugging every curve, and revealing a plentitude of cleavage. She reached up to the base of his throat and started to undo the knot of his tie.

"Are you planning to rip my shirt open as payback?" he asked, regaining his confidence.

She looked up at him through her long eyelashes and grinned. "It wouldn't be nearly as impressive as what you just accomplished."

"I'll say..." the teen said wistfully.

"Hey!" Tyler said in a warning tone as he pointed to him. "Be respectful."

She seemed surprised at his authoritative tone as she slid his tie free from his collar and looped it around her own neck. "I hope you don't mind me borrowing this, but I'm headed to a meeting." A shadow crossed her face, but it quickly faded and a slight smile lifted her mouth. "I'd rather not be mostly naked for the appointment."

Horror washed through him. "God. I'm so sorry."

She shrugged, then sighed. "*C'est la vie.*"

Other than her sudden shock at being drenched in coffee, then stripped in public, this was the first time he'd seen any sign that she'd seemed negatively affected by any of this. She'd definitely taken this far better than any other woman he knew would have done.

He reached for the tie and gently brushed her fingers away as he took over tying the knot. "I really *am* sorry."

She kept her gaze down. "It's hard to fault you for trying to save me from scalding burns."

He finished with the knot and resisted the urge to smooth the silk between her breasts.

"Of course, you helped only because you tossed your coffee on me, but I can overlook that part." Her smile was back in place as she looked up at him. "I'll be sure to give the jacket and tie to Brittany. Hopefully, she can get it back to you before the wedding."

He started to tell her that he'd see Brittany on Saturday, but the cashier was holding out her coffee. She grabbed it and took a step back.

Tyler reached for his wallet again. "I insist on paying."

The cashier shook her head and handed him a new cup with a sheepish look. "We remade yours, and both are on the house."

"Thanks," he said as he stuffed his wallet back into his pants. When he turned around to ask if he could walk her to her car, he did a double take. She was gone.

And he *still* didn't know her name.

Chapter Six

‿

Lanie hurried toward the elevator, sure she was now late for her meeting with Randy, but at least she had her coffee and what was left of her dignity. She was no prude, but flashing her bra in front of half a dozen people was pushing her limit. Still, she thought she'd recovered well, even after the shock of seeing Tyler again.

And that *had* been a shock. Especially since she'd just been thinking about him. She had no idea why she was so intrigued by him, but there was no denying that she'd loved his reaction. While she inherently knew he was a player, she'd completely knocked him off his game. Watching his horror when he realized he'd torn her shirt open, then the appreciation of what he saw...

She really did wish she *had* worn her Agent Provocateur bra.

She'd found his floundering amusing, and then the way he took charge when that kid had tried to sneak a peek...

If only she could ask Brittany about him without tipping her off that she was interested.

The elevator opened to the twelfth floor, and her phone began to ring. She considered letting it go to voice mail, but Stephanie had been anxious about possibly starting the interviews without Lanie. After her wardrobe malfunction, Lanie would need to go home to change, making her even later to the interviews.

But to her surprise, the number said Aiden, and she answered the phone with a grin. "Aiden, as usual, you have terrible timing. I haven't heard from you in months, and you call me just as I'm about to go into a meeting."

She glanced down at the end of the foyer to the reception desk with the name Goldman, Taylor, Hughes, and Evans plastered on the wall. Randy stood at the desk and did a double take when he saw her get off the elevator. She lifted a finger to tell him she'd be with him in a second.

"I'm dropping into the land of barbecue myself, Lane," Aiden said.

"When?" she asked, giving Randy a nervous look. The receptionist was already giving her an odd stare. Clearly "menswear chic" wasn't going to be the next fashion trend.

"This weekend, and I have tickets to the Royals game on Sunday. Come with me." He laughed. "And don't tell me you have to work. I'm not falling for it. No self-respecting construction crew is going to work on Labor Day weekend."

She *did* have work, but she could let Stephanie handle things for a few hours. Still, she had to give Aiden a hard time. "You know I hate baseball."

"All the more reason for me to make you come. I have something I'd like to talk to you about."

She hesitated. "Okay…I'm intrigued."

"Great, I'll pick you up at noon. Text me the address."
Then he hung up.

Shaking her head, she dropped her phone into her purse.
It was just like Aiden to call her out of the blue and expect
her to drop everything to see him. Not that she minded.
She'd met Aiden in college. They'd dated a few times until
they discovered that they worked better as friends than
lovers. Still, Aiden was one more person to add to her growing list of neglected friends. She needed to change that.

"Sorry about the delay," she said as she walked over to
Randy. "Thanks for seeing me."

"I know Britt says part of the perks of your job is that you
occasionally get designer clothes, but this wasn't what I expected."

She'd seen her reflection in the stainless-steel walls of
the elevator. Tyler's jacket covered enough of her skirt to
make it look like the only thing she was wearing was the
jacket and his tie. "It's a long story, but let's just say I'm
planning on going home to change as soon as we're done."
If it were anyone else, she would have cancelled, but he was
family now, and he'd squeezed her into his schedule. She
could deal with it.

He led her down the short hall and into his office. Shutting the door behind them, he led her to a chair in front of
his desk.

"Brittany tells me you're dealing with some legal issues
with your job—your secret job that I can't know about," he
said, sitting in his chair. "However, since you're here seeking
my legal advice, I'll point out that you can confide in your
attorney."

"Honestly, at this point it doesn't matter," she said wryly.
"I told Britt about my job years ago, so I'm surprised *she*
hasn't told you."

"You should know by now that Britt's a vault when it comes to secrets."

She used to be, Lanie thought. It was good to hear that hadn't changed. Lanie gripped the arms of her chair and looked him in the eye. "I'm not a time management consultant. I'm here opening a store on the Plaza, and yesterday we received an injunction that shut down the work site. But late last night I got word that corporate already has their legal team on it. They're positive they can reverse the injunction today, and we should be back to work by the end of the day."

Randy laced his fingers together on his desk. "But you're still here, so tell me what I can do for you."

Reaching into her purse, she pulled out her folded contract. "I need to figure out if it's in my best interest to let my VP fire me or turn in my notice."

She handed it over his desk, and he took it from her. "I'm guessing the question is over any severance package you might receive."

"Actually, a bonus package. If I leave in good standing I'm entitled to stock and a nice cash bonus. This store is scheduled to be completed in four weeks, then I'm supposed to move to Phoenix. If I lose my job, I don't have anything else lined up. I need to make sure I'm compensated. I've made good money over the last ten years, and I've saved a lot, but..."

"You don't want to leave any money on the table. That's smart." He studied her and asked, "What makes you so sure you're going to be fired? From what little Britt says, you're very good at your job."

"Let's just say I've been investigating my new VP's employment history, and she likes to go in and make a clean sweep of things. She's made it obvious she doesn't like me, so the proverbial handwriting's on the wall. I'd rather be proactive rather than reactive. I know my contract has several clauses for both scenarios. I need to know which one is to my advantage, especially since I know my company will be doing the same."

Randy glanced down at the contract and nodded. "Do you have any idea what you'll do?"

"Not a clue. I've worked for Montgomery Enterprises since I got out of college, which probably means I'm due for a change anyway," she said. "No one sticks around in one place too long anymore."

"Maybe you'll find something here," Randy said. "Brittany would love for you to be closer."

"Yeah," she said, surprised the thought hadn't even occurred to her. She'd been too busy worrying about a possible exit strategy to think about where she'd land. She stood and started to reach out to shake Randy's hand, but his averted gaze as he stood and took her hand reminded her that she'd let go of her blouse.

"I have a spare shirt you can put on if you like." He walked over to a closet, pulled a pale blue shirt off a hanger, and handed it to her. "I have meeting with some clients in about fifteen minutes. How about I go check to make sure everything's on track? That will give you time to change."

"I'll take off when I'm done. Thanks." She held up the shirt. "For everything."

"No problem." He stopped at the door and paused, his hand on the knob. "Britt thinks the world of you."

"I think the world of her too."

"I'm not sure you know how much she appreciates you doing all these wedding activities." He grinned. "It's excessive; trust me, I know. But I'd give her anything she wants. And she wants this."

Lanie was surprised at the twist of jealousy in her gut. "She's lucky to have you."

Randy's eyes twinkled as he pulled his phone out of his pocket. "Can you say that again, only this time to the camera?" Then he laughed and walked out the door.

* * *

Tyler headed up to the twelfth floor, trying to get in the right head space for his deposition, but he kept thinking about the sexy brunette from Britt's shower. He was trying not to dwell on the fact that she was walking around with his jacket and tie next to her creamy skin. He was no romantic, but he couldn't deny it kicked his imagination into overdrive.

Maybe he was ready to start seeing women again. Nothing serious, but maybe it was time to get back in the game.

His thoughts drifted back to his phone call with his father. Did his father have a point? When was the last time he'd made any effort to spend time with his family?

He stopped by his assistant's desk to pick up a file for his deposition, but as he headed to his office, he saw Victor heading toward him and thought of a way to start things in the right direction with his brothers.

"Hey, Victor," Tyler said as he started to walk by. "Does your offer include your Royals season tickets?"

Victor's smile wavered. "Yeah. What day?"

"Sunday?"

"Sure. I'll give them to you by the end of the day." Victor waved and continued down the hall.

"Thanks."

Randy walked up behind Tyler and released a low whistle. "Was I hearing things? Did Victor willingly hand over his Royals tickets?"

"I gave him some legal advice, and he said he owed me. I just had to name the price."

"*Nice.* You *do* know we have a photo shoot Sunday night too, don't you?"

"The game starts at one. I'll make it."

"I'd beg to come along, but Britt would kill me."

"And any other time I'd take you, but I'm going to ask my dad and my brothers."

Randy's eyes widened in surprise, not that Tyler blamed him. Randy knew he wasn't close to his family. "Do you think your dad will come?"

"No. But at least I've made the offer." Time for a subject change. "Are you ready for the deposition?"

Randy stopped and did a double take. "Yeah, but where's your tie? You usually wear one when we're meeting with clients."

"Yeah." Tyler sighed. "Long story."

"There's a lot of those going around."

"What?"

Randy shook his head and grinned. "Never mind. I have a spare in my office if you want to borrow it."

"You have a spare tie?"

He shrugged. "You never know when you'll have a fashion emergency. Do you want it?"

Tyler grinned. "*Fashion emergency.* You never used to say things like that before Britt. It's not purple or covered in flashing lights, is it?"

"No," Randy said in mock disgust. "You think I'd actually let you steal the limelight more than you usually do with a blinking tie?"

Tyler laughed. "I can't help it if the women love me."

"Yeah, they love you a little too much." But Randy cringed after he said it. "Sorry, Tyler. Not so funny."

"Hey, if you can't laugh about a woman stalking you and tying you up in your own bed, then what can you laugh about? Nina was harmless."

"Maybe so, but it was still scary as shit."

Tyler shrugged, but it had scared him enough to swear off women for a while.

"You'll find a good woman. Look at me and Britt. And Kevin and Holly."

Tyler curled his upper lip and said derisively, "Who the hell says I want *that*?"

"Everybody wants someone."

"Not me." Tyler shook his head. "Look, I'm not knocking what you and Britt have, but it's not for everyone."

Randy looked dubious. "Maybe so, but you're not even dating casually right now, unless you consider your romantic relationship with your hand dating."

Tyler released a mock laugh. "Ha, ha, funny guy. I've already endured my fill of uncomfortable situations this morning. Just give me the damn tie."

Randy gave him a strange look, then led him to his office and rapped on the door.

"You need to knock on your own office door?" Tyler asked suspiciously.

"I left someone in there and I want to make sure she's okay with us walking in."

"Do you have Britt tucked away in there with an overcoat and nothing underneath?"

Randy frowned and shot him a look that said *Don't think about my fiancée that way*. "No." He pushed the door open a crack and looked around before opening it all the way. "It's clear."

"What's going on? You're acting like you're hiding Donald Trump's tax returns."

"I just had a client this morning who was...a little shy."

"And you locked her up in your office?"

Randy shot him a grin. "Long story."

Tyler shrugged. "Fair enough."

Randy handed him an ice-blue tie, and Tyler looped it over his neck and began to tie the knot, trying not to think about knotting his tie on the sexy brunette.

"Why do you suddenly look constipated?" Randy asked.

"What the hell?" Tyler said in disgust. "I do *not* look constipated."

"Well, you looked weird. Stop it or you'll scare the clients."

"I never scare the clients. *You* scare the clients."

"Well, in this instance, if you show them that look, they'll run for it. So stop it."

"Being in love is screwing with your brain, Randy. Now, let's go to the deposition."

But as Tyler walked out of the room, he couldn't help wondering if the sexy brunette was screwing with *his* brain.

Because he would have bet money that he smelled her perfume in Randy's office.

Chapter Seven

⟋

Late Saturday afternoon, Lanie groaned when her phone dinged with another text. Britt was driving her crazy.

Don't forget we're meeting at seven!

As though she could forget. How many brides had a full wedding attire photo shoot one month before their wedding? This was the fifth reminder in the past three hours. But this was only the beginning. There were three more photo shoots after this one, along with several other bridal party activities.

"I really liked the last interview. Patricia," Stephanie said as she tapped on her tablet. "She has experience as a manager *and* she seems eager. What did you think?"

Lanie sent a quick text to Brittany—Thanks for letting me know that the time hasn't changed. AGAIN—then she glanced at her assistant. "It's my crazy cousin."

"The one who suggested I take her yoga class? She didn't seem that crazy."

"She's getting married. That's clue enough that she's

crazy, don't you think? Not to mention that she's having multiple photo shoots before the wedding. Remember?"

"You're going to the Nelson-Atkins Art Museum tonight, right?"

"Yeah, we're taking photos in front of the giant badminton birdies."

Stephanie looked her up and down. "You've been in a weird mood since you came back from meeting your cousin's fiancé yesterday. What happened?"

Lanie scrunched her nose. "What are you talking about? I'm fine."

Stephanie tilted her head and studied her. "No. You're not. You met a guy."

Lanie froze. Was she that transparent? "What? Why would you think that?"

Stephanie's eyes lit up. "You're hiding something. Spill it."

Dammit. Stephanie had been fishing, and Lanie had fallen for it. "There's nothing to tell." There was no way she was going to tell Stephanie about her run-in with Tyler...For some reason, knowing his name only increased her interest. She reminded herself that she was far too busy to get involved with some self-centered guy who was interested in a quick lay...but when she thought about it, she wondered what the downside of that would be. Maybe that's what she needed to distract herself from her current career crisis.

"Lanie, we've worked together for five years," Stephanie said with a grin. "I know when you're lying. Now, what happened yesterday?"

"Isn't our next interview in five minutes?"

"Plenty of time to tell me about your guy."

Steph could be relentless when she wanted to be. Better to throw her a bone and get her off the scent. "I already told you. I took my contract to Randy for him to look it over."

Rolling her eyes, Stephanie put her hand on her hip. "Is that the best you can do?

What could she tell her? Then it hit her. "Aiden's coming to town. He wants to go out tomorrow afternoon."

"A date? I thought you two were just friends."

"We are…It's just a Royals game. He said he needed to talk to me about something."

Stephanie frowned. "Sounds ominous."

"I know."

Lanie's phone rang. She was trying to decide if she was going to send Britt to voice mail when she saw the California number and cringed. "Shit. It's Eve."

Worry filled Stephanie's eyes. "Why would she be calling on a Saturday afternoon?"

Lanie gave her a wry look. "You're one to talk. We're working at four on a Saturday afternoon." She walked to back of their rented office space and answered. "Hello, Eve."

"I don't like what I'm hearing, Lanie."

That was no surprise. "Tell me what you're hearing, and I'll tell you if you should worry."

"I don't appreciate your attitude. The store is behind schedule, and you're being flippant."

"With all due respect, Eve, I've done this twelve times. I know what I'm doing."

"I hope you do, because we have a lot riding on this opening."

Lanie wanted to say, "No, *you* have a lot riding on this opening," but she wisely kept it to herself. "My reputation is on the line too. We'll open, and it will be on time."

"We'll see," Eve said. "I'm working on some reports and I need your August financial report to me by nine."

"Tonight? They're not due until the fifteenth. Today's the second." Pulling the data together would take several hours, and she'd promised Britt she'd be at the photo shoot at seven.

"Your delays are making me nervous, so I need that report. Tonight. And that's nine central time, not Pacific...Is this a problem?"

Lanie was silent for several seconds as the truth hit her. Eve was setting her up to fail. "No."

"Good. I'm looking forward to it." Then Eve hung up.

Lanie released a groan as a young woman walked through the door. The woman gave Lanie a startled look, and Lanie held up her hand. "I'm sorry. Ignore me."

Stephanie glanced up, obviously dying to ask questions, but their next interviewee kept her silent.

Lanie walked over to the table and picked up her purse. "I have to do something for Eve, so I'm going to let you handle the last few interviews."

Stephanie looked worried, so Lanie gave her a reassuring smile, even if she wasn't feeling reassured herself.

Lanie walked over and shook the young woman's hand. "I'm Lanie, but I'm going to leave you in Stephanie's capable hands. If you impress her, then I'll see you again next week." Then she headed out the door to walk the four blocks to her apartment.

It was the Saturday of Labor Day weekend, and the heat was still oppressive. She normally liked walking to and from work, but her nerves were shot after her phone call and wisps of her hair had plastered themselves to her forehead. She decided to make sure wherever she ended up moving to wouldn't be so humid. Maybe she should look out east. But then she stopped in her tracks as the reality of her situation hit her.

Her entire life could be about to change.

Putting her hand on her stomach, she took a deep breath and told herself everything would be okay. She'd never been one to run from hard work. She'd find a new place in the world. But the thought was overwhelming and coated with loneliness. Stephanie wouldn't be going with her this time.

Lanie was drenched in sweat when she reached her apartment, so she took a quick shower, put on shorts and a tank top, and got to work. She was deep in a spreadsheet when Stephanie called.

"What's Eve got you doing?"

"She wants the August financial report by nine."

"You're kidding?" she asked, sounding indignant. "They're not due until the fifteenth."

"Well, now it's due today." Which was ridiculous and unrealistic, but because Lanie was a dedicated employee, she was killing herself to get it done anyway.

Why?

She'd busted her ass for this company for ten years, and things weren't going to change. Maybe it was time Lanie made things change.

Was she seriously thinking about quitting?

"What about your photo shoot?" Stephanie asked.

Lanie's stomach twisted. How was she going to get the report done? "I've got about another hour or two of work. So now I have an excuse to come home early."

"Lanie, that's never going to work. The shoot starts in twenty minutes, and the report's due in at nine. Let me work on it."

"*Twenty minutes?* I'm not even ready." Shit. How had she lost track of time? Brittany was going to kill her.

"I can help," Stephanie said in an authoritative tone. "You

get ready and go to the photo shoot, and I'll finish the report, then when you finish with the photo session, we can meet at O'Dowd's for drinks."

"Steph..."

"Come on. If you don't let me do this, I'll just go back to my empty apartment and watch pathetic rom-coms while I eat pizza and drink a whole bottle of wine by myself. Don't think I'm doing you a favor. I'm doing this all for me."

Lanie grinned. "Well, when you put it that way..."

"So just send me the files you've worked on, and I'll take over. Now, go get ready."

"Thanks."

She ran to the bathroom and touched up her makeup, but left her hair down, since Britt wanted a more natural look. After she got into her dress, a quick check of the time told her she needed to hurry. The art museum was only several blocks away, but it was too hot to walk.

She found her phone on the table and requested an Uber. Just as the request went through, a text from Britt popped up.

Do you happen to have any insect repellant?

What? No.

Okay. Never mind. We'll take care of it.

Well, crap. Was the lawn of the Nelson-Atkins Art Museum infested with mosquitoes? Lanie had half a mind to stop for some spray, but she was going to be late as it was.

Lanie didn't do late and it was grating on her nerves. She was also oddly nervous about seeing Britt and Randy together again. Her reaction at the shower had been unsettling. She'd never yearned for relationships. Her career had been enough. But suddenly all she was seeing was what she didn't have.

Wallowing did not become her.

She opened the refrigerator and pulled out an already opened bottle of Riesling. Unscrewing the cap, Lanie put the bottle up to her lips and took a big gulp. While she could bring herself to admit that she was jealous of Brittany's life, she could think of about a thousand things higher up on her list of problems. She took another generous gulp.

Her phone rang, and she was sure it was Britt calling to ask why she wasn't there yet, but she was relieved to see it was Aiden.

"I'm in town, Lane," he said when she answered, "and you still haven't sent me your address."

She took another drink from the bottle. "I'm a little busy, Aiden."

"You said that when I called yesterday. You could give a guy a complex."

Her car was going to be there any minute, and she still wasn't ready. She needed to find her shoes. Britt had had three-inch-tall pumps dyed to match the lilac-colored bridesmaids' dresses, and she could have sworn she'd brought them to the living room. "I promise to give you my full undivided attention tomorrow. Right now I need to go my cousin's wedding photo shoot."

He laughed. "Oh my God. You're a *bridesmaid*? You used to make fun of that shit."

"And wine coolers used to be my drink of choice. But then I grew up."

She sloshed the wine in her bottle and wondered how much pregaming was too much. The more the better. She gulped down another drink as she spotted her shoes next to the sofa.

Her phone buzzed in her hand, probably alerting her that her Uber driver was waiting in the no-parking zone in front of her apartment, and she still wasn't ready. "I have to go. My car's here. I'll text you my address when I'm on my way."

"Go play Bridesmaid Barbie. I'll see you tomorrow."

Lanie grabbed the bottle and took one last drink, shocked when she realized how little wine was left.

She'd drunk over half a bottle of wine in less than five minutes.

Well, crap. There was nothing she could do about it now.

It was showtime.

Chapter Eight

Tyler stuffed his finger between his collar and his neck. The app on his phone said it was eighty-nine degrees, so it could have been worse, but that didn't mean shit when sweat was dripping down his back. Of course, it was more than the heat making him sweat. He hated weddings and went out of his way to avoid them. And now he was *in* one.

"Okay," Britt said, lifting her hands in surrender. She looked out of place standing on the grass in front of a twenty-foot-tall shuttlecock in a wedding dress. "Guys, you can take off your ties for now."

"Just our ties?" Randy's brother, Rowdy, asked in dismay.

"We'll get the formal photos, then you can take off your jackets and we'll do some informal ones."

"So why haven't we started yet?" a whiny blonde asked. She wore a long, sleeveless lavender dress that, unlike a lot of bridesmaids' dresses Tyler had seen, actually complemented her figure. What no one else realized was that Tyler already knew her. He hadn't remembered her when he'd seen her at the shower, when she'd walked up to him and flirted, hinting that they should hook up *again*. It hadn't been until later that night that he'd figured out that he'd dated her four years ago. And he used the term *dated* loosely. Hooked up a few times was more accurate.

But amazingly, he hadn't been tempted when she'd approached him at the shower, and she had *definitely* been his type of girl. Maybe the Bachelor Brotherhood had ruined him for life. Maybe a life of celibacy was in his future. But all he had to do was think of Britt's sexy brunette friend to know that wasn't true. His taste had changed. Maybe half of his problem with women was that he'd gone for the flash instead of the substance.

Women like his mystery brunette.

He didn't really know much about her, but he instinctively knew she was different. Was it because *he* was different now? She'd been the only woman to affect him in months. When the photo shoot was over, he planned to ask Brittany about her.

But unfortunately, the blonde bridesmaid hadn't caught on that he wasn't interested. She gave him a seductive look as she sidled up next to him and clutched his arm. "Tyler's melting."

"I'm fine," he said, pulling his arm away from her grasp. He turned to Brittany, doing a poor job of hiding his aggravation, and said, "But Celia's right. Why haven't we started yet?" He wanted to get this over with as quickly as possible.

"*Celesta*," the blonde said with a hint of irritation.

Hell, he'd slept with her multiple times and he couldn't even remember her name. What a prick. Still, he didn't feel bad enough to start something with her again, so Tyler took another step to the side.

Brittany held her hands out and gave him an apologetic look. "My cousin's not here yet, but she's on her way." She held up her phone. "I just texted her, and she said her driver took a wrong turn."

"She has a driver?" Tyler asked in surprise.

"Uber," Randy said offhandedly, then turned to his brother, cajoling him into leaving his jacket on.

Holly had been standing in the periphery, but all the whining must have gotten to her because she moved into the middle of the group and gave them a big smile.

"Since our last bridesmaid is on her way," Holly continued, "why don't we start setting up the first photo?"

Celesta shrieked, and a loud slapping sound followed. "I just got bit!"

Tyler looked around for a stray dog or toddler. "What bit you?"

"A mosquito!" she said, rubbing her arm.

Sure enough, a welt was already starting to raise on her bicep.

Brittany's eyes grew wide, but Holly patted her arm. "Not to worry. The photographer can Photoshop that out."

The photographer nodded her agreement.

"But it still itches! I can't work under these conditions."

Work? Was she a model? He honestly couldn't remember what her profession had been, but she was already on his last nerve. Tyler gritted his teeth. Please dear God, don't let him be stuck with her at the wedding.

"We have some insect repellant on the way, Celesta," Randy said with a plastered-on smile. "If you like we can make a human shield around you until it arrives."

Anyone could hear the sarcasm in his voice—anyone except for Celesta. "Would you?" she asked hopefully.

Holly stared at the bridesmaid in disbelief, then ignored

her as she continued. "Brittany and I have paired everyone off, and we're about to read the list. This person will be your partner from now until the wedding's done."

Britt winked at Tyler. "Of course, if you choose to stick with your partner after the wedding, that's okay, too."

Oh, God. It was just like Britt's friend had warned him. Britt *was* playing matchmaker. He eyed the distance to the street where his car was parked. Could he make a break for it?

But Kevin had just appeared at the edge of the group, and while Tyler initially felt relieved to see him, his friend now caught Tyler's attention and held his gaze. Kevin knew him well, and the message was clear. Tyler wasn't going anywhere.

"But," Randy said as he scanned the group with a big grin, "that only applies to you *single* people."

Everyone laughed, but Rowdy didn't laugh as much as the others, and Tyler wondered if it was because he and his wife were having marital problems—not that he was supposed to know. Randy had let it slip the week before at the office.

"Kevin's back with the insect repellant," Holly said, giving her husband a look of relief. "So we'll get everyone covered first."

Kevin walked through the group, handing out cans of repellant. Celesta ran over and snatched one from him and began spraying a cloud so thick it gagged Tyler from ten feet away.

"You look like you're waiting for your walk to the gallows," Kevin teased as he came up beside Tyler.

"You know I'm allergic to weddings." He glanced over at his friend. "All of this reminds me that I never thanked you for getting married without any of us around. I'm not sure I could have handled being in two weddings within three months."

"If you can't handle being in a wedding, how are you going to handle your own wedding someday?"

Tyler snorted. "I'm never getting married. I thought I'd made that pretty clear."

Kevin crossed his arms and scanned the group.

His nonresponse was a response of its own, which rankled Tyler even more. "Watch out for the blonde bridesmaid. I suspect she has a thing for heroes."

"Looks like she only has eyes for you." Kevin chuckled. "She's drooling like you're an ice cream cone on a hot summer day."

"She's liable to turn her attention to you when she realizes you've saved her from a mosquito attack."

Kevin chuckled again and shook his head. "Ha! Holly would put a stop to that."

"Sweet little Holly?" Tyler asked.

"Never underestimate a woman in love, my friend."

Memories of his crazy Nina flooded Tyler's head. If that's what love did to women, he wanted no part of it.

"She wasn't in love with you," Kevin said quietly. "She was obsessed. There's a difference."

Tyler whipped his head around in surprise.

"I could see it on your face." Kevin paused. "You know, the Bachelor Brotherhood seemed like a good idea at the time, but now I'm not so sure."

Tyler snorted. "Says the man who lasted one fucking day."

A wicked grin lit up Kevin's eyes. "Which maybe proves my point even more. The thing is, you and I are a lot alike. We've spent most of our dating life going after the easy catch. It was when I took a risk that it worked out for me. When Holly and I met, for the first time in my life, I had no idea how it would turn out. Did she want me? Did she even *like* me? I actually had to work for it."

Tyler shook his head, becoming irritated with this conversation, mostly because Britt's friend from the shower kept popping into his head. The image of her in the coffee shop, with her open shirt and the pale blue bra, had quickly taken over. Where did she fit into Kevin's theory? Did it even matter? "Don't you have better things to do on a Saturday night? I thought your fake wedding-planner-assistant job only applied to the actual weddings."

Kevin laughed. "And miss out on the chance to watch you suffer in the ninety-degree heat in a monkey suit? No way. Besides, the pay is crap—but the benefits are *totally* worth it."

Tyler cringed, then changed the subject. He didn't want to hear about his best friend's sex life. "Since *your wife* has the list pairing the bridal party, please tell me that I'm not stuck with that nightmare."

"Which one?" Kevin teased.

"Oh, God. There's more than *one*?"

"I hear Britt's cousin is a firecracker."

"She obviously can't be bothered to show up on time." Tyler looked over at Celesta, who continued eyeing him with undisguised interest. His anxiety grew when he realized that Holly had already announced a groomsman and a bridesmaid, pairing Rowdy and some other woman, before she got interrupted by the photographer. That left Kevin and one other groomsman and the *very* interested Celesta. And the missing firecracker cousin.

"Okay," Holly said as the photographer opened her camera bag. "The next pair is Tyler and—"

Britt released an excited squeal. "There's Lanie!"

The wedding party stood between Tyler and the trees next to the street, but he could see glimpses of a woman in a lavender dress weaving a path toward them.

She stumbled as she tripped on her dress, and her long, dark hair fell forward into her face.

"What the hell?" Kevin muttered. "Is she drunk?"

Tyler had to wonder which of his two bridesmaid choices was the lesser of his evils.

Celesta gave him a seductive smile, making a production of licking her bottom lip.

Well, that answered that.

He took off jogging toward the brunette bridesmaid just as she semi-righted herself and kicked off her shoe. It flew through the air, and he ducked out of its path, congratulating himself on his quick reflexes. But as soon as he straightened, the other heel hit him square on the forehead, and he stumbled back a step.

Brittany gasped loudly enough for him to hear twenty feet away, but he was in too much shock to think about the stinging over his eye. He was more stunned by the woman in front of him.

Holy shit. The woman he'd been obsessing over was Brittany's cousin. He wasn't sure if that was a good thing or a complete disaster.

His brain was too shocked to figure it out, but his body decided it didn't need his brain to get on board with this new development.

Maybe this was fate. He scoffed at the idea, wondering where *that* thought came from.

But his thought process was interrupted as Lanie looked up at him and recognized him too. Her eyes widened in horror.

He realized that she was probably horrified to see him after he'd ripped her shirt open. Or maybe she was worried he was going to tell everyone and embarrass her more, although she hadn't acted very embarrassed at the time. Her reaction now was confusing him.

She rushed toward him, her face still covered in fear. Was she going to verbally berate him? Slap him across the face?

But she did neither, stopping in front of him and looking around frantically.

How drunk *was* she?

She bent down to pick up the hem of her skirt, then dropped it and reached for his tie, before finally grabbing the handkerchief out of his jacket pocket. She jerked it out and pressed it to his forehead, using a lot of pressure.

"Thank God," she said. "If that had dripped on your tux, Brittany would have killed me."

He shook his head, and her hand followed. "What are you talking about?" But he smelled alcohol on her breath, giving support to his assumption that she was drunk.

"You're bleeding." She cast an anxious glance over to her cousin. "Don't make a big deal over this, okay? I know men can be big babies, but if you play this off, I'll make it worth your time."

A jolt shot right to his crotch, and a grin stretched his lips.

"Oh my God," she said in disgust. "Not *that*." She was about to take a step away from him, but another look at Brittany stopped her.

Brittany was rushing over to them, so he lowered his voice. "I think we can work out a deal."

She gave him a wary look. "I'm listening."

"If you insist on being my partner in this groomsman/bridesmaid thing until the end of the wedding, I'll act like it's a scratch." For all he knew, it was. It stung, but it couldn't be that bad.

"What happened?" Brittany asked, sounding breathless as she reached them.

"I tripped on this dress," Lanie said, then she sounded

indignant. "And my heels sunk in the grass. Why are we wearing heels in the grass?"

"You were supposed to wear flats and put the heels on when it's time to take photos. Didn't you get the text?"

A guilty look washed over Lanie's face, but then it faded. "You sent me ten million texts today, but I'm pretty sure I didn't get that one."

"Is he *bleeding*?" Brittany asked in dismay.

"Brittany," Holly said, walking up behind them. "I've got it covered. Randy, come help your bride back over to the group, but pick up her dress so she doesn't get grass stains." Then she glanced up at Tyler's forehead and grimaced. "Kevin, can you bring over my bag?"

Tyler tried to turn back to see what Kevin was getting, but Lanie grabbed his chin and held him in place.

"Stop. You're going to bleed on your tux!" she whisper-hissed and gave Holly a worried look. "If Brittany realizes I maimed him, she's going to kill me. You have to fix this."

"Maimed?" Tyler asked in confusion. "From a shoe?"

Kevin approached with a small canvas bag. He set it down, pulled out a first-aid box, then removed several packages of gauze.

"Lanie," he said, ripping the packages. "You release the pressure when I tell you to."

"But drop the handkerchief in the grass so you don't get blood on your dress," Holly added.

Tyler gave Kevin a questioning look, but his friend ignored him as he put a piece of gauze under Holly's hand.

"I've got it," Kevin said, blocking Tyler's view of Lanie as he dabbed at the wound.

Tyler flinched. "Shit. That hurts."

"I bet. I'm pretty sure you need stitches."

"Stitches? From a shoe?"

Kevin shrugged, and a smirk lit up his eyes.

"No!" Lanie whispered loudly. "He can't need stitches. Brittany is going to kill me!"

"*Brittany?*" Tyler asked in disbelief. "I'm the one who's maimed."

"Shh!" Lanie waved her hand in dismissal as she turned to Holly. "Do you have any butterfly bandages in that first-aid kit?"

"Probably," Holly said, picking up the box and examining the contents.

"He's still going to need stitches," Kevin said. "And the bandages are going to show in the photos."

"Oh, for Christ's sake." Tyler groaned and held out his hand. "Give me a damn mirror."

Holly gave him a sympathetic look. "I don't have one."

Shaking her head, Lanie swiped the screen of her phone. "Here. Use this." Then she handed it to him, open to the camera app in selfie mode.

He held it up in front of his face, pushing Kevin's hand away. When he saw the cut, he groaned. Sure enough, there was a half-inch gash, and one part looked fairly deep.

"Well, shit."

Lanie looked worried when he handed back her phone. "I'm so sorry. I'll pay for your medical bills, just please don't act like this is a big deal until we're done."

"How do I act like this isn't a big deal when I'm bleeding to death?"

"Not to mention it's going to show in the photos," Kevin reminded them.

"The photographer can Photoshop them out," Holly said. "Just like Celesta's mosquito bite."

"But I—" Tyler started to say before Lanie rolled her eyes and cut him off.

"*Please*. I promise you're not bleeding to death. We'll patch you up with a couple of butterflies, then when we're done, you can go get your stitches." She gave him a sardonic smile. "We'd hate for that pretty face to get scarred."

A bad-boy grin spread across his face. "I hear women like guys with scars. It makes them look more dangerous."

"Of course, a guy like you would say that."

"How's it going over there?" Brittany called over.

"Fine!" Holly shouted. "We're just cleaning it up, and then he'll be good to go."

Just then the blonde hurried over and draped her hand possessively on his arm. "You poor baby. I can't believe that woman kicked her shoe at you!"

"I didn't do it on purpose," Lanie countered, sounding indignant.

"No worries, Celesta," Tyler said, shifting his stance to shrug off her hand. "It's just a scratch."

"She's Celesta?" Lanie began to giggle.

What in the hell was she laughing at? She really *was* drunk. "What's so funny?" Tyler asked.

"Nothing." But she was still giggling as she eyed the blonde woman.

Celesta shot her a withering glare. "Look at all the blood! You could have killed him."

"He'll be fine, Selestra," Kevin said, turning Tyler so the woman couldn't see his wound. "I think the photographer's looking for you."

"My name is *Celesta*. Why can't anyone get it right? And I can't do anything without my partner."

Tyler caught Holly's attention with a wild look, but before the wedding planner could say anything, Lanie put a hand on her hip and made a shooing motion, still wearing a grin. "Then run on over and claim him. He looks like he's waiting for you too. Tyler's mine."

Randy's gangly teenaged cousin waved to Celesta.

Lanie gave Holly an expectant look. "Celesta is Alvin's partner, right?"

She nodded. "Yeah. That's right."

Celesta's face turned red, and she started to protest, but Holly stared her down. Celesta's anger faded, and she grudgingly stomped toward Alvin.

Holly handed Kevin a butterfly bandage, and he applied it to Tyler's forehead. "This is holding it really well, but since it's on your forehead, you should still get stitches. I suspect it's going to scar either way, but it's likely to scar less if you see a professional."

Guilt washed over Lanie's face.

"Kevin," Holly said, "he still has blood smeared all over his forehead."

Lanie snatched an alcohol pad from the kit and ripped it open. "I'll clean him up."

Holly lifted her eyebrows as she waited for Tyler's answer.

"Yeah," he said. "You need to get back and boss everyone around. Since this is Lanie's fault in the first place, she can finish up."

Lanie started to protest, then closed her mouth and looked like she was biting her lips to keep from saying what was on her mind.

Tyler laughed.

Kevin glanced between the two of them, then clapped Tyler on the shoulder. "Drinks later. You promised."

"That was before my trip to the ER."

Kevin waved him off as he walked away. "Hell. You've got something like six hours before it's too late for stitches. Don't be a wuss."

Lanie moved closer as they walked away. "Are you really going to wait to go to the ER?"

"I don't know yet," he said, watching her in amusement. She was acting guilty as hell. "Are you going for drinks?"

She looked up into his eyes. "Yeah, I am." A grin lit up her face. "But not with you. It's a work thing."

"On a Saturday night?"

"No rest for the wicked," she murmured as she gently swiped his skin.

A warm feeling spread throughout his body. This woman intrigued him more than she should. He was suddenly looking forward to all of Britt's wedding craziness.

"How much did you have to drink?" he asked with a grin.

"Who said I've been drinking?"

He chuckled. "Your entrance and your breath."

She rolled her eyes. "So I had some wine before I came, but in my defense, how was I supposed to face Celesta sober?"

She was lying. It was obvious the two women hadn't known each other. Maybe being here made her just as anxious as it made him.

He laughed. "Bring me some next time. You owe me after this." He pointed toward his forehead.

She cocked an eyebrow. "You think there's going to be a next time?"

"I know for a fact there's a next time. Tomorrow night at Loose Park, the time to be determined. And whatever other places Britt chooses for her crazy photos. We're stuck together until this wedding is over." His grin spread. "How do I know more about this wedding than you do?"

Guilt washed over her face again, then her grin was back. "I can always call Celesta back over. I'm sure she can be very entertaining if you're adventurous."

He was about to ask her what she was talking about when he heard a loud whistle come from the group.

"Hey," Randy shouted. "Are you two going to keep flirting for the rest of the night or are you going to join us for photos? You can flirt over here, you know."

Tyler looked behind him and realized the entire wedding party was watching them with intense interest.

"We're not flirting!" Lanie replied as a deep red blush stained her cheeks. "I'm making sure he's presentable for photos."

The snickers from the group suggested no one believed her.

"You can't act like you're interested in me," she said, sounding desperate.

"Who says I'm interested in you?"

She rolled her eyes. "Remember the shower? Britt's meddling matchmaking? If Britt finds out, she'll pull out the big guns to get us together."

While Tyler wasn't sure how disastrous that would be, Lanie obviously knew better. "So how am I supposed to play this? Ambivalent? Disgusted? Outraged over the maiming?"

"Take your pick, and I'll follow your lead." But as soon as she uttered the words, he could see she regretted them.

This was going to more fun than he'd expected.

Chapter Nine

Lanie couldn't believe her cousin hadn't walked over and wrung her neck.

This was her own fault for drinking so much wine, but at least it had worked—she didn't have to worry about hiding her jealousy anymore. Her embarrassing entrance and the subsequent maiming had taken care of that.

But even worse was that she was now partnered with the man who had inspired some very vivid daydreams, and from the mischievous look on his face, she was about to become even more uncomfortable. He was definitely sticking close.

"Okay," Holly said. "Let's get everyone standing underneath the giant shuttlecock."

"That's something you don't hear every day," Randy's brother joked.

The phone vibrated in Lanie's hand, and she saw a text from Stephanie.

I can't find the invoices for the display shelves. We ordered them, right?

She typed out a quick message. Yes, but we couldn't order those electronically. I think the invoice is in the file cabinet.

"Lanie!" Brittany called out. "Please tell me that's not work."

Lanie gave her an innocent look, and Britt shook her head, but at least she was smiling.

Holly and the photographer started to position everyone in some complicated staging, and Lanie realized Tyler wasn't next to her; he was headed toward the street.

"Lanie," Holly said. "Over here."

She started to mention Tyler's escape, but Holly was looking over her chart. "We'll get Tyler situated after you're in place."

No reason to call attention to the fact that she'd chased off one of Randy's groomsmen.

Holly and the photographer looked at their chart and had her stand in the place they wanted her, then Holly said, "Okay, Tyler. You stand behind her."

Tyler walked around the two women and stood in front of her with her shoes hanging from his fingertips.

How had she forgotten those damn shoes?

He handed her the shoes and flashed another mischievous grin. "You'll be wanting your weapons."

The group laughed, and she couldn't help grinning as she dropped them to the ground. Tyler took her arm and steadied her as she stepped into them.

"And put your phone away," Brittany said.

"Unless you want to Photoshop that out too," Celesta said with a smirk.

Lanie looked down at the phone, hesitating. She knew she

couldn't hold it during the photos, but if she put it in her purse, Brittany would give her grief for checking it. What if Stephanie had more questions?

"I'll take it," Tyler said, holding out his hand. Then he lowered his voice. "That way I can let you know if you get a call or message."

Lanie narrowed her eyes as she studied his face. Was this some kind of trick to pay her back for injuring him? More like his way of trying to hit on her. But he seemed genuine, so she handed him the phone, chiding herself on her paranoia.

She'd been in the dog-eat-dog corporate world too long. There was always someone out to one up her or thwart her— her new VP and the stupid injunction were just one of a long string of issues she'd had to deal with. She'd become jaded. Too jaded. The world was not out to get her. She needed to start trusting people more. And as stupid as it sounded, handing her most prized possession to a man she barely knew was taking a step in that direction.

His solemn expression as he slid her phone into a pocket inside his jacket suggested he realized the significance of what she'd done.

"Your tie," Lanie said. "It's undone." She started to reach up to tie it but quickly dropped her hands.

What was wrong with her? Helping a guy fix his tie was no big deal. What was it about this man that got under her skin?

She told herself that Brittany and Randy were the problem. This whole wedding had made her question everything in her life, but if she was honest with herself, she knew she'd felt unsettled for months. She could admit that she was ready for a change in her career, but was she ready for a real relationship too? In the past, all she had to do was think about

her parents' relationship and any thought of something serious flew out the window, but now she was considering
rethinking her stance against a real relationship.

And that scared the crap out of her.

Still, Tyler was no threat. She knew his type. She'd attracted them for years. There was nothing more appealing to
a no-strings guy than a woman who came with no expectations of her own.

She watched him knot his tie, then turned away as her fingers itched to reach up and straighten it for him. He was a
temptation, and that wasn't such a bad thing. But she wasn't
sure how Brittany and Randy would feel about her having
a casual fling with their friend. Still, they couldn't be that
close. He said he'd only known her cousin about a year.

"So what's your connection to Britt and Randy?" she
asked, trying not to think about what else he could do with
his nimble fingers.

"Friend of the groom." He finished the tie and glanced up
at her. "How's it look?"

Her mouth twisted into a grin. "It's crooked." She
reached up to straighten it at his neck, spending more time
than she'd intended, but his eyes had captured hers and
she felt like she was going to combust. Maybe they could
make it a secret fling. What Britt didn't know wouldn't hurt
her, right?

She ran her fingers down the length of the tie, making
sure it was straight, but she stopped where it tucked into his
jacket, even though her imagination ran wild thinking about
where it led.

"Penny for your thoughts," he said in a husky tone, but
there was a teasing glint in his eyes.

She couldn't very well tell him the truth, so she said the
first thing her mind latched onto. "I still have your jacket.

From yesterday." Then she glanced around to see to see if anyone had heard her.

Everyone was watching an animated Celesta try to convince Holly that she had a better idea for a pose.

But Tyler kept his amused gaze on Lanie. "You can bring it to me next time."

A wave of lust washed through her. Would *he* be open to a secret fling?

For the next twenty minutes, Holly and the photographer positioned them in various traditional poses, and the entire time Tyler chatted with Lanie and the rest of the wedding party and remained on his best behavior. But several times she caught him staring at her, and the look in his eyes heated her blood.

The sun had set behind the trees, casting a soft glow over them. Lanie knew Britt had chosen this time of day specifically for the lighting, but she couldn't help worrying about Stephanie tackling the financial reporting all on her own. She cast a nervous glance at Tyler's jacket, where she knew he'd tucked her phone. Could she get away with checking it without hurting her cousin's feelings?

Tyler moved to her side, blocking Britt's view of her as he reached into his jacket, then handed her the phone. "Go ahead and check it while Celesta tries to pretend she's in charge."

"Am I that easy to read?"

"Like a book."

She glanced up at him with a grin. "Do you even read?"

He laughed. "I've been known to read a book or two."

She started to scroll through her texts from Stephanie, but her stomach twisted into knots at the last text Stephanie had sent.

CALL ME STAT!

Oh, shit.

She was about to send her a text when her phone vibrated with a call from Stephanie.

"Go ahead and answer it," Tyler said, glancing over his shoulder. "Holly looks like she's about to strangle Celesta, and you'll lose all hope of a distraction if she takes her out."

Lanie forced a smile, but she was trying not to panic when she answered, "I'm making this call in secret, so we have to do this quickly."

"I lost it all." Stephanie sounded like she was about to cry.

Lanie covered her other ear with her hand so she could hear better. "When you say you lost it all . . ."

"The file. The program crashed. And when I reopened it, half my work was gone."

Her stomach dropped to her toes. "Okay, don't panic."

"How can I not panic? Hours of work are gone. I'll never finish in time."

Lanie glanced over at her cousin, who was still distracted. "It should have an auto-recovery file, but the computer might have stored it in a different folder. You pulled it out of the cloud, right? Check your documents and desktop. Or better yet, do a search of your entire computer with the first part of the name of the file. Maybe that will pull it up."

"Good idea."

"That's why I get paid the big bucks," she teased, although she was secretly flipping out. If the file was really gone, she would either have to accept that the report wouldn't be turned in on time or tell Britt she had to leave so she could help Stephanie. A voice in her head told her there was no shame if they couldn't get the report done on time. It was an unreasonable request, purposely set up to test

Lanie. But she was too stubborn to let Eve win, even though Stephanie was paying the price.

"Steph," she said, trying to keep the defeat out of her voice. "It's okay. Eve purposely set us up to fail, so maybe we should just throw in the towel. At least we tried."

"I found it!" Stephanie squealed in her ear. "It was on my desktop."

"Oh, thank God." Lanie sighed and rested her forehead on Tyler's chest. "But that doesn't change what I said earlier. She can't assume we don't have a life and assign unrealistic deadlines."

"But we don't have a life," Stephanie said in a much more chipper tone than before. The two of them had joked endlessly about the fact that their career was their life, but tonight it seemed totally pathetic.

"Maybe it's time we did."

"Lanie!" Brittany called out, and Tyler grabbed her arm.

She glanced up, realizing that not only had she rested her head against his chest, but the rest of her body was pressed against him.

"I'll come by the office when I'm done," she said as she hung up.

Lanie spun around to face her irate cousin.

"Seriously, Lanie. It's a Saturday night. Can't you let your job go for *just one night*?"

"It's my fault," Tyler said, taking the phone from Lanie and putting it back into his pocket as he walked toward Britt. "I asked her to make a call for me."

Brittany put her hands on her hips and gave him a pointed look, clearly not buying it. "Right..." She turned to Lanie. "Who did you call?"

"Um..." Who *did* she call? "Are you really going to invade Tyler's privacy like that?"

"Lanie."

Lanie cast a glance at Tyler, who made a gesture to his head. But she blurted out, "I was calling his date."

"What?" Brittany asked in shock.

Tyler's eyes widened, and Celesta looked upset. *That* was interesting.

"Yeah. I was calling his date...because of his head. He can't meet her at the bar for drinks because he has to go get stitches."

Tyler looked like he was enjoying this too much.

Brittany's eyes narrowed. "So why did *you* call her?"

Lanie glanced over at Tyler, then her cousin. "He said she'd never believe him if he called, so since I was the one to maim him, I thought that I should call and cover his ass."

"And did it work?"

Lanie released a short laugh. "What do you think? She thinks he's spending the night with me and trying to get out of their date."

Britt swung her gaze from Lanie to Tyler, then back again. "I don't believe it for a second. You're having Lanie cancel the first date you've had since April?" she asked in disbelief.

And that was even more interesting. One, how was Britt so familiar with Tyler's dating life? And two, Lanie had seriously misread Tyler as a womanizer. No self-respecting player would have gone five months without sleeping with a woman, let alone a date.

"Britt," Tyler said in a tight voice. "Believe it or not, I don't clear my social life with you."

Britt wasn't buying it. She turned back to Lanie. "What was her name? Both of you say it at the same time."

This was ridiculous. Lanie was a grown woman. Why

was she having to justify a freaking phone call? But damned if she didn't still want to salvage this.

Tyler stood behind Britt and he mouthed something she couldn't make out. Something with an M, and then drawn out. Marshmallow?

Seriously? He was naming his fake girlfriend Marshmallow?

"Marshmallow," Lanie said.

"Marsha," Tyler said.

Oh, crap.

Brittany narrowed her gaze. "You called his girlfriend *Marshmallow*?"

Lanie waved her hand in dismissal. "It's a long, painful story I was forced to listen to while you were hamming it up with your fiancé."

Celesta shot her a look of disbelief. "It's the least you could do, after scarring him for life."

"I didn't scar him for life!" Lanie shouted, clenching her fists at her sides, starting to get ticked off. She was already dealing with her bitchy boss, and now she was having to defend a phone call that could have saved her job, temporarily at least. But she was also wrestling with the guilt that she likely *had* scarred Tyler for life.

Tyler stepped between them, holding up his hands. "Ladies, ladies. I'm fine. It's not that bad, and even if it does scar, it will only add to my rugged charm."

Celesta stared up at him like he was a martyr calmly accepting his fate of being burned at the stake.

Lanie just rolled her eyes. "We'd probably better finish this up. You're losing the light."

"She's right," the photographer said. "We have a half hour, tops."

"Then let's get started," Holly said with a plastered-on

smile. "We're feeling good about the photos we've gotten and we're ready to move on to some more fun shots."

Tension hung in the air as Holly and the photographer started setting them up, but after a few photos, everyone seemed to relax, including Lanie. Some of the goofy ideas the women suggested were fun.

Holly instructed all the bridesmaids to stand in a line, then positioned the groomsmen behind them before she instructed each couple to hold a different pose.

"Tyler," Holly said, standing in front of the pair, "I want you to put your hand on Lanie's side. And Lanie, you lean your head to the opposite side, exposing the side of your neck, then Tyler, you lean in to her ear, like you're whispering a secret."

His hand settled on her hip in a possessive hold, and he pulled her back to his chest. "Like this?"

Lanie fought to catch her breath as an electric spark jolted through her body, a blaze of want following in its wake.

"Perfect," Holly said, oblivious to Lanie's dilemma. "But Laney, tilt your head and let Tyler tell you his secret."

Lanie felt like a fool as she complied, both because she was sure she looked ridiculous, and she was insanely turned on by just his hand on her hip and his hard chest pressed against her back.

He lowered his mouth to her ear and whispered in a seductive voice, "You have a *very* sexy ass."

His statement caught her off guard, and she whipped around to face him, but the back of her head hit him squarely in the chin.

He dropped his hold on her and put his hand to his chin, shaking his head cautiously as he stepped away from her.

"Oh my God! Are you okay?" she asked, trying to ignore the throbbing in the back of her head.

"Why is she paired with him?" Celesta demanded in outrage. "It's like she has some personal vendetta against him! Put me with Tyler and I promise not to hurt him."

Alvin shook his head frantically, his eyes round with fear. "No. I don't want to be paired with her."

But a slow smile spread across Rowdy's face. "I'd be willing to take on Black Widow."

"Black Widow?" Lanie asked in disbelief.

Holly released a sigh of frustration. "You're not switching!" She turned to Lanie. "Can you please try to stop disfiguring the groomsman? We need his pretty face for the photos."

"Hey," Tyler said, still rubbing his chin. "I object to the word *disfigured*."

Lanie started to protest, but fell silent when Tyler's arm slid around her waist and tugged her hip to his. "I committed to being Lanie's partner 'til death do us part, or the wedding, whichever comes first. I'll just brush up on some self-defense moves before our next session." Then he winked and gave her a sexy grin. And damned if she didn't melt a little.

"Okay," Holly said. "I know we're all hot and a little cranky, but we only have a few more photos and then we're done. So just hang in there with me." She glanced over at Tyler. "Tyler? You good?"

"Great," he said without sarcasm, and Lanie had to wonder why he was taking all of this so well. She'd dated a couple of guys who would have lost their shit over the shoe incident.

Tyler leaned in to Lanie's ear and whispered, "You're cute when you get pissed."

"I'm not cute," she said. "*Cute* is for little girls, and I am definitely *not* a little girl."

He stepped closer, close enough for her to see the red welt rising on his chin. "No," he said in a husky tone, low enough so that only the two of them could hear. "You are definitely all woman."

Lanie's body flushed, and she stood frozen in place by his mesmerizing eyes. Crap, this man was dangerous.

He grabbed her waist and spun her around, steering her to their spot. "We need to practice our pose."

Her heart rate sped up at his touch. "Aren't you afraid of physical injury?"

His hand rested on her hip again, and his mouth lowered to her ear. "I'll take my chances."

His warm breath tickled her neck, and a shiver ran down her spine, and she felt her resolve weakening.

She was lost in the moment, about to do something stupid like kiss him, when she heard a shriek and jolted upright.

Celesta stomped her foot. "This is impossible!"

"Let me explain it one more time," Holly said in a controlled voice, cluing in everyone but Celesta to the fact that she was about at her wit's end.

Holly wanted Celesta to stand in front of Alvin, then have the boy dip Celesta backward and to the side, while Celesta kicked up a foot.

"Now try it again," Holly said.

The scrawny teen struggled to hold Celesta upright in their practice of the pose.

Celesta jerked out of his hold. "I need a new partner! I need Tyler!"

Holly's mouth pinched, and Kevin, who had been standing in the background, took a few steps forward. "Just switch the poses. Have Tyler and Lanie try it, and Celesta and Alvin do the other."

"What?" Celesta shrieked.

"Sure," Tyler said, then wrapped his arm around Lanie's back and dipped her backward. He grinned down at her. "You're supposed to kick up your foot, but I humbly request you keep it away from my groin."

The group chuckled, and Lanie felt herself flush with embarrassment this time.

"Perfect," Holly said after Lanie complied.

Tyler set her upright, and Holly moved on to Britt and Randy's pose, but Tyler's hands lingered on her hips. She should shrug him off—it was pretty obvious this wasn't a casual pose—but she couldn't bring herself to do it. His touch felt right.

He leaned close to her ear. "You just got three calls in a row."

Like a bucket of cold water, that brought her back to reality. Stephanie. "Crap."

"It's obvious that you're dealing with something that needs your attention. I can be the bad guy and end this thing if you want."

She glanced back over her shoulder at him. "Why?"

"Why end it? Maybe it's not all about you, killer. Maybe I'm dying from a head wound."

"*Killer?*"

He winked. "You *did* try to kill me... twice."

She rolled her eyes. "If I'd tried to kill you, you'd be dead. Do. Or do not. There is no try."

Appreciation filled his eyes. "You quote *Star Wars.*"

"*Return of the Jedi*, to be more precise."

Chapter Ten

⟋

At nine thirty, Lanie and Stephanie sat at a table for two in a crowded bar on the Plaza. Lanie couldn't help wishing she'd just gone home. It had been a stressful day and evening, and the chaos of the bar scene was the last thing she needed, but Stephanie had insisted and Lanie couldn't tell her no after her assistant gone above and beyond to cover her ass the last couple of days.

Lanie lifted her vodka tonic and clicked it into Stephanie's cosmo. "To kick-ass women getting shit done."

"Hear, hear," Stephanie said with a huge grin.

Lanie had been like twenty-seven-year-old Stephanie once, she thought, full of energy and ready to take on the world. But she was only thirty-two years old, for God's sake. She was too young to be so jaded.

"You're brilliant," Stephanie said. "FaceTiming Eve at eight forty-five to personally walk her through the report, line by line, was a nice touch." She laughed. "Especially when you pointed out that, given how important it must be—

since she needed it at an unusual time in the middle of the weekend—you thought it best to walk her through it so there weren't any questions."

Lanie's mouth lifted into a wry grin. "I can be a bitch when I need to be."

"I still say you should have worn your purple bridesmaid dress during the call."

"Nah." Lanie laughed. "It would have been overkill." It had been a damn good thing that she'd had a spare skirt and blouse at the office in case of disaster. She glanced down at the grass-stained lilac pumps. Too bad she'd never foreseen needing shoes.

Stephanie clicked her glass into Lanie's. "To being bitches."

"Damn straight," Lanie said before she took a sip. But she'd realized something else during that call. She didn't want to work for people who didn't value her opinion and her expertise. She was going to turn in her notice.

A wave of terror had washed through her, but a wave of excitement quickly followed. She was going to change careers.

But how was she going to tell Stephanie?

"So how did the photo shoot go?"

Tyler's profusely bleeding forehead came to mind, then the way he'd set her body on fire followed quickly after.

"Oh!" Steph exclaimed in excitement. "There's a story behind that look, and I want to hear it."

Stephanie knew Lanie's modus operandi when it came to dating, so she wouldn't be all that surprised if Lanie was interested in a sexy groomsman. Since she and Lanie rarely spent more than six months in any location, a serious relationship was pretty much off the table. A year ago, Steph had fallen in love in San Francisco. But she'd quickly gotten her heart broken when her boyfriend had insisted she quit her job when it came time to for her to move on to Seattle. It had been a tough choice, but Steph had chosen the job.

For Lanie it was never a choice. She *always* chose the job. Even before she said hello to the guy. But she wondered if she was being too black-and-white. From what she could see, Randy was a great guy who loved and worshipped Brittany. Even as cynical as Lanie was, she knew there were good men still out there. Maybe when the dust settled with her career, she should consider looking for one.

Steph leaned back in her seat and crossed her legs. Her eyes lit up with excitement. "I want all the details."

"About?"

"That look. The guy who incited it."

Lanie told her about Celesta and the poses, carefully skirting any mention of Tyler.

Stephanie shook her head. "You're holding out on me."

"What are you talking about?"

"The guy who put that look on your face...I want to know about *him*."

Fighting a grin, she took a sip of her drink. "There's not much to tell. I scarred him for life. It doesn't get much better than that."

"I know you can be *intimidating*..."

"No, Steph, I mean a *literal* scar. On his face." She pointed to her own forehead. "I took your advice and drank before I went, but I drank straight from the bottle, and then Aiden called and I got distracted while I was searching my apartment for these damn shoes—bottle in hand—and by the time I'd found them, I'd almost drunk the entire thing."

"Oh my God! You drank an entire bottle of wine?"

"No." She shook her head with a frown. "Just half a bottle. And when I got there, I struggled to walk across the lawn in my three-inch heels—"

"I'm sure the fact you were drunk didn't help."

"I was holding my own—until my heel sank in the dirt. I stumbled, and when I righted myself, I kicked off my shoes, and one of them hit a groomsman in the forehead."

Stephanie burst out laughing. "Are you serious?"

"The wedding planner and her husband looked him over, and the husband patched him up with butterflies to get him through the photo shoot, but then he was going to the ER for stitches."

"You're *kidding*."

"I wish to God I was."

"But what about the photos? Didn't the bandages show?"

Lanie frowned. "The wedding planner said the photographer could Photoshop them out."

A grin spread across Stephanie's face. "So you like this guy?"

"The wedding planner's husband?" She shrugged, and her mouth lifted with a mischievous grin. "He seems okay. They make an attractive couple."

"Ha, ha," Stephanie teased. "You *do* realize the less you reveal, the more curious I become. Not because I'm desperate for details—"

"*There's* a first," Lanie interrupted with a laugh.

"But because the fact you're *not* sharing is very telling," Stephanie continued. "Guys never get under your skin. But then, I guess you did put a gash in his."

"Very funny."

"So why the hesitation? Oh! There's something wrong with him." Stephanie's eyes widened. "He's *married*."

"What? No!"

"Then he's sixty years old and rich." She grinned. "I

always knew you were a gold digger underneath that feminist exterior."

"He's not old."

"Homeless?" Stephanie tilted her head. "I can do this all day."

"You're acting like a five-year-old."

"He's a polygamist."

"Okay, okay." Lanie downed the rest of her drink. "He's...funny. And he's..." She shrugged, trying to look nonchalant. "Sexy."

"Funny looking, or he has a sense of humor?"

Fighting a grin, Lanie pretended to be offended.

"Sorry. Couldn't resist. But if he's sexy and has a sense of humor, I don't see a problem." Then she added, "Unless he's one of those practical joke guys."

"Not that I know of."

"Again, I fail to see the problem."

"He's Britt and Randy's friend. And I've told you that she likes to play matchmaker. If we started something, and she found out...she would be ruthless."

Stephanie seemed to give it some consideration. "I can see how that could be a problem. But what about seeing him on the sly?"

"Trust me, I've considered that."

"Is he scared off because you injured him?"

"He doesn't seem to be, which should be a warning sign. Any sane man would run."

Stephanie shrugged. "Sanity's overrated." She bit her lower lip, then said, "I bet the problem is that you're rusty. It's been over a year, but the longer you wait, the harder it will be to hop back on and *ride* that horse."

Grinning, Lanie shook her head, but she couldn't help thinking Stephanie was on to something. Lanie was just off her game. "Okay. The next time I see him, I'm going to invite him over to my apartment."

"That's right. Hop back on."

This conversation was making her squirm. Lanie finished off her glass. "I'm going to get another drink. Do you want another?"

Stephanie lifted her half-full glass. "No. I'm good."

Lanie pushed her way through the crowed to get to the bar. The noise and the chaos were beginning to give her a headache, and she wondered how long Stephanie needed to hang out before she was ready to call it a night. She ordered a vodka tonic then scanned the room, envious of the tables full of people having fun. How long had it been since she'd hung out in a bar with friends who didn't include business associates?

The bartender placed her drink in front of her. "Eight dollars."

She started to tell him to put it on her tab, but a man slid up to the bar next to her and said in a deep voice, "I've got it. And I'll take another Boulevard IPA. Put them both on my tab."

"That's not necess—" she said as she spun to face him, then gasped.

Tyler.

It was time to get back on that horse.

Chapter Eleven

Hey," she said with a grin that lit up her brown eyes.

She was gorgeous. He'd dated a long string of beautiful women, but none had intrigued him like Lanie. Maybe his five months of abstinence were getting to him. If he was going to move back into dating, Lanie was definitely the woman to start with.

Her gaze drifted up to the bandage on his forehead. "Did you go to the ER?"

"Three stitches."

She grimaced. "Sorry."

He laughed. "Hey, it's not every day I get attacked by a shoe. Great war story. Kevin did two tours in Afghanistan, so I need all the help I can get." He winked. "But he got married this summer, so now I don't have to worry about the competition."

"For what it's worth," she said, running her index finger up and down her glass as she looked up at him with a smile, "you were doing just fine before the war wound."

His gaze drifted to her finger. Jesus. He was getting turned on just watching her rub the condensation from her drink. Then he focused his attention on her mouth. He'd had a few fantasies about that mouth after watching her drink from the beer bottle in the garage.

Down, boy. If he came on too strong, he was going to scare her off. And he definitely didn't want to scare her off. "Did you get your business taken care of?"

"I did, thanks to you. You're still wearing your tux," she said in a sultry voice, setting her glass on the bar and giving his tie a tug. "It looks good on you. I particularly like the half-knotted-tie thing you've got going on."

"And you changed." Tyler's gaze drifted from her face down to her body. Her silky blue blouse clung to her generous breasts, and the gray skirt hugged her hips in all the right places. She looked better suited for a board meeting than a Saturday night at a bar. A grin tugged at his lips when he saw her purple bridesmaid shoes at the end of her long, sexy legs. "But I see you're still wearing your weapons."

She laughed and leaned her hip into the bar. "A girl should always be prepared to defend herself from predators."

"Do you have any predators on the radar?"

She picked up her glass, and her eyes twinkled. "The jury's still out."

The bartender brought his beer, and he picked up the bottle and took a long pull. Other than the night in the garage, he hadn't had this much fun with a woman in ages.

"So who are you here with tonight?" she asked. "Your girlfriend Marshmallow?"

He rested his elbow on the counter. "Nah, you blew my night with Marshmallow. She thinks I'm spending the night with you."

"Is that so...?" Her grin suggested she had a secret.

Lust flooded his veins and shot straight to his groin. *Jesus*, he wanted her.

"So you're just out trolling the bars?" she teased.

"I'm here with friends. What about you?"

"My assistant." She lifted one shoulder into a half shrug. "But we're friends too."

"What do you do?" he asked. "I think I remember Britt saying you travel with your job."

She hesitated, and her smile wavered for a moment. "That's right. I'm a retail time management consultant. What about you?"

"An attorney, but we're a dime a dozen." He leaned closer to her. "I've never met a time management consultant before. Tell me how that works. People pay you to come in and evaluate their business?"

She took a sip of her drink. "I've had enough business talk today. I'd rather talk about you. Where are these friends you're with?" She glanced around the bar, then grinned when she spotted Kevin at a table across the room.

Tyler wasn't surprised Matt and Kevin were watching with interest. He hadn't said a word when he'd seen Lanie at the bar. He'd just taken off and headed straight for her.

Wearing a grin, she waved at them, and they waved back, Matt with a look of confusion that faded as Kevin said something to him.

"I figured out that you knew Kevin at the photo shoot," she said. "But who's the other guy?"

"Matt. The three of us have been best friends since we were kids."

She grinned. "That's cute."

"Cute?" he asked with a chuckle. "*Cute* is for little boys and I'm *definitely* not a little boy."

Her voice turned husky. "No. You definitely aren't."

His hand was itching to touch her, but he told himself to let her take the lead.

She glanced over at his table. The amusement left her eyes, and her smile softened. "I think it's amazing that you guys are still close. Brittany and I used to be best friends, until I moved away." When she saw the questioning look on his face, she added, "I grew up in Lee's Summit, before I left and went to school out east—Columbia University—and then I got a job and got busy..." She looked down, and her finger drew a line through the condensation on her glass, then she shrugged and glanced back up at him. "You know the story."

"Kevin left after college and joined the Marines. He drifted from us for a while, but then he came back home this summer. You're here now. It's not too late."

A sly grin spread across her face. "I'm only here for another month, and then it's time to move on to the next city. Unencumbered."

"And where's that?"

She lifted the glass. "Not sure yet." Then she took a drink.

He thought that was unusual, but she didn't seem concerned. But the way she'd looked up at him when she'd said she was only here for a month and was leaving unencumbered was definitely a signal that she had no expectations.

Could she be any more perfect?

He was about to ask her how long she'd been back in Kansas City when someone bumped into his side.

"*Tyler Norris?*" a woman squealed. "Is that you?"

"*Fuck,*" he cursed under his breath. *Nina.*

Lanie's eyebrows rose, and she looked amused as she turned to face the woman next to him.

He had to get her to leave without creating an incident.

"You're not supposed to be here, Nina," Tyler said. "In fact, you're supposed to be fifty feet away."

The perky blonde tossed her hair over her shoulder. "It's a free country, Tyler."

"Actually, Nina, it's *not* when you have a *restraining order*."

Nina gave him a sweet smile. "Can't we put all of this misunderstanding behind us and start over?"

"Nina," he groaned. While she really was harmless, she was like a cockroach—impossible to get rid of.

Lanie turned to face Nina and wrapped her hand around Tyler's bicep, leaning into him. "Tyler's currently not on the market."

Nina's face hardened. "And who are *you*?"

"Tyler's girlfriend."

Nina started to laugh and cast a quick glance to Tyler. "Tyler doesn't do girlfriends."

Tyler slipped an arm around Lanie's back, and snugged her against his side. "I do now. I guess I was just looking for the right woman."

Lanie cupped the side of his face and turned him to face her, then her lips covered his, soft and gentle. Although she took him by surprise, it took him less than a second to catch up. He turned so that she fit between his spread legs, and he slipped his arm behind her back, pulling her close as he took over. Then he remembered who was watching.

Shit.

He kept his arm around Lanie's back and turned to face his crazy ex. "Thanks for coming over to say hi, Nina, but we'd like to get back to our date."

Tears welled in Nina's eyes, and she turned and ran out the door. Two women who must have been her friends quickly followed behind her.

"A restraining order?" Lanie asked. Tyler took it as a good sign that Lanie was still in his embrace and making no effort to get away.

"We dated. Last spring." He tilted his head, trying to downplay the incident. "Things got a little intense on her end, and I had to have the court intervene." He knew he should tell her more, but the truth would probably fuck with her head, and he hadn't missed her surprise earlier when Britt had announced that he hadn't dated in five months. After that kiss, he definitely didn't want to scare her off.

Brittany be damned.

She released a soft laugh. "You make it sound like it happens all the time. Does it?"

"No. And I haven't seen her since last April."

She lifted an eyebrow. "In court, I presume." She studied him for a moment, then took a step back. "It's been a long day, and I think I'm ready to call it a night."

Shit. Maybe he could still salvage this. "Lanie—"

"Will you take me home? You can get the jacket and tie you loaned me."

That was the last thing he'd expected. A grin spread across his face. "It depends. Do I need to worry about you disfiguring me again?"

Her eyes danced. "No promises."

"Then I guess I'll take my chances."

"Good answer." She leaned forward and gave him a soft, lingering kiss. "I have to get my purse and tell Stephanie that I'm leaving. I'll be right back."

"Your assistant won't mind?"

A knowing grin spread across her face. "In this instance, no."

"Okay."

He watched the sway of her hips as she walked to a table in the back. He shifted to try to ease the throbbing in his pants.

"Earth to Norris."

Tyler turned to see Matt standing next to him. "Hey. You just saved me a walk to our table to tell you I'm leaving."

"With Lanie?"

Tyler looked at him in surprise.

"Kevin told me who she was. I also saw Nina."

"Yeah, but Nina left without any drama."

Matt looked uncomfortable. "Hey, I know this is the first woman you've been interested in since the whole Nina thing, but she's Brittany's cousin. Maybe you should stop and think that one through. What happens when it all crashes and burns?"

"Who says it's going to crash and burn?"

"It always crashes and burns, Ty," he said without malice.

Matt had a point. Matt had seen it all—the good, the bad, and even the ugly last spring.

"Look," Tyler said. He wanted this too much to admit there might be a problem. "Lanie's short term. *She* made that clear. She's here for a month and then she's moving on to the next job. *Unencumbered.* Her word."

"Believe it or not, I'm worried about *you*."

Tyler started to laugh, then realized Matt was serious. "Me? What the hell are you talking about?"

But Lanie was walking up to them with her purse hanging from her arm.

"Everything good with your friend?" Tyler asked.

"She's summoning an Uber even as we speak." She smiled up at Matt. "Hi, you must be Tyler's best friend."

"Lanie," Tyler said as he slapped a hand on his friend's shoulder. "This is Matt. And he knows we're leaving." He stepped away from the bar, wrapped an arm around her lower back, and ushered her toward the door.

"Bye, Matt," Lanie called over her shoulder, then glanced up at Tyler with a grin. "What's the hurry? Worried I'll change my mind?"

He stopped on the sidewalk and turned toward her, keeping his hand at the small of her back. Her breasts pressed against his chest, and a jolt of electricity shot straight to his crotch. "Should I be?"

She grinned, looking mischievous. "What's life without a little mystery?" She pressed a lingering kiss to his lips, then leaned back and smiled. "Take me home, Tyler."

Chapter Twelve

They'd been silent during the short drive to her apartment, but when he parked in the small lot behind her building, he was dying to touch her—yet he was still determined to let her take the lead.

By the time he'd gotten out of the car, she was already halfway up the sidewalk to the door. She punched in a key code to enter the building and opened the door.

He wasn't sure if she was in a hurry or if she was testing him, but he followed her into the small entry and watched her push the button for the elevator. When the door opened, he snagged her hand and tugged her inside. He pressed her back against the elevator wall and kissed her, his mouth devouring hers. So much for letting her take the lead.

She clung to him, kissing him back with a raw hunger that excited him more. He tried to put his leg between hers, but her tight skirt kept her legs from spreading far enough apart.

When he lifted his head, she stared up at him, dazed and breathless.

It was then that he realized that even though the elevator doors had closed, they were still on the ground floor. "What floor?"

She blinked. "Fifth."

He leaned to the side and pressed the five button, then kissed her again until the door dinged.

He took a step back, thinking they were on her floor, but the three light was illuminated over the open doors. An elderly woman stood outside the elevator, her mouth parted. Then she grinned and stepped inside. "Don't stop on my account."

A playful look filled Lanie's eyes, and she buried her face into his chest as she tried to hide her giggles.

The door closed, and they stood in an awkward silence. Tyler slipped his arm around her back and held her close. While he'd missed holding a woman, Lanie felt different. There was no denying that she was beautiful. But he realized there was more to her appeal than just her physical beauty. She was smart, and witty and driven, and confident. While a lot of men would have found her confidence intimidating, it only turned him on more. He found the whole package irresistible.

The door opened again, this time on the fifth floor. Tyler practically pushed Lanie out of the elevator and into the hall.

She grabbed his hand and tugged him to the left. "I'm in 505." They stopped in front of her door, and she searched her purse. "Oh, shit."

He froze. "What's wrong?"

Pushing out a sigh, she looked up at him with a hopeful gaze. "How good are you at picking locks?"

He laughed and ran his hand over his head. "I'm not sure there's a right way to answer that."

She pressed her hand to her temple. "I was running late when I left for the photo shoot—obviously—and I must have left my keys on my kitchen counter." She dropped her hand and looked up at him. "I can call a locksmith, but I'd rather not wait. If you can unlock my door...you can get your jacket."

He considered suggesting they go to his place, which was less than five minutes away, but then she'd still have to deal with unlocking her door. But more important, she might change her mind. And he *really* didn't want her to change her mind. He'd kick the door open if he had to. "I'm game."

She stepped out of her shoes and squatted to pick them up, then glanced up and saw his amused grin.

"Is this the part where you threaten bodily harm if I don't open your door?" He flicked a finger toward the heels dangling from her fingers. "Using intimidation tactics?"

Laughing, she gave him a saucy grin. "Will that give you more incentive to try?"

He stepped closer and pressed a kiss to her neck below her ear. His hand rested on her waist and slowly skimmed up her side, stopping just below her breast. He was aching to touch her, but he wasn't sure molesting her in the hallway was a great idea. "I usually respond better to positive reinforcement."

"I'll keep that in mind for future reference," she said in a breathless voice.

He took the shoes from her hand as he took a step back and tossed them into the corner of the hall. "I feel better if you're disarmed."

She laughed, and he was even more eager to get that damn door open.

She gestured toward the doorknob. "So you have experience picking locks?"

"I plead the fifth." He'd picked a few locks in his youth, not for burglaries, but all for mischievous purposes. "Do you have any hairpins?"

"Thanks to Britt's trial hair appointments, you're in luck." She dug into her purse and produced several.

Taking two from her open palm, he knelt in front of her doorknob. "Then let's give it a try." It only took a few seconds before he had the door unlocked and open.

"Wow," she said with a chuckle. "I'm not sure whether to be impressed or terrified."

He got to his feet and handed her the bent pins. "Would it help if I told you that I only use my devious powers for good?"

She took a step backward and grinned. "I'd rather you use them for wicked."

A bolt of lust shot through him as she turned and walked into the dimly lit apartment. He followed her inside, his gaze falling to her ass again. His mind ran wild as he imagined what she might be wearing underneath that tight skirt.

"Do you want a glass of wine?" she asked as she walked into the small kitchen of the open layout space. Her apartment was small and tastefully decorated. It was open concept, with the living room and tiny kitchen occupying a small space. A short hall looked like it led to a bathroom and bedroom. A lamp sat on an end table in the living room, illuminating the space in a low light.

Lanie lifted a wine bottle out of the sink, then tossed into a nearby trash can. She opened the refrigerator and looked inside, then quickly closed the door. "I'm out of wine. I have some vodka, but nothing to mix with it."

He took several slow steps toward her. "I'm not feeling very thirsty."

"Oh?" she asked with a grin. "Are you hungry?"

"Very."

"I don't have any food."

"It's not food I'm hungry for."

*   *   *

When he pulled her to his chest, she melted into him as he kissed her with an intensity that weakened her knees. But she was hungry for him too.

One of his hands grabbed her ass and pulled her even tighter against him. She rested her hands on his shirt, feeling his rippled chest underneath her fingertips. His mouth skimmed down her neck, nipping at the tender skin, while his hand traced the side of her breast, then made slow circles around her nipple over her silky blouse.

"Is your plan to drive me crazy before you even get my clothes off?" she asked breathlessly. "Because it's working."

He lifted his head and grinned.

"Don't look so pleased with yourself," she teased. "I'm waiting to see how the rest of this goes before I offer a critique."

He laughed and then brushed his thumb over her nipple. She arched her back as she squirmed, and his grin spread. "How am I doing so far?"

"Still reserving judgment."

"Tough sell."

His mouth covered hers again, his tongue parting her lips and searching her mouth.

She released a soft moan, and he started to work on the top button of her blouse while he continued to kiss her, but then seconds later, he lifted his head and ripped her shirt open.

She laughed. "Seriously. *Again?*"

"I'll buy you a new shirt," he said in a husky voice that made her shiver as he focused on her white lacy bra. "I'll buy you a truckload of shirts." He pulled her shirt free from the waistband of her skirt, then rested his hands on her waist.

The touch of his hands on her bare skin sent a wave of heat through her body. "Patience is a virtue," she said breathlessly.

His hands skimmed up her sides. He slowly pushed the blouse off her shoulders, letting the fabric fall down her arms to the floor. He lifted his gaze to hers, his mouth twisting into a seductive smile. "I have to warn you, Lanie. I'm not feeling very virtuous."

An ache burned low in her pelvis. "Neither am I."

Taking a step back, she grabbed his hand and tugged him to her bedroom. She flipped a switch on the wall, turning on a bedside lamp. She turned toward him, looking up into his lust-filled eyes.

She started to unknot his tie, but he brushed her hand away and pulled it over his head, then tossed it on the floor.

She released a soft laugh.

His jacket was next, and he tossed it onto the chair in the corner, while she started to work on the buttons of his shirt.

He reached behind her and unfastened her skirt. A quick tug pulled it over her hips, and it fell to the ground at her bare feet.

His hands slid down her back and over the rise of her ass as she finished with the last button of his shirt and spread it open.

"You're too slow," he said with a grin as he started to undo his pants.

"I can't help it if you're a cheater."

He stepped out of his shoes, then let his pants drop to the floor. She barely had time to study the impressive bulge in his briefs before he pushed her onto the bed.

Holding her arms over her head, he leaned over her, kissing her as though he had all the time in the world. His thumb made lazy brushstrokes across her cheeks and down her neck, tracing her exposed collarbone.

"I thought you were in a hurry," she said as his mouth lowered to her neck, nipping and sucking across her collarbone down to the rise of her breast.

"I changed my mind," he murmured against her skin. "I want to taste *all* of you." His hand cupped her other breast, the weight filling his hand. His mouth made its way to her nipple, licking the tip through the lace as his thumb teased her other breast.

Lanie gasped, and Tyler murmured his approval as he reached behind her and unhooked her bra, then pulled it free and tossed it to the floor. His lips skimmed across her breast before he sucked her nipple into his mouth. Her pelvis lifted involuntarily, and his hand slipped under the band of her panties, then slid between her folds.

"God, Lanie. You're so wet."

Her response was a low moan.

His mouth skimmed down her abdomen, stopping at the edge of her panties. He rose to his knees and pulled her panties over her hips and down her legs. He lowered his mouth to her inner thigh as he spread her legs, then licked and sucked a path higher and higher toward her core. He buried his face between her legs as he pushed them wider, his tongue finding the spot that made her cry out this time.

A slow, burning ache filled her pelvis, the pressure building until he pushed her over the edge. She cried out and he kissed his way up her body, lingering over her breasts.

She pushed him up, then leaned to the side and opened her nightstand drawer. She pulled out a condom and ripped it open as he pulled off his briefs. She paused when she saw how large he was, and she flushed with excitement and anticipation.

A wicked gleam filled his eyes as she pushed him onto his back, and she grinned at him. She rolled the condom over his throbbing erection, then straddled his waist. She let her hands roam his body, studying him as she explored his arms and chest, then his hard abdomen. He watched her, cupping both breasts and brushing her nipples with the pads of his thumbs. The heat was building in her core.

"I want you, Lanie," his said in a groan. "*Now.*"

She lifted over him then slowly lowered onto his shaft as she stretched to take him in, letting him fill her. When she was fully seated, she leaned her head back and reveled in the sensation. She moaned, then whispered, "You feel so good."

She rose then slowly lowered herself again, taking him fully.

He sat up and pulled her legs around his back. His hands dug into her hips, and he began to move her, picking up the pace. She took over, mimicking his pace.

He captured the back of her head in his hand and kissed her hard, his mouth punishing as his tongue coaxed hers.

The pressure was building again, and she clung to his shoulders.

Tyler grunted, then still inside her, flipped her to her back.

She gasped, but it only turned her on more as he pinned her wrists over her head and slowly thrust inside her.

"God, Lanie," he forced through gritted teeth.

"How am I doing?" she teased, but her voice held a desperate sound that brought a satisfied look to his eyes.

"I'm reserving judgment," he grunted.

She wrapped her legs tighter around his waist, and he quickened the pace, leaning on his elbow as he grabbed her hip and pumped into her faster. He took her higher and higher until she reached the top and fell, calling out his name as she tightened around him. His grip on her ass tightened as he gave one last deep thrust, then buried his face in her neck.

They lay together for several seconds, catching their breath. Grinning, he lightly kissed her. "You are amazing."

"You're not so bad yourself."

He rolled to his side and draped his arm across her stomach, then leaned over and gave her a long lazy kiss. "You're beautiful."

She lay her head over his heart, feeling the rise and fall of his chest against her cheek. His arm curled around her, pulling her close, and she felt more relaxed than she had in forever. Her eyes drifted closed.

His lips brushed her forehead, and he shifted from underneath her, and then she realized she'd fallen asleep. She rolled to her side and watched him as he got out of bed and reached for his underwear on the floor.

"Sorry, I woke you," he said as he stepped into his briefs, then pulled on his pants. "Go back to sleep, and I'll let myself out."

She almost invited him to stay the night, then stopped herself. She rarely had men spend the night, and certainly not after the first time they'd slept together, but the bed felt strangely empty without him. "Don't be silly," she said, sitting up and leaning over to her dresser to pull out a long

T-shirt. She pulled it over her head while he slipped his arms into his sleeves and buttoned his shirt.

He sat on the bed and slipped on his shoes, then stood, pulling Lanie to her feet. He gave her a slow, lazy kiss, then lifted his head and grinned. "Thank you for an interesting night."

She reached up and touched the edge of his bandage. "Does it hurt very much?"

"Some," he admitted. "Which is partially why I got up. I need to take more ibuprofen."

Guilt washed through her. "I'm sorry."

A smile stretched his lips. "Strangely, I'm not." He grabbed his jacket off the chair, then walked toward her front door.

As he started to open the door, Lanie stopped him. "I guess I should have mentioned this earlier, but if it's okay with you, I'd like to keep this secret."

Surprise filled his eyes, then he grinned. "You want me to be your dirty little secret?"

She laughed. "Yes. That's exactly it." Standing on her tiptoes, she cupped his cheek and gave him a kiss. "No, it's because of Britt. If she found out we slept together, she'd be merciless with her matchmaking."

He nodded but sobered. "Yeah, you have a point." He slid an arm around the small of her back and pulled her flush against him, then kissed her senseless.

When he lifted his head, she realized she'd melted into him. She quickly dropped her hold on him before he thought she was one of those clingy-after-sex women.

He opened the door and walked into the hallway, then stopped and grinned. He picked up her lilac shoes in the corner and handed them to her, toes first. "Wear these wisely. With great power comes great responsibility."

She laughed as she took them. "I'll keep that in mind."

He walked backward down the hall, still watching her as he moved to the elevator and pushed the down button. The elevator dinged and opened, and he gave her a wave.

She leaned her temple into the door frame. "See you tomorrow night."

A smile covered his face. "I'm counting on it."

Chapter Thirteen

⌒

Tyler had picked his younger brother up around noon, and Eric hadn't said a word about Tyler's bandage. In fact, Eric hadn't said more than two words since he'd gotten into the car. But when they met their brother, Alex, outside the stadium, he commented on it right away.

"I'm not sure if anyone's told you this," Alex said, "but you're not supposed to shave your forehead."

Tyler grimaced. "Very funny."

After they went through the security checkpoint, Eric got ahead of them, and Tyler used it to his advantage to talk to Alex. "We're here to have fun. No lectures."

Alex gave him a look of disbelief. "Then what the hell's the point?"

Alex hadn't been happy that Principal Carter had called Tyler instead of him. Not surprisingly, they disagreed on the best way to handle the situation. Tyler thought Eric just needed to be reminded that he had brothers who cared about him. Alex thought he needed tough love. Apparently their father thought he didn't need to do anything. He couldn't even be bothered to join them for a baseball game.

"The point is, he's our brother and we've ignored him. You know Dad doesn't give him the time of day. So today we're just three brothers enjoying a ball game together and that's it. If you can't get on board, then go the hell home."

"What are you guys talking about?" Eric asked as they caught up to him.

"Nothing," Alex said, sounding grumpy. "Just Tyler bragging about some big case he won."

As they walked around the stadium toward their section, Tyler couldn't help thinking about Lanie. He'd actually been tempted to stay with her the night before, but he'd never been one to sleep at a woman's place. It got too personal that way. He couldn't help wondering if her reason for keeping their hookup a secret was genuine, but he had to admit it seemed reasonable. He could see Britt making a bigger deal of this than it actually was.

Alex continued his whining as they climbed the stairs to their nosebleed seats, high up in the upper deck behind third base. "Do they provide oxygen with these seats?"

"Yeah," Tyler said. "But only to people who can't afford to lose brain cells. They'll bring your mask first."

Eric shot him a grin behind Alex's back, and Tyler was filled with relief. So it had taken a jab at their brother to get that grin, but he'd take it.

The sun beat down on their section, and Tyler was thankful there had been a break in the heat. The temperature may have been cooler than the past week, but the tension between the three brothers was heating up.

They'd made it to the first half of the second inning before Alex got in his first quip. "Looks like Melton's pitching with as much effort as you put into your schoolwork, Eric."

"Alex," Tyler said in warning.

"What would you know about effort?" Eric demanded, leaning around Tyler to face down his brother. "You were born perfect, Alex. No effort required."

Tyler got to his feet. "I'm going to get some food. Eric, why don't you come with me?"

"Might as well," he muttered under his breath as he slid past Alex. "No sense watching Melton pitch. Since he's just like me, we know it's pointless to expect anything of him."

Tyler was pissed. When they got to the aisle, Eric headed down the stairs, and Tyler turned around and pointed his finger toward Alex in warning, mouthing, *Cut the shit!*

Eric was slow descending the steps, and his shoulders hunched in a defeated pose. Tyler wanted to knock Alex upside the head.

When they stood in the back of the line at the concession stand, Tyler said, "Alex has always been an ass. Don't let his Mr. Perfect persona fool you."

Eric's head jerked up in surprise.

Tyler smirked. "Don't look so shocked. Alex sees the world as black-and-white, and everyone has their role to play. According to Alex, I'm Peter Pan."

Eric shook his head, keeping his gaze down, but a grin tugged at his lips. "I'm not sure you could pull off the tights, dude."

Tyler burst out laughing, and Eric stood just a little bit straighter and looked just a little bit happier.

Tyler leaned his head closer to his brother's. "Once when the two of us were little, Alex decided he wanted to make a cake."

"Alex made *a cake*?"

"Oh, it gets better. Mom had made Mississippi Mud Cake, and Alex wanted to replicate it. Mom and Dad were

still at work, and Alex went out back and turned on the
hose, drenching Mom's flower garden. Next thing I knew,
the house smelled like burning dirt. He'd scooped the mud
into cake pans and put them in the oven at four hundred fifty
degrees. The house stunk for weeks."

"Did he get in trouble?"

"Nah," Tyler said. "But I got in trouble because I wasn't
watching him."

"Alex didn't get in trouble at all?"

"Nope."

"What happened to you?"

"I lost Sega privileges for a month."

"What? That's not right!"

Tyler shrugged. "I was supposed to be watching him. The
house could have burned down."

"How old were you?"

"Eight."

"Jesus. You were babysitting at eight? Isn't that, like, il-
legal?"

He'd told this story before—always for the laugh—but
the significance had never hit him until now. "Yeah, I guess
so," he said absently.

Now that he thought about it, his parents had always
forced him into a pseudo-parenting role long before he'd
been ready or even capable. He'd never been allowed to be
a kid, and there'd been days when he'd felt like he was suffocating. When he'd hit high school, he'd rebelled hardcore.
And then, in college, he'd gotten a taste of what real freedom
felt like—no responsibilities, no one depending on him to do
or be something he wasn't, and he'd never looked back.

That gave him pause. Maybe there was something to
Alex's Peter Pan theory after all. Tyler wasn't sure which
to be more shocked over: that he'd actually given serious

psychobabble consideration to his childhood or that Alex might actually be right about something.

Eric gave him a curious stare. "Dude, are you all right?"

"Yeah," Tyler said, trying to recover and not look like an idiot in front of his younger brother. Wasn't he supposed to be an example of having his shit together? So he hastily asked, "How's school going?

The smile on Eric's face fell, and defiance stiffened his jaw. "So that's what this is about. *I knew it*. This is just some trick to interrogate me."

Shit. Tyler ran his hand through his hair. "No. It's not. I swear." *Dammit*. "But you have to realize it's one of those conversational topics. How's your job? Nice weather we're having. How's school?"

"How about school sucks ass? Is that the answer you're looking for? Gee, it sure is a hot one today. Won any big lawsuits lately?"

"You don't want to talk about school?" he said. "That's fine. Give me a list of topics that we can and cannot discuss. I take it school is on the don't ask, don't tell list."

"How about we just stick to the list of things I've fucked up?" Eric asked in disgust. "That seems to be Alex's favorite."

"Language," Tyler barked, glancing at a little boy who was watching them from several feet behind them in line.

"See?" Eric said, his eyes glassy. "I can't even get my *shucks darn* list right."

Tyler let out a long breath. This wasn't going at all as he'd planned.

When they reached the counter, Tyler ordered a beer and a hot dog while Eric ordered some hot wings and a Coke. After they got their food, Tyler headed over to the condiment table to doctor up his hot dog.

"Eric," Tyler said, giving his full attention to the ketchup dispenser, "believe it or not, I want to be your friend."

"Yeah, I've noticed. You want to hang out with me all the time."

Fuck. The kid was right. "I've been a dick. I've got no excuse."

Eric grinned, but he continued to look down and started rubbing the tip of his sneaker on the concrete floor, bending back a loose piece of rubber.

Why was he wearing piece-of-shit shoes?

Upon further inspection, Tyler realized Eric's jeans were worn, and the T-shirt he was wearing had multiple tiny holes.

Sure, Eric was seventeen, but he still needed parenting, which included basic necessities like clothes and shoes.

"You ready?" Tyler asked, picking up his hot dog and beer, then heading the opposite direction from where they'd been seated.

"You're going the wrong way," Eric said.

Tyler turned around and took a few steps backward. "Am I?" Then he kept going, heading down the escalator.

"Tyler!" Eric called after him, walking down the escalator steps to catch up. "Where are you going?"

Tyler stopped outside the entrance to the lower section directly behind home plate. "Hold this," he said, pulling two tickets out of his pocket. "Let's go get our seats."

"But we already have seats," Eric said, following behind.

Tyler took his food from his brother, then headed down the stairs. He stopped in front of an usher and handed him the two tickets. While he waited for the usher to look over the tickets, he glanced up at the section where they'd left Alex. His brother could enjoy the nosebleed seats alone.

"Just down these stairs," the usher said.

Tyler turned back to face him, but as he did, he stopped, sure he'd seen Lanie walking with a guy. He did a double take and scanned the area, certain that he was losing his mind.

The usher handed him the tickets, and he and Eric walked down to the fifth row behind home plate. They maneuvered past several people before Tyler sat in one of four empty seats.

But Tyler kept thinking about Lanie. He was dying to see her tonight and hopefully convince her to let him come over again. He'd forgotten to get his jacket from her. He could always use that as an excuse.

Eric sat next to him, glancing up at the section they'd originally sat in. "What's going on?"

For a brief moment, Tyler thought he was talking about Lanie, then he realized Eric was talking about the seating change.

"*These* are our seats," Tyler said, taking a bite of his hot dog as he looked out at home plate. "The tickets belong to an attorney in my law firm. His uncle is one of the bosses, and sometimes they take clients to these games. They wouldn't let clients sit in the crap seats we were sitting in."

"So where did the other seats come from?"

"Oh, I got those for Alex," Tyler said with an evil grin.

"What?"

"That was to see if he could play nice. Since he couldn't, now he gets to sit in time-out. Once he learns to behave, he can come sit with the screw-ups."

Eric laughed. "He's going to kill you."

Tyler shrugged.

"Isn't he going to wonder where we went?"

He shrugged again, then started shouting at the Royals' outfielder, who missed a fly ball.

"Should we text him?"

Tyler looked his brother square in the eye. "That's up to you, Eric."

"Me?"

Tyler turned serious. "I invited *you* to this ball game. Alex is just along for the ride. I thought it might be fun to have all the brothers together, but this is about *you* and what *you* want. So you tell me, do we leave him sitting in the baking sun or do we let him come over to these choice seats?"

Eric seem to consider it for several seconds. "I feel kind of bad leaving him there. He's been kind of a dick lately, but he used to..." His voice trailed off, and he sounded embarrassed.

"Be there when I wasn't?" Tyler finished. "That's okay. It's true." He turned in his seat. "Let's you and me make a deal, okay? We only tell each other the truth. The world often doesn't want to hear the truth because it's hard, hard as hell, and they can't handle it. But we Norris guys can, and I respect you too much to lie to you. Deal?"

Eric studied him as though looking for signs that he was being tricked. Finally, he said, "Deal."

Tyler lifted the hand holding his beer. "I'd shake but my hand's a little full."

Eric shot a glance up at the section where they'd left Alex, still sitting all by himself.

Tyler set his beer in the cup holder and handed Eric his hot dog. "Don't look so guilty. I'll text him." He pulled out his phone, then sent Alex a text.

Look behind home plate.

"He's definitely going to kill you," Eric said as they waited for Alex to respond.

"He shouldn't have made fun of my shaving skills."

"What's under that bandage, anyway?" Eric asked.

"Three stitches."

Alex was watching the game, but then shoved his hand into his front pocket and pulled out his phone. His gaze turned toward them.

"Wave," Tyler said and started waving his arm in big sweeps.

Eric laughed and waved Tyler's hot dog over his head.

Alex held his arms wide as though saying *What the hell?*

Tyler pointed to Alex and then at the empty seat next to him.

Alex tapped on his phone, then held it to his ear, and Tyler wasn't surprised to feel his phone vibrate. "I'll be right back," he told Eric as he squeezed past the people in the seats toward the aisle. "I've got his ticket."

He was walking up the stairs when Alex answered.

"What the hell?" Alex demanded.

"Just shut up and listen. Eric and I are in our real seats. While I hoped we could have a good time, I had a feeling you'd act like a dick. So you're sitting up there until you can behave."

"Who the hell do you think you are, Tyler?"

"I'm an idiot who hasn't spent enough time with his brothers, especially his youngest. And while I probably deserve every dick move you want to throw at me, this is bigger than both of us. Eric needs us to be friends."

"You realize that's like asking for a unicorn to shit rainbows," Alex muttered.

"Then pretend. Eric's clothes look like they should have been thrown away last year, and his shoes are falling to pieces. Does Dad do *anything*?"

"He's tired," Alex said. "He's ready to be done raising kids."

"Well, tough fucking shit. He's still raising one. He can't

just check out because he's tired." His father had always been an ass, but this was inexcusable.

A loud cheer went through the stadium, and Tyler plugged his ear. "Eric needs us," he said when the crowd quieted. "Not to lecture. He needs someone to talk to. He needs to know we give a shit. Can you do that for him?"

There was no hesitation. "Yes. Of course I can do it. I *want* to do it."

"Then get your ass down here. I'll text you the section and meet you with the ticket."

He stood at the top of the section, waiting for Alex to come down, but a large group showed up, asking the usher for help. Tyler walked down several steps to make room for them on the landing, then turned around to watch for Eric. From his peripheral vision he saw a man in the row one up from him lean over to kiss a woman in a straw hat, and when the guy sat back in his seat, Tyler's mouth dropped open. Lanie.

Lanie was at the game on a date.

What the hell?

Chapter Fourteen

⌒

Lanie had hoped Aiden would change his mind about the baseball game, but he'd shown up at her apartment at noon dressed for the part.

"Why are you wearing a Royals shirt?" she asked after she'd given him a warm welcoming hug. "You're from Atlanta."

"Never hurts to wear the enemy colors when in enemy territory," he said with a grin. Then he handed her a shirt too. "Now, put this on."

She glanced down at the royal blue shirt with the Kansas City Royals emblem. "You're kidding me."

"When in Rome, Lane," he said. "Now, go change."

So she went to her room and changed from her cotton dress to the T-shirt and a pair of white shorts, but she insisted on bringing the straw hat to keep the sun off her face.

When she emerged from her bedroom, Aiden had found Tyler's jacket on a chair in her living room, and was holding it up with a look that suggested she was about to be interrogated. "Please tell me this means you're dating someone."

"Define dating," she said as she grabbed her keys off the kitchen counter and put them in her purse. She doubted Aiden had Tyler's lock-picking skills. "If you're going to make me go to this game, then let's go."

"You make it sound like a death sentence, and don't think I didn't miss your evasion of the question," Aiden said as he followed her down the hall to the elevator.

She groaned and pressed the down button. "There's a guy, but it's nothing serious. You know me, Aiden. I don't do serious."

The elevator opened and they got inside and pressed the button.

"But you've brought him home," Aiden said. "How well do you know him?"

She reached up and patted his cheek, smiling up at him. "I'm a big girl. I can take care of myself."

The elevator stopped on the third floor and the older woman from the night before got on. The silver-haired woman did a double take when she saw Aiden, then turned to Lanie and winked. "Why stick to one man? Good for you, honey."

Aiden gave Lanie a questioning look, but remained silent.

They made small talk all the way to the stadium, and Lanie took advantage of the fact that he'd known the full details of her career since she first accepted a position with Montgomery Enterprises, and told him everything about her current situation and that she was considering turning in her notice. He remained silent, offering no advice or insight, and hopped out of his car in the stadium parking lot. Even stranger, he evaded her questions about his job, which was a first. He loved talking about his work.

When they got inside the stadium, he insisted they have the full baseball experience and got them both hot dogs and beer, then led her to what she presumed were expensive seats since they were so close to the field and home plate.

She made it halfway through the second inning before she asked, "Are you going to tell me what in the hell is going on here?"

"What?" he asked, taking a big bite of hot dog.

"Aiden."

He finished chewing and chased it down with a gulp of beer. "I lost my job about five months ago."

Lanie gasped. "Why didn't you tell me?"

"Because I was figuring out my shit."

"You thought I'd interfere with that?"

"No…maybe?" Then he shook his head. "I knew I had to make the change on my own, so I didn't tell anyone until I'd made the transition."

"Where did you land?" she asked. "Are you still in Atlanta?" She grinned and gestured between their shirts. "Or is this your way of telling me you're moving to Kansas City?"

He laughed. "I'm still in Atlanta. I considered moving, but I have too many contacts there to throw them away."

"So who did you end up with?"

"Me," he said. "I opened up my own firm."

"You opened up your own advertising firm?" she asked in surprise.

"Yes, but it's more than that. We provide full support to small businesses and upstart companies, helping them with everything from finances to marketing to branding. Anything and everything to help them grow their business."

She squinted up at him. " 'We'? You have employees?"

"I have three so far. To offer so many services, I need to have people on my team who know what they're doing." He paused. "And that's why I'm here to recruit you."

"Me?"

"Hell, yeah, Lanie. You've opened how many stores, in how many cities, over the past seven years? You know about zoning, and permits, and hiring contractors, and a whole host of crap I don't even know about. You could be a consultant for retailers who are starting out or looking to expand their business."

She snorted. "People are going to pay for that?"

"They already are. I have five clients, and it's just the start. One of those clients needs exactly what you have to offer."

Dazed, she sat back in her seat. "Wow. This is unexpected."

"I know you, Lanie, you were born to be your own boss. And this opportunity would be just that. I'd be hands-off. Are you open to considering it?"

"Well, yeah..."

"Awesome! I thought I was going to have to give you the hard sell to make you jump ship. Thankfully, the hard work was already done for me. You're unhappy with your job, and you're looking for a change. This seems like divine intervention for both of us."

He definitely had a point. "Do you think it's a good idea for us to work together?" she asked. "Since we're friends?"

"I'll be focusing on branding and marketing, so I'm sure our work will overlap to some extent, but you would be autonomous. As long as you're bringing in clients who are paying their consultation fees, you can do whatever you like. You're answering to yourself."

This seemed too good to be true.

"I know a lot of this hinges on salary," Aiden said, talking over the rising cheers of the Royals fans when a batter hit a double. "And we can talk specifics after the game—salary, a bonus structure, benefits, a relocation package."

"A relocation package?" She shook her head. "You know I hardly have anything to relocate."

"I know, and I know you're getting tired of your nomadic life. This will give you the opportunity to finally put down roots." He smiled. "You can stop running, Lanie."

"Stop running? What does that mean?"

He gave her a sad smile. "We've known each for twelve years now. I know why you've liked moving around, but it sounds like you've finally decided maybe you've had enough."

She shook her head in confusion.

"Most people would hate your job. Little opportunity to make any kind of lasting relationships. Haven't you ever wondered why you're so good at it? But earlier you admitted that you're getting tired of it. That you want a personal life. Come to Atlanta. You'll already have a friend to get your personal life jump-started."

His words stung, but she had to acknowledge that he spoke the truth. She *had* been running, but she didn't know why. She needed to figure that out too.

"Don't give me an answer, right now," Aiden said. "I don't expect it, and I wouldn't trust it. I know you need time to analyze all the data, so after the game, we can go to an early dinner, and I'll crunch the numbers for you. Then I'll leave you alone to think it over."

"It's not like I have a string of job opportunities lined up, Aiden."

"You haven't even looked, and I promise you, I don't want you working with me out of desperation. It's only going to work if you really believe in what we're doing."

"I'm really flattered you thought of me. Came all the way here to recruit me." She grabbed his hand and squeezed. "Thanks, Aiden."

He leaned over and kissed her cheek. "Always, Lane."

But when Aiden sat back in his seat, Lanie was shocked to see Tyler less than four feet away. He stood on the steps, staring at her with a blank expression.

"Tyler," she gasped in surprise. "I didn't know you were coming to the game." She glanced around. "Are you here with Kevin and Matt?"

"No. I'm with my brothers."

"Oh." She smiled, trying to figure out why he was acting so aloof. But then, he was a player, even if he had just jumped back into the game. She was pretty sure being a player was like riding a bike. While she'd had no expectations after last night, she *had* hoped to see him again.

Aiden stood and reached out his hand. "Aiden Collins. Are you a friend of Lanie's?"

Tyler shot Lanie a strange look then took Aiden's hand. "Tyler Norris. We're in her cousin Britt's wedding together."

"I thought her cousin was getting married next month," Aiden said, and he sounded smug. As if he thought he'd caught Tyler in a lie.

Lanie stood, confused by the strange undercurrent rolling between the men. "Britt's making us take photos at several places before the wedding," she said, glancing up at Aiden. "Tyler and I are partners...in the wedding. He's a groomsman, and I'm a bridesmaid."

Aiden wrapped an arm around Lanie's shoulder and continued his stare-down with Tyler as he gestured to the bandage on his forehead. "Were you in an accident?"

A smile ghosted across Tyler's face. "I was attacked by a shoe."

"Must have been one hell of a fight. I hope you won."

"The jury's still out."

The silence hung between them until Aiden said, "Well, it was great to meet you, Tyler. We'll let you get back to your brothers."

"Yeah." His gaze to shifted Lanie, but she still couldn't read him.

"I'll see you in a few hours," she said. "Loose Park. Britt's already texted me half a dozen times with the address and reminders about what to wear."

"You know Britt," he said evenly. "She likes to be prepared." Then he smiled, but it looked forced as he turned his attention to Aiden and then back to Lanie. "She wants us there at six thirty. Do you need a ride?"

"I'll take her," Aiden said, his hand squeezing her upper arm. "It's not a problem, since we're going out after the game."

Tyler nodded then headed up the stairs.

Lanie pushed off Aiden's hand and turned to watch Tyler walk toward a man standing at the top of the landing.

"What the hell just happened?" she asked as she sat down.

"That was the guy who owns the jacket in your apartment?"

"Yeah. What has gotten into you?" she asked in confusion. "Since when do you care about the guys I date?"

He grinned. "Looks like you're switching up your dating life too—going for a more serious relationship."

"What on earth gives you *that* idea? Tyler is just a no-strings, short-term relationship. Just like all the other guys before him."

Aiden laughed. "Lanie, I love you like the sister I never had, and you are one of the most brilliant, business-savvy people I know. But sometimes you can be so obtuse."

"What are you talking about?"

The crowd went wild as a Royals player hit a home run, and Aiden got to his feet, cheering with the crowd.

Serious relationship? And Aiden thought he knew her so well...

Chapter Fifteen

Tyler was irritable the rest of the game, and Eric had finally figured out that his brother had seen a woman he knew. Mostly because he kept glancing over in her direction every two minutes.

"Is that your girlfriend?" Eric asked.

Tyler snorted. "Girlfriend? I don't do girlfriends."

"Then who's that woman?"

"She's in the wedding I'm in. I'm a groomsman. She's a bridesmaid. That's all."

"So you don't care that she's making out with that beefy guy next to her?"

"*What?*" He jerked around to look, but both Lanie and Aiden were in their chairs, their eyes on the game, although they looked like they were in an animated conversation.

Eric burst out laughing. "I *knew* you liked her. And all this time I thought you were a lady's man who only liked to play the field."

"Lady's man? Who the hell says that? I thought you were seventeen, not seventy-two."

"Turn this back on me all you want," Eric said with a grin. "But it looks like the player lost his rule book."

Tyler shot him a glare, but Eric was surprisingly quiet.

* * *

Tyler arrived at Loose Park a full fifteen minutes early. He told himself he was just being punctual for Brittany's sake, but he knew better. He was hoping to catch sight of Lanie and her date, although he had no idea why. Holly was already there with the photographer, and Celesta was there early too. Thankfully, Holly took pity on him and gave Celesta some busywork task on the wooden bridge where they'd be posing.

Brittany and Randy looked more relaxed this time, chatting with their friends. Maybe they figured anything bad that could have happened already had.

At 6:25, Lanie still hadn't shown up, and Tyler was feeling anxious. *Why wasn't she here yet? Was she in bed with Aiden?*

Just the thought of her in her bed with Aiden made his stomach clench. His chest tightened, and he wanted to punch the shit out of something.

What the fuck was wrong with him?

A dark sedan pulled up, and Aiden got out, then walked around to the front of the car. Lanie was already getting out, but he reached down and helped her out the rest of the way. He pulled her into a tight embrace before kissing her on the cheek and waving good-bye.

Lanie walked over to the group, then stopped next to Britt and stared at Tyler.

God, she was beautiful. The deep V of the neckline in

her bridesmaid's dress exposed her cleavage, and the loose folds of the skirt clung to her full hips. Her hair hung down her back, and all he could think about was her naked in his arms, underneath him while he pushed deeper inside her.

An overwhelming need shot through him. *Fuck*.

The look in her eyes suggested that she wanted him too, but it bothered him that she had just left Aiden and now she was looking at him like she wanted a replay of last night.

Jesus, he was a hypocrite. Hadn't he done the same thing more times than he could count? But none of those women had really meant anything. Did that mean that Lanie did? He snorted to himself. What a load of bullshit. He hardly knew her.

She walked over to him, and he pounced on her. "You're late."

She glanced at her phone. "I'm two minutes early."

"The rest of us were at least ten minutes early."

She stared at him like he'd grown a second head. "What the hell is wrong with you?"

He wished he knew. He reached up to rub his temple, but accidently touched his bandage, sending a shooting pain through his head. "Shit."

"That bandage has to come off," Holly said as she walked by.

Lanie gave him an appraising glance, then motioned to a concrete picnic table. "It looks really taped on. Why don't you let me take it off?" When he started to protest, she added. "It's the least I can do, since I caused it."

He nodded and followed her to the table, letting her gently push him down on the seat.

"Did you and your brothers enjoy the game?" she asked

quietly as she started to gently pick at the tape on his fore-head.

"Yeah. Did you enjoy the game with your...?"

She smiled. "Aiden and I had fun."

He'd purposefully made the question leading, and he swallowed his frustration that it hadn't worked.

"Do you go to Royals games together very often?" she asked.

"No. A guy I work with has season tickets."

"An attorney?"

"Yeah. You?"

"Never been to a Royals game. I'm not a baseball fan," she said, slowly prying off the bandage. "But Aiden insisted, and I hated to tell him no."

He stifled the question he was begging to ask: How could she go on a date with another guy after the mind-blowing sex they'd had the night before? If she hated telling Aiden no, did that mean she'd told him yes when he'd wanted to sleep with her? Because there was no way in hell Aiden hadn't wanted to sleep with her.

But then a new thought hit him, making the blood rush to his feet. What if last night hadn't been as good for Lanie as it had been for him? What if she'd faked it?

Oh, God.

Was he that out of practice?

He jolted on the seat, making her brush his stitches. He grunted from the pain.

"Tyler," she grumbled, "I know this hurts, but you need to be still."

"I can take it," he said through gritted teeth.

"Of course you can," she said with a grin as she removed the last of the tape.

She wasn't being awkward, so why was he? She was

like a dream come true—they slept together, and she wasn't clinging to him like a dryer sheet. He would have killed for a woman like her before Nina. What was different now?

He didn't have time to dwell on it because Celesta stood in front of him and gasped as she pointed to his forehead. "Oh my God!"

"What?" he asked, trying to stay calm. Was the wound infected? Was it oozing with pus? Was an alien trying to escape? But Lanie was staring at it and not freaking out.

"You have a huge white patch on your forehead!" Celesta said in horror.

He looked up at Lanie for reassurance.

She gave him a hesitant smile. "You obviously got a little sun, but it's not that bad. I promise."

Holly walked over and cringed. "I'm sure that can be Photoshopped."

"Pretty soon they'll just have to Photoshop your entire head," Rowdy teased.

"Very funny," Tyler grumbled as he stood and moved away from Celesta.

"Okay," Holly said. "Let's get started. Now that we know what we're doing, hopefully this will go faster."

Tyler pulled his phone from his pocket and opened the camera app. Sure enough, there was a two-inch-square white spot on his forehead where the bandage had been.

Lanie glanced up at him with a grin. "You should have worn a hat."

But her comment only reminded him that *she'd* worn a hat to the game. With Aiden.

Why the fuck did he care about that shithead Aiden?

"Let's start moving to the bridge," Holly said, herding everyone in that direction.

But Tyler didn't follow. He was too busy trying to deal with his raging emotions. If he didn't know any better he'd think he was . . .

Oh my fucking God. He was jealous.

"Tyler?" Lanie asked. "Are you okay?"

No. He was far from okay, but there was no way in hell he was going to admit that. He'd slept with her one time. One fucking time. Why was he feeling this way?

But she was watching him, waiting for an answer.

"I'm fine," he said, reaching his hand up to run it over his hair, but he hit his gash and sent a spike of pain through his head. "Son of a bitch."

"When was the last time you took anything for the pain?" she asked, digging in her purse.

"This morning." He started to pace, his chest tightening. He needed to pull himself together.

She handed him two tablets and a bottle of water. "Here. This should help."

He swallowed the pills and chased them down with a gulp of water.

Lanie studied him with worried eyes, and he resisted the urge to haul her to his chest and kiss her. She'd kill him if he did. For one thing, she wanted last night to be a secret, but for another, he had no idea if she still wanted him. For all he knew last night was a one-time thing for her.

When did he start second-guessing himself?

"Lanie," he said, then paused. "About . . . I mean . . ."

"Tyler! Lanie!" Holly called. "We need you."

Lanie gave him a worried smile. "We can talk after the shoot."

"Yeah."

They walked over to the thirty-foot wooden bridge that spanned over a narrow section of a small lake in the park.

Holly had already positioned everyone else on the bridge, leaving Lanie and Tyler for last, although they were between Celesta and Alvin and Rowdy and Mindy, Brittany's maid of honor.

"This is a romantic location," Holly teased, "so let's have some fun with it."

A romantic location, he thought.

Tyler decided he'd never been one to sit around and whine. If he had, he'd be working as a mechanic in his father's auto shop. He'd always taken matters into his own hands, and that's what he was going to do now.

He was supposed to stand behind Lanie for the pose, and as he pressed his chest into her back, he got a fantastic view of her breasts. "I've thought about you today," he whispered.

Her breath hitched. "Oh, yeah?"

"Great smile, Lanie," the photographer said.

Tyler laughed behind her, rested his hand on her hip and watched the rise and fall of her breasts, getting more turned on by the second as he remembered her in her white lace bra the night before.

"Tyler!" the photographer shouted. "Can you look at the camera?"

Lanie chuckled as the photographer took several shots.

But when they changed positions, Tyler caught Celesta's glare.

He always had attracted the crazy ones, although Lanie didn't even come close to that category. Maybe that was why he was obsessing over her.

Holly moved them into a new position, and Lanie stood at Tyler's side. She instructed Tyler to put his arm around the small of Lanie's back while she put both hands on his shoulder. He held her closer than necessary, but she didn't seem to mind, glancing up at him with a knowing smile.

He leaned close and whispered, "I loved watching you come last night, while my tongue licked your—"

"Tyler!" Holly shouted. "You're supposed to be looking at the camera, and Lanie, what happened to your smile?"

Tyler shot Lanie a grin, feeling satisfied with himself when he saw the lust in her eyes. Her chest rose and fell, pressing her breast into his arm, and it was taking every last thread of willpower to keep from kissing her. Sure, his plan to drive her crazy was working, but it was working on him, too.

They changed positions again, this time with the women facing the men, then glancing over their shoulders at the camera. Tyler's fingers dug possessively into her hips, holding her tightly against him. He glanced down at her chest, catching a glimpse of the edge of her bra, then back up into her eyes. "Black? I bet you'll look gorgeous sprawled out on my bed wearing nothing but your black bra and panties."

She stared up into his face, her eyes hooded, and her breath shallow. "Are you purposely trying to drive me crazy?"

"Is it working?" he asked with a bad-boy smile.

She lifted her eyebrows and answered him with her own wicked grin.

"Lanie!" Holly called out. "You're supposed to be looking back at the camera."

Lanie's eyes gleamed with mischief, then she turned around and did as she was instructed.

The next pose was with the men sitting sideways on the edge of the bridge, and the women standing to their side with their hands on the men's shoulders. Holly had given the men fishing poles, and had Britt on the bank of the small pond directly underneath Randy so it looked like he was trying to catch her.

Lanie stood next to Tyler and leaned into his ear. "You got to taste all of me, but I didn't get to taste all of you."

He glanced back at her and she licked her upper lip with the tip of her tongue.

Thinking of what she could do with that tongue drove nearly all the blood in his body to his groin. "*Shit*," he murmured under his breath as he shifted, trying to relieve the pressure as well as hide the evidence of how turned on he was at the moment. He held the fishing pole over his rapidly increasing erection.

"Oh," Lanie cooed in his ear. "Do you have another booboo? Do I need to kiss it and make it all better?"

Fuck it all. He turned, about to pull her between his legs and kiss her right there in front of everyone, when a policeman walked up.

"You all got fishing permits?" he asked as he pointed toward the fishing poles.

Holly looked startled. "They're not really fishing, Officer."

Tyler secretly thanked the police officer, even if he was currently a pain in Holly's ass.

The police officer gestured to the men who had fishing pools extended over the side of the bridge. "Looks like they're fishing to me."

Tyler stood and gave himself a moment to settle down, preparing himself to intervene if necessary, but he questioned how convincing he'd be with a tent pole in his pants.

"That's because they're props," Holly said. "We're using them for a photo shoot. The rods don't have any fishing line or lures on them."

The officer hooked his thumbs into his belt and scanned the group. "So none of you all have a fishing license?"

Randy started down the bridge toward the policeman, carrying his fishing pole. "I have a license, officer, but as Holly said, none of us are really fishing. You can see the pole."

"I'm still going to need your license, sir."

Tyler set his pole on the bridge and gave Lanie a grin. "Don't go anywhere."

She laughed. "I wouldn't dream of it."

Chapter Sixteen

~

Lanie watched Tyler walk down the bridge, grateful for the reprieve to catch her breath. Good Lord, she'd been about to toss caution to the wind and throw herself at him. The police officer had saved the day.

"He's an attorney, you know," Celesta said behind Lanie.

Lanie gave her a tight smile as the woman walked next to her. "So I've heard."

Celesta leaned closer. "He's down there with Randy arguing for our rights. It's heroic, don't you think?"

Lanie was pretty sure heroic didn't describe someone convincing a police officer not to hand out a fine, but then a quick glance to Holly made her reevaluate. It might be heroic if it kept the wedding planner from having a stroke.

Randy and Tyler stood next to each other talking to the police officer, gesturing toward Holly and the bridge.

"They work together, you know," Celesta continued. "In the same law firm."

"Really?" Lanie tried to keep the interest out of her voice, then felt stupid that she hadn't put it together. She'd seen Tyler at the coffee shop in Randy's building. But in her defense, when she'd looked at the directory in the lobby, she'd seen that the office building housed seven law firms.

Celesta moved closer and gave her a condescending look. "I saw the way you were looking at him, but you really shouldn't waste your time."

Lanie fought a grin. "Really? Why's that?"

"Britt says he's taking a break from women, but I know Tyler. He doesn't take breaks from women. After so many months, he's going to be starving. And I plan to be there— lying out on the buffet table when he decides it's time to eat again. He's had me once." She winked. "So he knows how good it is."

Lanie would have laughed if she hadn't been disgusted by the image in her head. "There are probably health codes prohibiting that kind of thing." Lanie plastered on a smile. "But lucky for you, Tyler's an attorney. Why don't we ask him?"

Celesta leaned closer and gave her a warning look. "Just stay out of my way." Then she walked down the bridge toward Holly and Brittany.

Wow. So Celesta was another of Tyler's crazy exes. How many did he have?

The police officer said something to Holly, then shook Randy and Tyler's hands before he headed back to the parking lot.

"Misunderstanding," Randy said as he came back onto the bridge. "But we're good."

"We have a few more shots, if you're up to it," Holly said, looking relieved and exhausted.

Everyone agreed, and Holly conferred with Brittany about what to do next.

Tyler walked toward Lanie, and she gave him credit for looking nonchalant. He stood next to her, keeping a respectable distance, but he turned his back to everyone and gave her a sexy smile.

"Someone thinks you're a hero," she teased. "Your admirer."

The hopeful look on his face fell. "You mean Celesta."

"You two had a thing."

"Lanie..."

"I don't care." She chuckled when she saw the surprise on his face. "Hey, I know you've been around, and I know it's in the past." She paused. "It *is* in the past, right?"

"Distant past."

"How distant."

"Four years."

"Okay."

Holly set them up in their next pose, and Lanie whispered, "Any more crazy exes I should know about?"

He paused.

"Okay...let me rephrase that. Any other crazy exes I need to worry about in the foreseeable future?"

"No."

She grinned up at him. "Good. Just wear a condom and we're good."

He looked surprised, but she laughed. She might worry about his exes if they were going for something long term, but this would last a few weeks tops, because she was leaving Kansas City by the first week of October. The question was where she would end up.

She and Aiden had left the baseball game early and gone to Gates Bar-B-Q. Between Aiden's complaints that Kansas

City barbecue had nothing on South Carolina dry rub, he'd laid out an impressive plan for his company and Lanie's part in it.

"I can't match Margo Benson's salary," Aiden had admitted, "but I can give you a percentage of the company." Then he grinned. "And a great dental plan."

She'd studied the figures on his laptop, and a knot had formed in the pit of her stomach.

"What's holding you back?" he asked. "Are you worried about us working together?"

She'd looked into his face. "No. I think I'd love working with you. But it's change, which makes it scary."

"From everything you've told me about your new VP, your days might be numbered anyway, so you're smart to turn in your notice. Have you got any other leads?"

"No. Honestly, I haven't had a chance to look."

"You might want to put a few feelers out."

Or just take his offer. It was a great one. She could afford the pay cut, but something was holding her back. She just couldn't put her finger on what.

But her career options could wait until tomorrow. She was going to focus on the distraction next to her.

Holly seemed thrown off by the police officer's appearance and soon told them they were free to leave after reminding them to meet at a specific location in front of the Royals' stadium for the next set of photos on Thursday night.

"Since Aiden dropped you off," Tyler said with a lazy grin, "you probably need a ride home."

Her eyebrows rose playfully. "Are you offering to make the sacrifice?"

"I could be bribed."

She resisted the urge to kiss him. It was a good thing she

only had a few weeks left or she could see herself possibly falling for him, which would be a disaster of epic proportions. She was sure the two women she'd run into from his past were just the tip of the iceberg. Tyler Norris had a shelf life. "Good," she said. "But I need to talk to Randy first...alone."

He looked momentarily surprised but said, "I'll help Holly load up her car."

"Great." She made a beeline for Randy, who was deep in a conversation with Holly and Britt.

"I still can't believe that policeman," Britt said, shaking her head. "Did he really think I was fishing wearing a wedding dress?"

"He was a little overzealous, but we worked it out," Randy said.

Britt noticed as Lanie stopped next to them, and grabbed her arm. "Okay, I need to know all about the total cutie who dropped you off."

Randy squirmed. "I'm going to help Tyler."

"Actually, Randy," Lanie said, "you're the one I need to talk to."

Understanding filled his eyes, and he tilted his head, gesturing over to a picnic table about twenty feet away from the group.

"You're not getting out of giving me details that easily," Britt said in warning.

"I'll tell you after I talk to Randy," Lanie said. "Although I suspect you'll be disappointed."

Britt started to protest, but Lanie rushed over to the table Randy had already moved to.

"You know she'll break you down," he said with a grin. "Resistance is futile."

"She'll truly be disappointed. He's just a friend."

The look he gave her suggested that he didn't believe her. "Hey, what you do with your personal life is your own business, but I suspect you didn't ask me over here to talk about your love life." He took a deep breath then looked uncomfortable. "I meant to talk to you Friday night, but things got a little chaotic, and I didn't want to tell you on the phone."

Her heart sank. "You have bad news."

"Not really…More like a good news, bad news scenario." His mouth twisted to the side. "First I have to make it very clear that everything you and I discuss is purely unofficial. Just me talking to my fiancée's cousin. You are *not* my client."

Why was he acting so weird? "I don't have any qualms about paying you, Randy."

"No." He paused. "No. You can't pay me…The company that filed the injunction hired my firm."

"*What?*" She realized she'd nearly shouted the word, then turned her back to the group.

He leaned closer and lowered his voice. "I didn't have anything to do with it, another attorney in the firm is handling the case, but me officially consulting with you could be seen as a conflict of interest. As far as I'm concerned, we never met in my office, and I'd prefer you keep it to yourself."

"Britt—"

"Britt knows that our discussion wasn't official, and I've reminded her the whole thing is confidential."

"But does she know about your firm filing the injunction?"

"No, and I prefer to keep it that way."

Lanie was still trying to wrap her head around the fact that his firm was helping try to shut down her store, let alone the fact that he didn't want his fiancée to know. "Are they going to try something else?"

"Lanie, even if I knew I couldn't tell you."

She pushed out a frustrated breath. "They're screwing with my job, Randy."

"That's the good news."

"It's good news they're screwing with my job?" she asked in disbelief.

"No, but I've looked over your contract, and as long as you've had exemplary conduct during the course of your employment, you'll receive a significant bonus when you leave. Have you had any disciplinary demerits in the past?"

"No... But if anything stops this opening, I'll get fired. That's a pretty big demerit."

"The contract states that you're required to give three weeks' notice. Your bonus becomes structured after that. If you get a disciplinary reprimand during that time, your bonus will go down."

Her eyes widened. "How is that good news?"

"They can't give you a reprimand for a *delay* caused by an outside force. It's in the contract. Only if it doesn't open on time."

"So I can get a million delays, but as long as I open on time, I still get my bonus?"

"A fifty-thousand-dollar bonus. So injunctions might still get filed against the store, but as long as the Margo Benson legal team keeps overturning them, you should be fine."

She sucked in a breath. "You figured out I'm opening a Margo Benson?"

He leaned closer and cast a sideways glance toward the group. "It spread like wildfire once a paralegal told an assistant. But the firm thinks it's contained."

"Thinks." If word got out... just one more thing to worry

about. "You realize you're giving me advice that's in conflict with your firm?"

"Now you know why we never met in my office about your contract. You were there helping me figure out a wedding gift for Britt." He hesitated. "So are you going to give your notice?"

All of this scared the crap out of her, but it was the smart thing to do. Still, she wasn't ready to pull the trigger just yet. "Yeah, in fact I have a solid lead on a new job. That's where Aiden comes in. He's an old friend and he offered me a job in Atlanta. We were discussing it this afternoon, and he offered to drop me off."

"You can't tell Britt that."

Lanie's jaw dropped. "What? Why not?"

"She wants you to stay here. She's already shed a few tears about you leaving."

"Randy, she knows I'm leaving anyway."

"Since you came to see me about your contract, she knows there's a strong likelihood that you're leaving...your company. She's conniving to keep you here."

Well, shit. "I'll keep it to myself for now, but if I take the job, I'm telling her."

"Fair enough."

She turned to walk over to Britt but saw Tyler watching her with undisguised interest. She stopped in her tracks as a new worry hit her.

"Randy," she said, turning back to him. "You said another attorney in your firm was working on the case—"

"Lanie—"

"Just tell me this: Is Tyler the attorney?"

"No. I can assure you it's not him."

She closed her eyes. Thank God. She gave him a quick hug. "Thank you."

"I wish I could do more."

"You've been great."

Tyler was still watching as she walked toward them, but so was Britt. "Is everything okay?" she asked.

"Great." Lanie gave her a big smile. "We were discussing your wedding present, so no questions."

Relief washed over Randy's face as he wrapped an arm around his fiancée's back. "Turns out Lanie is pretty terrible at this."

"I'll say," Britt teased. "Remember the juicer?" But then her eyes danced with excitement. "Now, about the man who dropped you off..."

"He's an old friend," Lanie said, playing it coy. "He's in town for the weekend on business and wanted to see me. So we spent the afternoon together. End of story."

"Friend?" Britt asked suspiciously. "You realize every guy you've had a relationship with since college has been labeled as a *friend*?"

Lanie grinned. "I would hope I wouldn't be fraternizing with my *enemies*."

"Lanie..."

She gave her cousin a hug. "Britt, I love you, but your matchmaking is never going to work. I'll have a relationship when I'm ready. And then I'll tell you about it when I'm sure it's solid."

"Most people introduce their significant others to their friends and families."

"Then how about this? If I ever get a significant other, I'll make sure you're the first to know." Her answer had been flippant, but something caught in her chest. She was thirty-two years old and she could honestly say she'd never had a significant relationship other than a yearlong relationship in college.

"Okay."

Lanie did a double take, surprised Britt had conceded so easily, but she knew better than to look a gift horse in the mouth.

"Is Aiden coming back to take you home?"

And there it was. "No, Tyler offered to take me home."

That caught Britt by surprise. "Really? Randy and I can do it."

Tyler picked up Lanie's purse off the picnic table and handed it to Lanie. "She lives less than a half mile from me, so it's not a problem, but we need to leave now or I'll be late for my dinner plans."

"And since he's being so generous, I don't want to keep him waiting," Lanie said. "So I'll see you at your barbecue tomorrow, Britt."

"Okay."

Britt was surprisingly quiet about their departure, which made Lanie suspicious as she walked with Tyler toward his car. "Why didn't she ask more questions?"

"Because we gave her a good reason for me taking you home...?"

He started to head toward the passenger side of the car, and she shot him a glare. "No. You can't open my door for me. You're just a casual stranger giving me a ride home."

He stopped and looked down at her with an amused expression. "News flash: I would open your door whether I wanted to take you home and sleep with you or not."

A tingle ran across her skin. "So you're claiming to be a gentleman as well as a player."

He grinned. "And how do you think a player gets the women?" He continued toward the car and opened the passenger door. "It will be more out of character if I *don't* open your door."

She started to get in but cast a quick glance toward Britt. Sure enough, she was watching with open curiosity.

Tyler shut the door after she got in, and when he got inside, she said, "Britt's suspicious. Not that I can blame her. She probably noticed us being all handsy. We can't do that again."

He backed out of the parking spot and laughed. "You really are paranoid about her interference, aren't you?"

"She's devious." The way he shook his head proved he didn't believe her, but she had no plans to let him find out firsthand with her.

"Then I'll have to be more careful." He rested his hand on her leg and began to caress her thigh through the lilac satin.

Electricity shot straight to her core, and she sucked in a breath.

"Besides, Britt was too busy with the photos to notice us."

She hoped so. She'd gotten so caught up in the moment with Tyler, she hadn't even considered who was watching, which was totally out of character for her. Sleeping with a guy two nights in a row also fit that out-of-character category. But then she remembered his excuse for their quick departure. "Do you really have dinner plans?"

"I do," he said as he focused on the road, returning his hand to the steering wheel. "I have lots of plans with you, and dinner is only one part of them." He turned to her and flashed her his sexy smile.

Her stomach fluttered and caught her by surprise. She couldn't remember the last time a guy had given her butterflies. "You're not taking me to my apartment, are you?"

His gaze turned hungry. "Not a chance in hell."

Chapter Seventeen

It was a fifteen-minute drive to his condo, but it felt like an hour. He wanted to ask her about Aiden, but he knew better than to broach the subject. Did he accept her statement that they were simply friends? According to what she told Brittany, she'd called all the men she slept with *friends*. But they'd set no parameters, and they definitely weren't exclusive, so did it matter? Strangely, it did, and he wasn't sure what to do with that.

"Tell me about your brothers," she said, shifting in her seat to look at him.

He shot her a look, then turned back to the road. "There's not much to tell. I'm the oldest. Alex is two years younger than me, and Eric's a junior in high school."

"That's a huge age difference," she said.

"I suspect Eric was a last-ditch effort to make my parents' marriage work. My mother took off a year later."

"Oh, God. I'm sorry."

He shrugged, pretending indifference, but this many years later, her abandonment still stung like a bitch.

"My parents are divorced too," she said. "But they waited until I graduated. They stayed together for me. But I wish they'd divorced back when I was younger. They made most of my life after I turned eight miserable with their fighting. I didn't have any siblings to commiserate with, so I used to spend a lot of time at Brittany's house."

He didn't want to talk about their parents' failed marriages. He pulled to a red light and turned to face her. "Are you hungry?"

A smile spread across her face.

"For food," he said with a grin.

"Are you?"

"I'm more hungry for you." He leaned toward her, cupping the back of her head and giving her a deep kiss. A car honked behind them, and he grinned when he saw the light had turned green.

"Do you see your brothers often?" she asked, shifting in her seat to face him.

"Not as often as I should," he said, as he rested his hand on her thigh again.

"But you went to the ball game with them."

He tugged the fabric of her skirt higher so he could see her bare thigh. "Delayed gratification," he said in response to her questioning grin. "I've been wanting to touch you all day, and now I finally am."

Lanie laughed. "I get the hint." She pushed his hand away and ran her fingertips up the inside of his thigh, stopping just before his crotch, then slid her fingers slowly down and back up again. "Do you like this topic better?"

"Much."

She found the bulge in his pants and covered the length

of him, rubbing him with the palm of her hand. "You're so hard already," she murmured in his ear.

Groaning, he grabbed her hand and held it still. "Jesus, Lanie." His erection throbbed, and he sucked in his breath. All their earlier foreplay had made him eager, but damned if he'd come in the car. He had other plans.

She laughed in his ear and nipped his earlobe with her teeth.

He barely held it together the rest of the way to his condo. When he parked in the dark parking garage, he unbuckled her seat belt and hauled her partially over the console. He captured her mouth and kissed her until they were both breathless.

"Part of me wants to fuck you right here in the car," he murmured against her mouth. "But I'd rather have you in my bed."

He got out of the car before he changed his mind, then opened her door and helped her out of the car. She leaned forward to kiss him, but he took a step back and grinned. "The next time I touch you, I might not be able to stop, so I suggest we wait until we get into my condo."

She grinned, that mischievous grin that drove him crazy, and he second-guessed his decision.

He put his hand on her lower back and led her to the elevator bank, thanking the stars above that there was an elevator waiting.

"Which floor?" she asked.

"Fifth."

"That's easy to remember since I'm also on the fifth floor." She pushed the button and pressed her back against the wall while he stood in the middle. "So you can't touch me, right?" she asked. "But I can touch *you*?"

"Lanie," he said under his breath.

She moved in front of him and put a hand on his hip, then slid it toward his groin, cupping him in her hand.

"Lanie," he growled through gritted teeth. "If you keep this up, I'm going to pull up your dress and take you right here in the elevator."

She reached up on her tiptoes and brushed her mouth against the side of his neck. "You're full of promises."

His erection throbbed even more, straining against his briefs, and all he could think about was burying himself inside her again. He pushed her against the wall and grabbed her leg, lifting it to his hip as he pressed himself to her core. She moaned into his mouth, and he was vaguely aware that the elevator door had opened.

He dropped her leg and took a step backward, bringing her with him. But her heel caught in the hem of her bridesmaid dress, and she stumbled. He bent and scooped her into his arms and carried her into the hall.

She wrapped an arm around his neck then said, "My shoe!"

"That damn thing is possessed. Leave it." Then he kissed her as he took several steps toward his apartment. It was only fifteen feet down the hall, but it felt like fifteen miles.

He stopped in front of his door and lowered her to the floor, still keeping his hand around her back while he fished his keys out of his pocket.

Get the door open.

He reluctantly dragged his lips from her and took a breath as he inserted his key into the lock.

"Britt is going to kill me if I lose that shoe," she protested.

"If you're still thinking about that shoe, then I'm neglecting my duties." He pushed the door open. "I'll buy you a new pair, Killer."

"You'll buy me an entire new wardrobe before this is over."

"Or keep you naked in my bed." Covering his mouth with hers, he dragged her across the threshold and slammed the door behind them. But thoughts of her naked in his bed only made him more impatient. He grabbed her zipper and tugged it down her back.

"It's a good thing you had your key," she said, pushing off his jacket and letting it drop to the floor. "I don't possess the badass skills you do."

He grinned. "Don't underestimate your own badass skills." He pulled her toward the bedroom, leaving her dress and remaining shoe on the floor.

She worked on the buttons of his shirt while he continued to lead her down the hall. By the time he reached his room, his buttons were free and she slid her hands inside his shirt, running them over his chest before moving to his pants. She made quick work of his button and zipper, then took a half-step back, her hands on his hips.

Her hooded eyes stared up at him, and he ached to be inside her. He started to pull her down on the bed, but she smiled at him as she pushed his pants over his hips and to the floor. When she dropped to her knees, he sucked in a breath of anticipation.

She slowly tugged down his briefs while she licked his tip. His blood rushed to his erection and he sunk his hands into her hair as she took him in her mouth.

"God, Lanie," he groaned, pushing deeper into her mouth.

Her hand cupped his balls, squeezing gently as she licked and sucked until he was so close to the edge, he barely pulled her away in time. He lifted her to her feet, unhooked her bra, and pulled off her panties before he pushed her down on the bed sideways, covering her with his body an instant later.

She wrapped her leg around his waist and lifted her hips

as she sunk her fingers into his hair and held him against her mouth.

He needed to slow down or he wouldn't last more than a minute.

Pushing up on his hands, her stared down at her, taking in the sight of her swollen lips, then lowered his gaze to her hard nipples and her bare mound. "You're so fucking beautiful," he growled before he took one of her nipples in his mouth.

She arched her back and gasped.

He shifted his weight to his elbow and reached between her parted legs, sliding his fingers into her wet folds.

Lanie gasped again, and lifted her hips as she released a soft whimper.

His tongue trailed across her cleavage to her other breast, circling her nipple with his tongue before he sucked it into his mouth.

Crying out, she dug her hands into his hair, holding him in place.

He slid his finger deep inside there, then rubbed her nub until she moaned his name. "What do you want, Lanie?" he murmured against her breast.

"You," she gasped, lifting her hips. "I want you inside me. Now." Then her eyes flew open. "Please, dear God, tell me you have a condom."

He laughed, then he kissed her because he found her utterly irresistible. "Gorgeous, we wouldn't be in this situation if I didn't have one."

"Then get it," she said, pushing him up. "Get it *now*."

He chuckled as he rolled over and reached into his nightstand drawer...and found nothing.

"Tyler..."

"I'll be right back." He jumped off the bed, bolted into his bathroom, and yanked the cabinet door open. He hadn't used a condom in months, but he knew he'd had a box under his sink.

"Tyler..." She sounded panicked.

He reached into the cabinet, behind the toilet paper, and found the box. He tossed it onto the counter and grabbed a handful of condoms. "Got it."

He went into the bedroom and stopped in his tracks. Lanie lay on the bed, her legs spread so he could see her in all her glory. Her fingertips skimmed the flesh of her inner thigh, moving slowly upward.

"Jesus, Lanie," he gasped as he tossed all the condoms but one on the bed. "Where the hell have you been all my life?" He ripped the condom open and quickly rolled it on.

She grinned as she reached for him. "Waiting for you to find a condom."

He lowered himself onto the bed, then lifted her as he filled her with one deep thrust.

She pushed herself against him and groaned.

He knew he wouldn't last long. He'd waited too damn long to be inside her, but he sure as hell wouldn't come before she did.

He reached between her folds and coaxed her higher as he thrust into her, his pace quickening. His balls tightened when he felt her tighten around him. "Come for me, Lanie."

She moaned his name as she clamped around him. He grabbed both of her hips, pounding into her while they both came. When he finished, he collapsed on his side and reached an arm around her, pulling her tightly against him. She slung her leg around his waist and she looked into his eyes, a slight grin tugging at the corners of her lips.

He couldn't remember feeling like this after sex. Satiated

yet still hungry for more. But it wasn't just his sexual hunger that was satisfied. Something else deep in his chest felt full.

He kissed her, a deep passionate kiss, and he felt himself hardening already while he was still inside her.

She looked up at him with her grin. "Again?"

"Killer, we're just getting started."

Chapter Eighteen

Tyler roused when he felt a jostle and reached for Lanie as she started to roll out of bed.

"Where are you going?" he murmured sleepily.

She grabbed her phone off the bedside table. "I have to go."

He bolted up right. "What?"

"It's late. I have to go. Don't worry. I'll get an Uber." She bent down and picked up her underwear off the floor and went into his bathroom to pee.

She was wearing her bra and panties when she came out. Tyler was sitting on the edge of the bed, still naked, but he stood when she emerged and pulled her into his arms. "Why are you leaving?"

She froze and looked up at him. "Because it's late. Because the only clothes I have is my stupid bridesmaid dress. And because..."

His hand cupped her cheek, and his thumb stroked her jaw. "And because...?"

She hesitated before she said, "Because I don't have a toothbrush."

"I have a toothbrush."

She scrunched her nose. "I'm not using yours."

He laughed. "I'm glad to hear that, especially since I have a spare."

"For all your other women?" she teased.

"No. For me. I like to have spares."

She pulled free and padded out to the living room, looking around his apartment.

"Lanie, it's late," he said, following her. "Just come back to bed and I'll take you home in the morning." Then he grinned and grabbed her hips, pulling her flush against his chest. She felt his growing erection against her. "If you need help going back to sleep, I have another condom on the nightstand."

She laughed. "I never imagined you had so much stamina."

"I'm watching you walk around my condo, barely covered in sexy lace. What do you expect?"

A war waged in her eyes.

He gave her a gentle kiss, pulling her bottom lip between his teeth while his hand caressed her firm ass.

She wrapped an arm around the back of his neck and opened her mouth to his probing tongue, releasing a soft moan.

Damned if he wasn't ready to take her against the door.

But she broke the kiss and leaned her forehead against his chest.

Why was she struggling to stay? Was she thinking about Aiden?

A fierce jealousy consumed him, and he fought to contain it. What the hell was going on with him? This was a short-term arrangement. Nothing more. A sexy woman who was just as sexually driven as him, who wanted no commitments. It was absolutely the perfect relationship for him. He attributed his feelings to going so long without sex, probably part of the reason he'd been able to have so many repeat performances since they'd come to his condo last night.

But because this was so perfect, he wanted it for as long as he could have it. Which meant he had to convince her to stay.

"Do I snore?" he teased. "I can wait until you go to sleep if you want."

She laughed again and glanced back up at him. "And how will you know I'm asleep?"

He lifted an eyebrow. "I'll watch you like that sparkly vampire in that movie."

"FYI, everything about that sentence is wrong." She pulled free and headed back to his bedroom.

Had she decided to stay? He followed her, and saw her picking up her purse.

She was still leaving. The thought of her walking out the door left a vacuum in his chest he didn't understand. He only knew that some deep part of him needed her to stay.

She tossed her purse on the bed and searched the contents, sighing in relief when she jiggled her keys. "That would have been a disaster, getting locked out of my apartment at three a.m."

"I would never let that happen," he murmured as he pulled her against him again. "And I would never let you take an Uber. Especially this late." Her stomach grumbled, and then he had a new plan. "Why, Lanie Rogers. Is the way to your heart through your stomach?"

A sultry look filled her eyes. "I guess it depends on what you're feeding me."

A wave of lust washed over him as he remembered

watching her take him into his mouth. He fought to keep his breathing normal. "We're both awake, so let me feed you some food before I take you home. And yes, *I'll* take you home. No goddamned Uber."

She hesitated for the longest three seconds of his life. "Okay."

* * *

This was an epic mistake, and she knew it deep in her gut, yet she found herself powerless to refuse him. Because leaving was the last thing she wanted to do. Which meant she really needed to go.

But the desire in his eyes as he watched her was magnetic, and the way he possessed her body was addictive. She could see that already. This wasn't smart. She needed to end this now, but she couldn't. She'd never had this intense, overpowering need for a man before, and it scared her that she'd never find it again. All the more reason to end it before she got too used to it.

All the more reason to keep it as long as you can, another part of her countered.

This was going to hurt like hell when she left.

She was surprised at the thought. She'd never had a problem walking away from a man before. Usually, she couldn't leave them quick enough. Maybe she'd be tired of him before the wedding.

But when she thought of his body over hers, filling her so completely...

She shivered as electricity ran over her skin.

"You're cold." He walked over to his closet and returned with a pale blue dress shirt, holding it open for her to put on.

She couldn't hide her amusement as she slipped her arms

into the armholes. "Most guys would offer a girl their T-shirt." She started to button it, but he brushed her hands away and rested his own on her hips.

"Then most guys are idiots." He stared down at her body, and she flushed from his appraisal. "You're gorgeous, and I couldn't see the view if you wore a T-shirt." His hands gently swept up her sides, then over her stomach before returning to her hips. "And I most definitely want to see the view. I barely had seconds to see you in your bra and panties last night. Don't deprive me of it now."

He looked at her with unadulterated desire, and she felt her knees weaken. How could she already want him so much?

"Now, let me feed you."

She expected him to throw her on his bed and take her again. The large, twitching bulge in his briefs proved he was ready. But he stepped back and grabbed a shirt out of his dresser drawer, then tugged it over his head.

She nearly complained that it wasn't fair that she was on display for him while he was hidden from her. But when she saw the way the soft gray fabric clung to the hard muscles of his upper arms and chest, she changed her mind.

A shiver ran down her back, and a now familiar heat pooled between her legs. Good Lord, how many times had they had sex last night? Four times? But she'd orgasmed many more. Tyler Norris was definitely a generous man. It was no wonder her stomach was grumbling. She'd burned countless calories in his bed.

He gave her a gentle kiss, then headed down the hall. "What are you hungry for?" he asked.

"Don't make anything," she said, padding into his living room. "Just get some crackers or something."

His condo had an open-concept floor plan. It looked like

a loft, with its tall ceilings, but had a much more finished appearance. Dark granite counters topped dark wood cabinets along one wall of his kitchen, but his living room called to her. A deep leather sofa faced his stone fireplace, with a large TV over the mantel. It was surrounded by dark wood bookcases filled with books. She fingered the spine of a paperback murder mystery. "So you weren't kidding when you said you'd been known to read a book or two."

He grinned as he opened the fridge. "Nope." He set a carton of eggs on the counter.

"Tyler, I'm serious. Crackers or something easy would be fine."

"I don't have any crackers and I'm hungry too. That pizza was hours ago."

She moved toward the drapes that covered the wall opposite the kitchen.

He took several steps into the living room and picked up a remote from an end table. "Check out the view." He pushed a button, and the drapes parted, revealing a wall of windows that overlooked the Plaza.

She gasped. "I bet this is gorgeous at Christmas—when the Plaza's lit up with lights."

"I had a lighting party last year on Thanksgiving. We watched the Christmas lights turn on from my living room."

"That sounds amazing." She wanted to see it for herself, but she'd be gone by then. She paused at the spike of regret, then pushed it aside. "Your condo is beautiful...and not what I expected."

"What did you expect?" he asked.

"You know, lots of steel and chrome and modern."

"I could never relax in that kind of environment. Give me my leather sofa to sink into and watch a game or a movie."

She heard him cracking eggs, and she walked over to the island and sat on a bar stool. "I'm envious of your place."

"Your apartment is nice."

"But it's not mine," she said. "It's a rental and came fully furnished."

He turned around to face her. "Furnished? You don't have any furniture?"

"It's easier that way. And corporate gives me a monthly stipend. I usually send my assistant, Stephanie, to the city we're moving to about a month ahead to pick out a place for each of us."

"That sounds so…impersonal."

She shrugged. "It is what it is. But that's about to change."

"Because you're moving in a month?"

She opened her mouth, about to come clean, but then firmly closed it when she remembered her chat with Randy. He'd been adamant that Tyler not know she'd talked to him about her contract, and it was probably better he not know at all. "I'm not sure what I'll be doing in a month. I'm turning in my notice tomorrow."

He turned around to face her, and she realized how it probably sounded.

"Don't worry. It has nothing to do with you. You don't have to add me to your list of crazy exes. This has been brewing for a month or two and came to a head this week."

"Will you get a job here in Kansas City?" he asked, sounding guarded.

"No. You don't have to worry about your no-strings fling turning into a cling-on woman. The chances of me finding something here aren't that great." She paused, wondering how much to tell him, but not wanting to share too much. Short-term relationships came with an unofficial set of rules, and while rule number one was don't be clingy, rule number two was don't overshare. Nothing screamed "desperate for a real relationship" more loudly than someone spilling all their secrets, quickly followed by their hopes and dreams. "That's part of the reason Aiden came to see me," she said. "To convince me to move to Atlanta and work with him."

Tyler kept his back to her and remained strangely silent. She quickly scanned what she'd said, worried that it fell into the TMI category, but it all seemed fairly innocuous. Slightly above cocktail party chat.

He grabbed two plates out of his cabinet and set them on the counter. "Would you do time management work for Aiden?"

Why did he sound so weird? She'd said something that had bugged him, but damned if she knew what it was.

"No. I'd be a consultant, working with businesses that are either looking to expand or open their doors. Kind of like a small-business admin consulting."

"So you'd be moving to Atlanta after the wedding?" He kept his gaze down as he scraped scrambled eggs onto two plates and set them on the counter.

"I told Aiden I'd think about it, but I'm still considering my options."

"Have you looked at other options?" His gaze held hers, but his eyes were guarded.

She picked up the fork he'd set on the counter then set it down, even though the smell of the scrambled eggs was making her stomach rumble even more. But she'd already freaked him out. Maybe she should chalk this up to middle-of-the-night craziness, and hopefully pick this back up with him again tomorrow night after Britt and Randy's barbecue or, if he needed more time, on Thursday when she met him at the next photo shoot. "Maybe I should just go home."

"What?" he asked in shock. "Why?"

"Obviously, I've said or done something wrong. You started acting weird when I told you about quitting my job and looking for another one. I know you don't want to share personal information, but that seemed benign enough."

He held up his hands. "Whoa, whoa. Back up. When did I say I didn't want to share personal information?"

"In the car, you didn't want to talk about your brothers."

The corners of his mouth twitched. "In my defense, no man wants to talk about his brothers when the gorgeous woman next to him is giving him a hand job over his pants."

She grinned and nodded, feeling slightly better. "Fair enough."

"What other evidence do you have to present?" he asked, with a twinkle in his eyes.

"Oh," she cooed. "You're sexy when you talk all lawyerly."

"I've got plenty more legal talk where that came from," he teased, then turned more serious. "But I still want to know why you think something's wrong."

"You got weird when I talked about quitting my job. This isn't some pathetic attempt to trap you," she said. "I swear to you that this is all coincidental. The week after the wedding, you don't have to worry about me showing up on your doorstep telling you I have no place to live and no job to support myself. Then the next thing you know, I'm mooching all your food and Internet and giving you lazy sex." She chuckled when she saw his stunned face. "Sorry. That was me back when I was twenty-six and stupid. I mean, *I* didn't do it. It happened to me." She lifted a shoulder into a half-shrug. "He sucked up all my Internet for his video games."

He started to say something, then stopped. She was surprised at the seriousness in his eyes. "Lanie, I know we haven't set any rules here. We just started this. But here's the thing—I've really liked being with you the last few days."

"You mean the amazing sex."

A wicked gleam filled his eyes. "I won't deny that sex with you is mind-blowing and probably the best I've ever had, but it's more than that." He paused. "Look, I know you're leaving after the wedding, and I think you've figured out that I'm not a long-term kind of guy. So this is perfect for both of us. So—if you're willing—I'd like to spend more time with you before you go. And I don't want you to worry about oversharing. I just want you to be yourself and tell me as much or as little as you want." He leaned closer and placed a gentle kiss on her mouth. "Because I want to hear everything you're willing to tell me."

Alarm bells went off in her head. Her brain wasn't totally on board with that suggestion, but it wasn't volunteering a reason why. But her heart was all in, and that was the part she chose to listen to. There was no denying he turned her on like no man ever had, and that she loved his sense of humor. And she just liked *him*. He wasn't anything like she'd expected. "Does that mean you'll share with me too?"

"I'm an open book," he said, picking up her fork and handing it to her. "The eggs are getting cold."

She took a bite and watched him, wondering how open he would really be. "Not only can we still not tell Britt, but we have to be much more careful. We were careless today. If Britt even sniffs a hint that we're seeing each other, on top of me looking for another job, she'll blow this thing between us out of proportion in an attempt to keep me here."

"And you won't consider staying here?"

"Would it make you feel better if I promised not to look?" Then she grinned.

He didn't laugh. "Lanie, I want you to do what's best for you. If that's here..." His voice trailed off and she wasn't totally convinced.

"The eggs are really good," she said after another bite.

He had to know she was attempting to change the subject, but went along with it anyway. "You must really be hungry, because they're just scrambled eggs," he teased as he turned her stool just enough to face him. He parted the opening of her shirt to expose her black bra and panties. "Ah...that's better. And my offer still stands to help you go to sleep."

"That's one of the perks of this arrangement," she teased. "I plan on taking advantage of it while I can."

* * *

Lanie woke up the next morning, warm and cocooned with Tyler's bare chest pressed against her back and his arm draped over her stomach. She stirred, and he snuggled her closer.

"No. Don't go," he mumbled.

"Okay."

He rolled her on her back to face him, and he smiled down at her. "Good morning."

She smiled back, surprised by this feeling of happiness. Usually she couldn't wait to leave a man's bed and get back to her own space, but she actually wanted to be here. "Good morning to you too."

He smoothed the hair from her face, his fingertips brushing her cheek. "How soon do you need to get home? Any pressing plans?"

Her smiled dimmed. "It might be Labor Day, but I need to get some paperwork done before heading to Britt and Randy's barbecue."

He searched her eyes. "And write your letter of resignation?"

"Yeah." Admitting it hurt more than she expected. "Are you going to the barbecue?"

His gaze softened, and he stroked her cheekbone with his thumb. "Yeah." Something shifted in his eyes. "You have to work on Labor Day? No wonder you're considering looking for a new job."

"What about you?" she asked. "Happy with your job?"

"Yeah." He shifted his weight and rested his hand on her bare shoulder. "I like what I do and, for the most part, I like the people I work with." He paused. "I specialize in contract law, usually corporate stuff. I work with Randy. I don't know if you knew that."

She was definitely on shaky ground, but she was genuinely curious about him. "Actually, he just told me last night."

His brows rose. "When?"

Oh, crap. "After the shoot. When we were talking about Britt's present. He mentioned it then."

"Where I work came up in a conversation about Brittany's wedding gift?"

She tried not to show any reaction. "Yeah, something about the shower, I think. I've forgotten."

The tension around his eyes softened. "So he didn't put it together that we've..."

She raised her eyebrows and laughed. "Become friends?"

He leaned over and kissed her shoulder. "Very *good* friends."

She expected him to continue seducing her, but he leaned back up and stared into her face again. "So tell me about the places you've worked."

"You mean the cities?"

"That too."

Her heart sank, but she stuck to her cover story. "Actually, it's mostly confidential."

He looked shocked. "Time management consultation?"

She had a stock answer for that too. "Proprietary formulas, you know."

A grin lit up his eyes. "Actually I *don't* know, which sounds like a good thing. I'd hate to discover your secrets and force you to kill me."

His easygoing nature made her relax. How many guys had she told her cover story? And what percentage had gotten pissed she wouldn't divulge more?

"So, if you can't tell me about your job, then tell me about the cities you've lived in. I'm somewhat jealous. I've only lived in three places—Columbia, Blue Springs, and Kansas City, and in reality, the last two count as one."

"It was exciting at first," she said. "Los Angeles, Denver, San Francisco, Seattle, and now here."

"Obviously Kansas City being the most glamorous."

She gave him a coy smile. "Hey, it's not so bad. The perks here are pretty amazing."

His face lit up and he kissed her. "If I'm included in the perks package, I'm feeling pressure to keep you happy."

"You're doing pretty well so far."

He turned more serious. "But I can see the downside. You said you live in furnished apartments so you don't even have your own things with you. Do you have a home base anywhere?"

"I used to have a storage unit in LA, but I got tired of paying the monthly fee when I didn't use anything in it."

"So you're homeless?"

In the whole five years she'd been doing this, she'd never looked at it that way. "Yeah, I guess I am."

He paused, and something shifted in his eyes. "Where will you live if you move to Atlanta?"

A wave of panic hit her and she sat up. "I don't know. I hadn't even considered that aspect of it." She wouldn't have Stephanie with her. She'd be alone. Suddenly, she felt like she was losing something important, and it gave her second thoughts.

He sat up with her and turned her to face him. "Hey. It's just logistics, Lanie. You'll figure it out."

"Yeah."

When he spoke next, his words sounded weighted. "What about Aiden? I thought you two were friends."

What was she thinking? She wouldn't be alone. She'd have Aiden and the people in his new company. From the way he talked it up, they often worked as a team and got along well. "Yeah."

Tyler pulled her into a deep, soulful kiss then lifted his head, searching her eyes. "Do you want to take a shower before I take you home?"

She shoved her distress to the back of her head. She didn't want her fear getting in the way of her time with Tyler. Giving him a sexy smile, she said, "Only if you take one with me."

He hauled her out of the bed and flush against his naked body. "It's one of those Kansas City perks."

Chapter Nineteen

W hat the hell had he gotten himself into?

Tyler watched his younger brother pack away two hamburgers, an order of fries, and a chocolate shake. And now he was snatching an onion ring off Tyler's plate.

After their shower, he'd tried to get Lanie to go out to breakfast with him, but she only had her bridesmaid dress and one shoe—they couldn't find the other anywhere, but he'd promised to check with the building manager on Tuesday. He'd suggested he take her home to change first, but she'd insisted she needed to get started with her paperwork, with writing her resignation letter at the top of the list, and said she'd see him at the barbecue.

So after he'd dropped her off, he'd thought about their conversation about his brothers and called Eric and invited him to Five Guys for lunch. And now he was about to go broke feeding the kid.

"Does Dad cook?" Tyler asked, finally caving in and shoving his tray toward the teen.

Eric laughed through a mouthful of food. "Yeah, right."

"What do you guys eat?"

"Frozen dinners. Takeout when Dad leaves money. He's at the garage most of the time. I'm trying to get a part-time job, but the car Dad got me broke down."

Tyler frowned. "Why doesn't Dad fix it? He owns a garage."

Eric shrugged and grabbed more of Tyler's onion rings.

Dammit. No one was taking care of his brother.

His chest tightened, and he felt claustrophobic even though they were in a restaurant with thirteen-foot ceilings and walls of windows. He knew it wasn't the restaurant making him feel closed in. It was memories of his childhood, when he'd been responsible for himself and Alex for as long as he could remember. Sure, his mother hadn't left until Tyler was nearly seventeen, but in reality, she'd checked out long before she'd gone.

Now Eric had no one taking care of him, and Tyler felt that old familiar noose tightening around his neck.

But anxiety or not, this was his brother, who hadn't asked for their shitty family any more than he had. "Say," Tyler said carefully, testing out the words as he said them, "I need to go to the mall and get a few new dress shirts and ties. Want to come with me?"

Eric glanced up at him as though there was a catch, and Tyler felt like a dick. He'd created this gap between them. It was up to him to repair it.

"I need some jeans, too," he said. "Maybe you could help me pick out a pair."

Eric snorted. "I thought you had swagger."

"Is that a good thing or bad?"

His brother laughed, relaxing a bit. "Good, but now I'm reassessing."

"Then obviously I need your help. What do you say?"

Eric studied Tyler's face, and Tyler purposely remained impassive. He suspected it might be easier to lure a bear into a cage than to get his brother to go shopping with him.

Finally, Eric shrugged. "Sure. Why not?"

Two hours later, Tyler had two shirts and ties he hadn't needed, along with a pair of jeans, a pair of shoes, and some T-shirts. But Eric had multiple bags of new clothes and shoes of his own. If it took pretending that Tyler needed new athletic shoes to convince Eric to go into the store and try a pair on and buy them, then so be it.

"I'm hungry," Eric said, after they left a trendy clothing store for teens. He was carrying a bag with several name-brand shirts and jeans. The only way Tyler could get Eric to let him buy them was by lying and telling him he'd gotten a coupon for 50 percent off at the register.

Tyler laughed. "Why am I not surprised?" But when he saw the smile fall from Eric's face, he quickly added, "But you read my mind. I'm hungry too. What will it be? I say we skip the food court. How about 54th Street Grill? I could go for their Gringo Dip."

Eric shrugged, trying to look indifferent. "Yeah. Sure."

They took their shopping bags to Tyler's car and put them in the trunk before they drove across the street to the restaurant.

After the hostess showed them to their seat, Tyler racked his brain for a subject to talk about. School was out. When he was seventeen, what was he interested in? Football and girls. Since Eric didn't play football, that left girls.

Shit. He was in trouble.

When the waiter came over, Tyler ordered Gringo Dip and Eric ordered a chicken strip platter. When the waiter walked away, Eric beat him to starting the conversation. "So why are you hanging out with me? Couldn't get a date?"

Tyler considered reminding him it was three o'clock in the afternoon on Labor Day, not exactly prime dating time, but said, "I haven't been dating lately."

Eric snickered. "Define *lately*. You mean the last few days?"

"Five months."

Eric's eyes widened, and he sat up, finally showing interest. "You're kidding? Alex says you have a new woman every week."

Tyler shifted in his seat. "Let's just say I had a situation that made me reconsider dating."

"Did you get someone pregnant?"

Tyler's eyes narrowed. "No. I know how to use birth control, moron. Do we need to have that talk?" The edge in his voice softened. Maybe they *did* need to have that talk. Their father had never given it to him when he was a teen. "I'm not sure what they teach you in school, but you need to use condoms every time, Eric. The girl might be on birth control, but it's not always 100 percent foolproof, and you need to protect you both against STDs."

Eric squinted his eyes closed and shuddered. "Oh. My. God. I am not having this conversation."

"Tell me you're smart when it comes to sex."

Eric pushed out a loud sigh. "Not everyone is like you, Tyler. We don't all have women falling at our feet."

Tyler studied him for a moment. Eric hadn't mentioned having a girlfriend, not that Tyler had ever told the family about the girls he'd dated back then either. But Eric wasn't Tyler—he seemed more sensitive and not as cocky. Maybe that was why his grades were slipping. Maybe he had an unrequited crush on a girl. "True, but sometimes that's a good thing. Is there anyone you're interested in?"

"I'm not talking about girls with you."

"Have you had a girlfriend?"

"What part of 'I'm not talking about girls with you' do you not understand?"

Defeated, Tyler picked up a package of sugar and twisted it in his fingers. "How's band?" When Eric didn't answer, he glanced over at him. "Are you still in band?"

Eric held his gaze. "What instrument do I play?"

Tyler dropped the sugar packet on the table, stalling. "Uh... the trombone?"

Eric's mouth pinched, and he crossed his arms, glaring out the window like he could catch one of the cars in the parking lot on fire if he concentrated hard enough.

Wrong answer, apparently.

The waiter brought their food, and Tyler realized this was his little brother, and he didn't know jack shit about his life.

"You were a cute baby."

Eric gave him a look that said he was sure Tyler had lost his mind.

"I remember one Christmas, Mom dragged us to the mall to see Santa. I protested that I was too old to see Santa, but she wouldn't take no for an answer. You were a baby. I was sixteen."

Eric's expression softened. "What was she like?"

Well, shit. She'd left six months later. Eric wouldn't remember her at all. "Sometimes she was nice. Fun when she was around and... herself. When she acted like our mom, she used to do the stupidest things, like dance contests and gingerbread decorating contests between Alex and me."

"I bet Dad hated that."

"He did." Looking back now, he wondered if his father had pushed her into her madness. He was a cantankerous, practical man. But she had been like Dr. Jekyll and

Mr. Hyde. When she was on the upswing, she was giggly, fun, and lit up the room when she walked in. He'd adored that mother. Worshipped her. But toward the end, she became the dark side of herself, especially when she became pregnant with Eric.

He hadn't understood it back then, but he'd talked to his grandmother and researched it later. Their mother had been bipolar, and when she became pregnant with Eric, she'd stopped taking her medication and refused to go back on it after he was born. She'd suffered a deep postpartum depression. She'd started doing drugs and hooked up with her dealer, and the next thing he knew, she was gone. They never heard from her again.

She'd abandoned them all. Even the bubbly baby that shared her temperament when she wasn't deep in her madness. Only there was no sign of that carefree temperament in Eric now.

She might have abandoned her sons, but Tyler had abandoned Eric.

The waiter came to check on them, and when he left, Tyler steered the conversation to the latest movies they'd seen. Before he knew it, Eric was telling him about marching band camp and a new video game he'd borrowed from a friend.

Watching him, Tyler smiled, trying to remember being seventeen and having his whole life ahead of him. He'd been more cynical and jaded, mad at the whole fucking world, and while he'd turned out okay in the end, he didn't want that for Eric.

Tyler glanced at his phone to check the time. The barbecue was in an hour and a half, which meant he had another hour or so before he needed to take Eric home. Just as he was about to return his phone to his pocket, it rang.

He almost let it go to voice mail, but was surprised to see Lanie's number. They'd exchanged numbers that morning, but he hadn't expected to talk to her until Britt and Randy's get-together. Maybe she wanted him to take her home after the party. He *hoped* she wanted him to take her home after the party.

He tried to disguise his excitement when he answered.

"Lanie." He glanced at his kid brother and decided he didn't give a shit what he heard. He liked Lanie, and while he planned to keep it from everyone else—at Lanie's request—Eric didn't know any of his friends to tell. "Did you get all your work done?"

"Yeah." She sounded hesitant. "But I'm calling about something else, and I hope I'm not out of bounds."

He tried to quell his anticipation. It was obvious she was still trying to keep this as light and easy as possible, and common sense suggested that seeing each other three nights in a row was too much, too soon, yet damned if he didn't want to see her anyway. "I told you I wanted you to tell me anything you feel comfortable sharing. No rules, Lanie. We're just going to enjoy this before you go."

She hesitated. "Tyler, I think Britt's on to us."

"What makes you say that?"

"She called me after you dropped me off this morning. She says Celesta cornered her last night and told her I was lusting after you."

Tyler nearly choked on his water. "She said that?"

"I heard it secondhand, but basically that's the story, and the word *lust* was definitely used. But Britt wanted to know if I liked you and is suggesting pairing us up at their shindig."

"Oh." Why didn't that idea sound as bad it should have? "So what do you suggest?"

"I think one of us should skip Britt and Randy's barbecue."

He blinked, sure he'd heard her wrong. "What?"

"There's too much chemistry between us to deny it. We might be able to get away with hiding it at the next photo shoot this week, but at a party? There's no way I'll be able to pretend I'm not interested in you if I'm with you for a couple of hours."

He suspected she was right.

"It will be easier for me to come up with an excuse than you, so I'm going to text her and tell her I can't get away from work. Which isn't actually a lie." She laughed, but there was no humor in her voice.

He was surprised by the wave of disappointment that he wouldn't see her. He rubbed his forehead, bumping his stitches. He flinched. "Shit."

"You're pissed."

"What? No. That had nothing to do with you." He rubbed his head again. "Lanie, I think you're right, but let me ask you this—if you weren't worried about her discovering us, would you still put work on the back burner and go to the barbecue?"

"Yeah, but that's beside the point."

"No. It's not." He pushed out a breath. "I'll bow out. You go. Britt misses you, and you're leaving in less than a month. She'll be upset if you don't show. I can see them anytime."

"Are you sure?"

"Yeah." He glanced over at his brother. "Believe it or not, I wasn't planning to go anyway. I'm spending the day with my brother Eric."

"Thanks," she said, her tone husky. "I know you're lying about not going, and I think it's sweet. I promise to make it up to you. I'm already thinking of several ways to show you my appreciation."

His groin tightened, and he shifted in his seat. "I'm looking forward to it," he said, but kept his tone conversational.

She laughed. "Your brother's with you now, isn't he?"

"Yep."

"Older or younger?"

"Younger."

"Too bad," she whispered. "I was going to tell you some dirty, dirty things, but it doesn't seem appropriate when you're next to a teenager." She laughed again. "Thanks, Tyler." Then she hung up.

He must have worn a bewildered expression, because Eric was grinning ear to ear. "I didn't think you had a girlfriend."

"I don't."

"Was that the woman you were obsessed with at the game?"

"I wasn't obsessed."

"Okay, the woman you stared at every two minutes."

Tyler grunted and shifted to relieve the pressure of his erection in his jeans. "That was Lanie."

"Lanie..." Eric's tone sounded suggestive.

Tyler turned on a dime. "You will say her name with respect."

His brother's eyes widened. "Wow. You really like her."

He could deny it, but he had to deny it with everyone else—he didn't want to deny it with Eric, too. "Yeah. I do."

"But she's leaving in a month?"

"Yeah." He sucked in a breath and leaned his elbow on the table. "Her job moves her around every few months."

"That sucks. What does she do?"

"She's a time management consultant for retail stores."

"Wow," Eric said taking a bite of his chicken tender. "How does that work?"

"I'm not sure. She doesn't talk about it much."

"Where is she going that she doesn't want you to go?" Tyler shot him a surprised look, and he grinned. "I could hear your side of the conversation, you know."

Might as well tell him everything... within reason. "I'm a groomsman in my friends' wedding—Britt and Randy. One of the bridesmaids is Britt's cousin."

"Lanie."

"Yeah."

"She doesn't want Britt to know about us because Britt tends to meddle." When Eric made a face, he added, "She means well, but Lanie doesn't want her to meddle with us. So she wants to keep it a secret. From everyone."

"Is she embarrassed by you?"

That caught him off guard. "No. I don't think so." He'd dwell on that later. "But I suspect Britt might not meddle the way Lanie thinks. I think instead of trying to keep us together, she'd try to split us apart."

"I thought Britt was your friend."

"She is, but she knows my... past." If Britt wanted Lanie to stay, setting her up with Tyler would be the last thing she'd do.

"You mean that you've slept around with a lot of women?" Tyler's eyes widened.

"Dude, you never made any secret of it, and remember, Alex fills me in."

He shook his head. "Yeah, you're right. I did until last spring." He gave him the condensed, PG version of his experience with Nina. "That was the situation I was referring to earlier."

"And you haven't dated anyone since?" Eric asked.

"Not until Lanie."

"That sucks." He devoured the last chicken strip. "You don't want her to leave."

He decided to be honest with this too. "No. I don't. I don't understand it—I barely know her—but I don't."

Eric nodded sympathetically. "The same thing happened to Ricky Henderson."

"Who's Ricky Henderson?"

"A guy in my English class. He fell for a foreign exchange student last year, Mei Ling. An older woman." He grinned and then it fell. "But then she went back to China, and he was left with a broken heart."

"Poor bastard," Tyler said with a frown. He was exactly like fucking Ricky Henderson.

"So what are you going to do?" Eric asked.

"I don't know. I guess I'll see her as much as I can before she leaves."

"Even if hurts when she leaves?"

"Yeah." And that's what surprised him the most.

Chapter Twenty

Lanie sat in Britt's backyard having major second thoughts about Aiden's offer. She was fairly certain Atlanta was even hotter and more humid than Kansas City. But now that she'd turned in her notice, she might not have a choice.

She wandered over to the drinks table and grabbed a bottle of water. Everyone else was drinking margaritas or beer, but she felt unsettled for some reason. Probably because she'd spent most of the afternoon giving Aiden's offer serious consideration. She'd worked for Montgomery Enterprises for nearly her entire adult life. If she took Aiden's job, her whole life would change.

Randy made a subtle motion to her from over by the grill. She took a drink of water as she headed toward him.

"I've been stewing about this for an hour," he said, keeping his voice low. "I can't believe I'm about to tell you this…"

"What are you talking about?"

"See that guy in the pink polo shirt over there?"

"Yeah…"

"He's the attorney representing the firm that filed the injunction."

She gasped.

"I know for a fact he's talking about the case to the other guy, who is also an attorney from our firm."

She glanced up at him in shock.

"I didn't tell you a thing. And I don't even know who you really work for. So if you happened to wander over there, how would I know that an interested party might hear some key strategy?"

"Randy Harris, I had no idea you could be so devious."

He gave her a wicked grin. "If you ever implicate me, I'll deny it until my dying breath."

"Understood."

He winked. "Go get 'em."

She headed back to the drinks table and poured herself a frozen margarita from the pitcher. With drink in hand, at least she'd blend in. Part of her wondered why she even cared what Randy's colleague had to say about his strategy. She was leaving Margo Benson. But she'd had a successful seven years opening the stores, and she wanted to end it on a high note.

The question was, how to play this? She decided to stand by them to see if she could pick up their conversation.

"Going with Nelson versus Neidermier, huh?" a man in a white-and-blue plaid button-down shirt asked.

"That's right. Try to go through the back door," the guy in the pink shirt said, then he looked up and saw Lanie. "Well, hello there. You must be Brittany's cousin."

She had no choice but to be direct now. "That's right." She stuck out her hand. "Lanie."

"Victor. I work with Randy." He shook her hand, holding on longer than necessary.

She tugged her hand free. "So you're an attorney?" she asked, feigning surprise.

"You like attorneys?" he asked hopefully. "People either love them or hate them."

Tyler instantly popped into her head. "I fall into the approval camp."

"Britt tells me you're single."

The interest in his voice made her shoot a quick glance to his left ringer finger. No ring. Thank God. Nothing worse than married guys hitting on her, which happened more often than she liked. But when she looked back up, she realized he'd noticed. She didn't feel like leading this guy on. "Actually, I'm seeing someone."

Disappointment filled his eyes, but he said, "He's an attorney."

She was never going to see this man again. What would it hurt? "Yes."

"Who is he?" he asked. "I might know him."

There were a half dozen reasons she couldn't tell him the truth. Why had she dug herself into this hole? "He's not from around here. He lives in Atlanta."

She was playing this all wrong. She should have pretended to be single and hung out with him for the rest of the evening, and found out everything she could to help the store, but the thought made her feel slimy. And strangely enough, she felt like she was being unfaithful to Tyler, which in itself was ridiculous. They had no commitment to each other at all. For all she knew, he was going out with some other woman tonight.

But she knew he wasn't. He was with his brother. He'd told her he hadn't wanted to come, but she knew he'd stayed away because of her.

She realized Victor had asked her a question, but she

shook her head. "I'm sorry. I need to go make a quick phone call."

He nodded, and she headed into the house, setting her drink on the kitchen counter then hiding in the garage like she had during the shower.

What the hell was going on with her? How could she be so taken with him? If she was going to fall for someone, it couldn't be Tyler Norris. He was a *terrible* choice.

She pulled a Stella out of the refrigerator and popped off the top. Hopping up on the work bench, she sipped her beer, feeling like something was missing.

Tyler.

Then, before she could stop to think it through, she pulled out her phone and snapped a photo of the bottle with the label showing and the garage in the background. She uploaded it to a message that read, Thinking of you.

Sipping her beer, she waited several minutes for him to respond, disappointed when she got no response.

She was a grown woman, moping around because the man she'd practically asked not to come to his friends' party didn't answer her text.

What the hell is wrong with me? she asked herself, for what had to be tenth time that day.

It was her professional life. It was in tatters and it was bleeding into her personal life. But then, who was she kidding? She had no personal life.

But that wasn't true either. She had Tyler.

"Enough," she said out loud, draining the last of the beer and throwing the bottle into the glass-recycling bin.

She headed outside, grabbed a new bottle of water, and flopped down in a lawn chair next to her cousin.

"I want to know more about Tyler driving you home last

night," Britt said as she sipped her frozen margarita through a straw.

Good Lord. She needed to play this casual. Leaning back in her lawn chair, Lanie gave Brittany a pointed look. "Britt, I already told you everything."

"No...you didn't. Not really." When Lanie didn't answer, Britt pressed on. "So he was...nice?"

"Of course he was nice. Why wouldn't he be nice?"

"Well...after the shoe incident..."

"In case you didn't notice, we got along fine when I took off his bandage."

"True, but he seemed tense."

"He was in pain." Which still made her feel guilty. "The tape was stuck to his skin."

"No. It was more than that. He showed up a good fifteen minutes early—totally on edge—and he paced like a lion at the zoo, watching the parking lot until you showed up."

Lanie tried to hide her surprise. "No offense, Britt, but he's probably not a huge fan of all these photos shoots. If I was the last one to show up, maybe he was eager for me to get there so we could get started."

"Maybe..."

Lanie didn't believe her own explanation for a minute, but damned if she could figure out another explanation for his behavior. There was no doubt he was eager to see her again, but why would he be tense? He knew she was coming.

"I think there's something between you two."

Lanie tried to look amused. "You're hilarious. There's nothing there. Celesta was imagining things. Imagine that."

"Why don't I believe you?"

"Because you're always trying to set me up. He took me home, and that was that. He had dinner plans, remember?"

"It's just weird," Britt mused. "He was acting strange last

night, then he took you home, and then he cancelled today, which is weird because he's been hanging out a lot with us lately. I just wondered if something happened with you two."

Well, crap. If Britt wouldn't accept denial, maybe she should try distraction. "When he took me home he mentioned seeing his brother today."

Britt perked up. "His brother? Which one?"

"Um...younger. Eric?"

"That's great," Britt said, getting excited. "I'm surprised he didn't tell me. What else did you guys talk about?"

"Are you trying to pair us off for real?" And why did the thought send a flutter through her gut?

Britt laughed and gave her a look that suggested she was ridiculous. "Of course not. Tyler's a self-proclaimed life-long bachelor, and you run from anything that even hints of permanency. There's no hooking you two up."

That's exactly what she wanted Britt to think, but she felt oddly insulted. And she definitely didn't like her explanation. "What are you talking about?"

"Tyler's made no secret that—"

"No, not Tyler," Lanie protested, setting her bottle of water in the cup holder in her chair. "Me. What do you mean *I* run from any hint of permanency?"

Britt sat up, incredulous. "Are you serious?"

Lanie frowned. "I wouldn't be asking if I weren't."

"Look at your life, Lanie."

"I don't have to look at it. I'm living it. And I've been with Montgomery Enterprises for ten years, and the...other division for seven. That sounds pretty long-term to me."

"But you move from city to city every few months—"

"For my job, which I've held for years."

"You don't own a home. Hell, you don't even own a stick of furniture or even a car. You live a nomadic life."

"And I've made a lot of money. Most people would applaud me for being successful doing a damn hard job, and doing it consistently over and over again."

"But the job's not faithful to you, is it?"

Now Lanie was good and pissed. "If this is about Saturday night—"

"No. It's more than Saturday night. Or Thursday at lunch. Or Tuesday at my shower. Or the times when you were with me over the last two months, but you weren't really with me because you were too busy thinking about your job." Britt paused. "You've given your everything for this job, yet it's screwing you over, and you just keep going back for more."

Lanie had no argument. As much as it burned her, Britt was right. "Fine. What do you want me to say? I know they've screwed me. Now I'm dealing with it."

"I wish you'd learn from this, but you're just going to run off to the next city, or if they fire you, you'll find another job that sucks you dry. You'll go through the same thing all over again."

"You don't know that, Britt. I'm trying."

"But are you really? You're still working for them. You haven't turned in your notice, have you?"

Part of her wanted to tell Britt the truth, but Lanie knew she'd get the hard sell to stay. Better to figure out what she was doing before she spilled the beans. "I can't just quit my job, Britt. I have to have another one lined up."

"Are you even *looking*?"

"Britt…"

"You're running from something, Lanie. And until you face it, you'll never stop."

Lanie'd had enough. She stood and glared down at her cousin. "I love you, Britt, but back off."

Britt set down her drink and stood to face her. "No, I love

you too much to let it go. Name one serious relationship you've had with a man."

Lanie realized they were drawing attention and dragged Britt over behind a trellis covered in flowering ivy. "Tony," she said, resuming where they'd left off. "We were together for an entire year."

"You were a sophomore in college, and *you* broke that one off too."

"Yeah. Because he liked Dungeons and Dragons."

Britt's brow rose. "That's not a reason."

Lanie clenched her fists at her sides. "In my defense, that's just plain weird. He was some kind of magic guy and started walking around in a black robe, getting pissed if I didn't call him Mage Llewellyn. How was I supposed to take *that* seriously? Could you imagine him at Thanksgiving dinner?"

"Were you in love with him?"

"What? Are you kidding me? I loved him at some point. Then he got too weird."

Britt shook her head. "No. Not love, I'm talking *in* love. You know, when you see a guy and you go weak in the knees, you can't take your eyes off him, and he's all you can think about."

"Sorry to be the bearer of bad news, Britt, but that's lust." She caught Randy in her peripheral vision. He must have walked over from the grill to see what was going on. "Love's different. Deeper."

"That's true. But let's focus on the first part. Name one man who's made you feel alive."

There was only one, and she sure as hell couldn't tell Britt, so she remained silent.

"See?"

"Storybook endings are for you, Britt, not me."

"You don't know that. You won't even try." She took a breath. "So instead you'll just stay with your job, or you'll get fired and find some other impersonal corporation to work for, pretending that you like being alone."

"You have no idea what you're talking about," Lanie said, tears stinging her eyes. She never cried, and that pissed her off even more. "That's why Aiden was here yesterday. He asked me to—"

"Britt," Randy interrupted and rushed over to step between them. "Do you know where the hamburgers are?"

Britt gave him an exasperated glare as she pointed in the direction of the grill. "There're over there where you left them."

He forced a laugh. "I must have had one too many beers." Then he moved over to Lanie and wrapped an arm around her shoulder, giving her arm a hard squeeze. "Britt, I think it's time Lanie and I came clean about Aiden."

Britt gave him a bewildered look, but Lanie shot Randy a glare. She didn't want Britt to know until she'd made a decision.

"Randy—"

Randy squeezed again and cut Lanie off. "Let me tell her."

"Randy," Britt said sounding confused. "How do you know about Aiden?"

Randy kept his arm in place. "She told me yesterday after the photo shoot. While we were discussing your gift... Isn't that right, Lanie?"

What was he up to? "Yeah, but—"

Britt put her hands on her hips. "Go on."

Randy continued. "As you know, Aiden is Lanie's old boyfriend." He shot Lanie a pleading look, then turned to his fiancée. "She wants him to come to the wedding as her date."

Lanie tried not to look relieved, but Randy mistook her reaction and squeezed again. "It's okay, Lanie. She's not going to be mad."

"Why would I be mad?" Britt asked.

"Because," Randy said, "the guest list is tight, and Lanie knows how stressed you are. So she asked me if I would check into getting him an invite. I just hadn't talked to you about it yet."

"Lanie," Britt said with a groan. "Your invitation was a plus one. Which means you didn't even read it."

Lanie was irritated because she *had* read the invitation. She'd actually planned to bring Stephanie as her plus one. But she also saw the silver lining. Aiden was a thousand miles away and out of Britt's reach. If Britt thought she was dating Aiden, that took the heat off her and Tyler.

Britt must have seen this as a positive development and dropped her antagonistic attitude. "You want to bring a date."

Randy turned to her with pleading eyes. He'd been a huge help to her and stuck his neck out on a limb, especially when he'd told her about Victor. He had to have some reason for lying to his fiancée, and he was obviously asking Lanie to trust him. She took a breath. What harm could it do to go along with Randy's lie, especially when it helped her too? It wasn't like Aiden would even know. She had three weeks for Aiden to "change his mind" to explain why he wasn't able to make it to the wedding.

She only hoped it didn't bite her in the ass.

"Yeah," she said, and Randy dropped his arm. "And I *did* see the plus one. I planned to bring Stephanie. But if it's okay, I'd likc to bring Aiden too."

"Well, of course he can come. Just give me his address and I'll send an invitation to him."

Shit. She hadn't thought that all the way through. "Don't worry about it. I can just tell him."

"Not a chance. He's getting an invite." Excitement lit up her eyes. "What does Aiden do?"

"He's an attorney," Victor volunteered from several feet away. "Sorry. I heard loud voices and came over to make sure everything was okay. You *are* talking about your boyfriend from Atlanta, right?"

Britt's gaze narrowed, no doubt pissed that Randy's co-worker had found out the "good news" before she had.

Lanie was in a world of shit, but she was more worried about what Victor had heard. Had she said anything to clue him in that she was associated with Margo Benson? Surely Randy would be freaked out if she had. But instead, he was over at the ice bucket, grabbing another beer.

Although that wasn't exactly reassuring.

But Britt was clueless to her inner turmoil and seemed to take it in stride, trying to pry as much information from Lanie as possible. For the most part, Lanie stuck to the truth. She and Aiden had dated in college and kept in touch over the years. They saw each other several times a year. He lived in Atlanta and had come to see her the day before.

And with every word, Lanie felt more and more sick to her stomach.

An hour later, Tyler still hadn't answered her text, adding to her growing anxiety. Had she pushed him away?

After they ate, Lanie helped clean up and cornered Randy in the garage, where he was dumping bottles into the recycling bin.

"Why did you tell Britt I wanted Aiden to come to the wedding?"

He spun around, his eyes pleading with her. "Just trust me, okay?"

"I hate lying, Randy. I *hate* it."

"I know. I'm sorry. But what's it going to hurt? Just go along with it and tell her he can't come."

"I already told her his address."

"Then he can come if he wants. Either way, it won't matter."

And yet it did, only she didn't know why. But that was a lie. She knew exactly why. *Tyler*.

This was a disaster.

Chapter Twenty-One

Tyler walked into his condo, feeling good about his day with his brother. After he'd skipped the barbecue, he'd asked Eric to see the latest X-Men movie with him, then they ate dinner before Tyler dropped him off at home, making plans to see him on Wednesday night for dinner.

He felt like a first-class asshole. When he'd asked Eric to lunch, it had been out of obligation, but now he realized how much he liked the kid and really wanted to be part of his life.

Someone had to step up and make sure he was taken care of.

He expected the familiar suffocating feeling to swoop in, the tightening around his throat that made it difficult to breathe whenever he thought of someone being dependent on him, but it never came. Instead, it felt good to be needed.

He wouldn't screw his brother over like their mother had screwed them all over.

He sat on his leather sofa and realized his mother had defined his life—not just his past, but his future, too. He didn't trust people because neither of his parents could ever be counted on to be there when he needed them. But he also realized he had let *some* people in—Matt and Kevin. Britt and Randy.

What about Lanie?

Lanie scared him. He suspected he was going to end up like that poor bastard Ricky Henderson. Earlier he'd thought it was worth the risk, but now he wasn't so sure.

She'd sent him a text while he'd been in the movie, but he'd discovered it as they'd walked out of the theater. He'd stared at it for several long seconds before he slipped his phone back into his pocket. He needed to figure out what he wanted first.

But a few hours later, he still had no answer. He wanted to respond to her text, but several hours had passed. What was he going to say?

He glanced around his apartment, trying to think of what to take a photo of. His bed seemed too crass. And truth be told, as much as he wanted her there, if she said she wanted to see him and not have sex, he'd be happy to have that too.

That realization washed through him, and he sank back into the couch. He'd never wanted to just hang out with a woman before without the possible reward of sex. He wasn't sure he could ever be just friends with Lanie—he wanted her physically too damn much—but so far, he enjoyed her company out of bed as much as he enjoyed her in it.

He stood and moved to the living room window, then took a photo of the city lights. He attached it to the text he'd agonized over before he hit send.

This beautiful view will have to do until I see you on Thursday.

Then he waited. Nothing.

He sat back on the sofa and turned on the TV, then flipped

through a couple hundred channels, finally landing on an old movie, but he felt unsettled and he was unsure why. Was it Lanie? Was it thinking so much about his mother?

He checked his phone in case he'd missed the vibrating alert. Nothing.

He'd gotten up to take a shower and go to bed when the phone rang. His heart sped up until he saw Matt's number. He moved to his window as he answered.

"Hey."

"How are you doing after your run-in with Nina Saturday night?"

"I'm fine."

"Are you sure?"

"Why don't you get to what you're really calling about?" Tyler barked.

"And what's that, Mr. Mind Reader?" Matt asked in a calm voice.

"Lanie."

"Hey, what you do with Lanie is your business. I'm more worried about you jumping back into dating after taking such a long break."

"Five months isn't that long."

Matt paused. "Look, I know we're guys and we don't talk about our feeling much, but I want you to know you're not alone. You have friends who care about you. You can talk to me and Kevin about anything."

"I'm fine. I promise." He paused. "I spent most of the day with Eric."

"I thought you were going to that party at Randy's."

"I changed my mind."

"So what prompted your visit with Eric?" he asked.

"He's having trouble at school, and then I realized my dad's not doing shit for him. He's just a kid. He needs someone who cares. Turns out he's a pretty cool kid. We're going out to dinner on Wednesday."

"Sounds like my baby boy's growing up," Matt teased.

"You haven't seen Eric in over a year."

"I'm talking about you."

"Me?"

"You shy away from emotional attachments like they're poison ivy. Why do you think you haven't spent much time with the kid? Or women, for that matter."

Tyler pushed away from the window in frustration. "Now you're a psychologist?"

"It doesn't take a genius to see that's what you do."

"If you've known this, why didn't you tell *me*?"

"Because you weren't ready to see it yet."

Tyler couldn't deal with this right now. He headed toward his bedroom. "I'm tired. I'm going to bed."

"Tyler. Wait." Matt paused. "How about we go out for drinks again. Friday night?"

Tyler hesitated. "Let me get back to you."

"Kevin says she's leaving in three weeks."

He pushed out a breath. "I know."

"Just be careful."

It was too damn late for that.

He'd hung up and plugged his phone into the charger when Lanie's text popped onto the screen.

I'm looking forward to it.

So was he. Maybe a little too much.

Chapter Twenty-Two

‿

Lanie was ready for a shit-storm on Tuesday, but she was running on little sleep and frayed nerves. How long until she heard from corporate? And she still needed to break the news to Stephanie. She was dreading that conversation. And even though she was quitting, she still wanted this opening to be a success. From what little she'd overheard from Victor at the barbecue, he had a plan—not that she was surprised. But now she was living in limbo, waiting for the ax to fall.

Had she been foolish for not trying to get it out of him?

When she walked through the back door to the store at eight, with two boxes of doughnuts, the construction crew was bustling. They might have only been shut down for about twenty-four hours last week, but it seemed to have set them back several days. They had a week and a half to get everything done so that Lanie and Stephanie had time to get the store set up, and the staff trained and ready for the opening.

"Hector," Lanie called out to the foreman when she saw

him across the room. She set the boxes on a table in the back and met him halfway. "What are the chances we can be ready for me to start putting the store together by next Monday?"

"Lanie," he groaned. "You know I'm pushing my guys hard, but I'm tellin' ya, we can't handle any more delays. Next Wednesday's deadline is already pushing it."

She ignored the growing knot in the pit of her stomach. "And if we encounter another delay, would your crew be able to work over the weekend to make up for lost time?"

He looked skeptical. "You're looking at overtime. The last time we talked, you'd used up your cushion."

Gnawing on her bottom lip, she scanned the nearly completed store.

"You're expecting another delay," he said, studying her.

"I've dealt with people like this before. They don't give up so easily. I'm just preparing for the worst."

He leaned closer and lowered his voice, but he was still loud enough to be heard over the whine of a drill across the space. "Look, it's none of my business, but you haven't even announced any kind of opening. What's the big deal if you're delayed a week?"

"Because it's a big deal to my boss."

"We've a had a string of bad luck. We were delayed three days after that inspector got sick and forgot to hand our inspection over to someone else. Then the two days we couldn't continue construction waiting on those back-ordered sprinkler sprockets. Then that damned injunction. None of those things was your fault. Surely your boss isn't that big of a hard-ass."

"There's no good excuse in her book." She saw the irritated look on his face and gave him a reassuring smile. He was a fair and honest man with both his employees *and* his clients. He'd become aware of the pressures she was facing and he'd helped her when he could. She'd made a good decision when she'd accepted his bid, but then, she usually had good instincts when it came to business. "Don't worry about it, Hector. All we can do is bust our asses and hope for the best."

"It still isn't right, and it sure isn't fair."

"We both know life isn't fair." He looked so worried, she patted his arm. "Don't worry about me. I'm good no matter what happens."

She pulled out her tablet and walked around the store, ticking off the items on her list of things that had been completed and trying not to become overwhelmed by what wasn't. When she was satisfied, she waved good-bye to Hector and walked the block toward their rented office space.

She arrived before Stephanie, so she sat at her desk and took a deep breath, allowing herself a moment to think about Tyler.

His text last night had bothered her more than she cared to admit. She'd hoped to see him sooner than Thursday. While she could dwell on it, she chose to think about the positive. He still wanted to see her. When he hadn't answered for hours, she'd concluded that he'd decided she wasn't worth the trouble. So she'd take what she could get in the little time she had left and be grateful.

Her phone rang, and she froze when she saw Aiden's name on the screen.

"Aiden, I didn't expect to hear from you so soon. How was your trip back to Atlanta?"

"Uneventful, just how I like it." He paused. "I'm calling to touch base with you on my offer and see if you have any questions."

"I do have a few. I forgot to ask you when you would want me to start."

"October first. But I know you're living in corporate housing, so I suspect you'd want to come up to a week early to start getting your housing situation taken care of. I have a real estate agent I trust who can help you find something.

"Thanks." She swallowed. "I'm still wrapping my head around the fact that I turned in my notice."

"You had a good run, Lane. There are only bigger and better things in your future, whether you come work for me or not."

"Thanks, Aiden. But while I have you on the phone, I need to warn you about something you're about to get in the mail."

"Is Margo Benson sending me a box of anthrax for daring to lure you away?"

She laughed. "No. Maybe worse…It's an invitation to my cousin's wedding." When he didn't respond, she continued. "It's a long story, but my cousin thinks we're a couple, so she's sending you an invite. Feel free to throw it in the trash."

"Okay." She could hear the grin in his voice. "Never a dull moment with you, Lane."

"Personally, I'd love to have a dull moment or two." She hung up as Stephanie walked through the door.

"Dull moments are overrated," Stephanie said as she dropped her purse on her desk.

Lanie's stomach turned flips. She couldn't remember the last time she'd been this on edge. "Steph, I have to talk to you about something."

"It better be all about what happened after you left with that hottie from the wedding."

Saturday night seemed like ages ago. She took a deep breath. "I'll tell you after I talk to you about this first."

Her grin fell. "That sounds ominous."

Lanie looked her in the eyes. "After all the crap Eve's put us through...I decided I was done. I don't know about you, but I'm tired of them giving us a new boss every six to twelve months and having to kowtow to their demands. So yesterday I turned in my notice. But don't worry," Lanie added when she saw Stephanie's shock. "I'm not deserting you. I'm staying until the opening. I wouldn't leave you high and dry."

Stephanie stared at her. "I can't believe it."

"I know," Lanie said, her stomach balling into a tight knot. "I'm just tired of fighting a losing battle, you know?"

Stephanie nodded.

"In any case, I looked over my contract, and it's to my advantage to quit rather than let them fire me. I'll get a bonus package."

Steph nodded, looking devastated. "No, that's smart. Do you know where you're going?"

Lanie gave her an apologetic smile. "Well...as luck would have it, the reason Aiden was here was to offer me a job."

"In Atlanta?"

"Yeah."

Stephanie turned to look out the window, then back at Lanie. "Did you take it?"

"No, I haven't decided yet. But it's a really great offer." She gave Stephanie the details, including the part about finally finding a place to call home.

"Wow," Stephanie murmured. "That's quite a change."

"The idea of working for someone who appreciates me is exciting."

Stephanie's eyes turned glassy. "I already have that."

"The hardest part of this is leaving you."

Steph smiled, but it looked forced. "I'll be fine."

"I'm still going to give this opening one hundred percent. I'm not going to drop this all on you."

"I know you won't."

Lanie took a breath. "I owe you, Steph."

"No. I owe *you* for not only teaching me just about everything you know, but being my friend, too. I don't think I could have handled the past three years without you. Phoenix is going to be lonely."

"You won't have time to be lonely," Lanie said in a light tone. "You'll be busy setting up a store. And then you'll have your own Stephanie."

She wiped at her eyes, grabbed her purse, and stood. "I'm going to head over in case the delivery guys are early."

"Okay."

After Stephanie left, Lanie took a few minutes to pull herself together. She felt like she was losing her best friend. She told herself that she'd still be in contact with Stephanie, but deep down, she knew it wouldn't be the same.

She sent an e-mail to a headhunter who had contacted her multiple times over the last three years, trying to lure her away from Montgomery Enterprises. Aiden was right. She should explore her options, especially in the Kansas City area. Britt would be thrilled if she found a job here, and Lanie couldn't ignore the part of her that wondered what would happen with her and Tyler if she stayed. Would it freak him out? Would he be willing to give them a chance at something long-term? Would she?

She glanced down at her phone and realized he'd sent her a text.

How are you doing after turning in your notice? If you need to talk, give me a call. I'm free all morning.

Her heart skipped a beat, then she felt stupid for getting so excited. She was thirty-two years old, not twelve.

Before she could change her mind, she called him.

"Hey," he said softly.

Something warmed in her chest. "Is this a bad time?"

"No. It's a perfect time. I'm looking over a contract that's about to put me to sleep. How was the barbecue?"

Guilt washed through her, but she decided to play it light. "It wasn't nearly as fun as hanging out with you in the garage at the shower."

He released a low chuckle. "It looked like you made a good stab at it."

"I'm still waiting for Randy to notice he's missing all those Stellas." She paused. "I'm feeling guilty that you missed the party."

"Lanie. It was no big deal. I promise. I went to a movie with Eric, and then we went out for dinner. I'm glad I spent the day with him."

"Are you sure?"

"I'm going to be honest, okay?"

Her pulse sped up. Here it was, the big *but*.. She swallowed. "Yeah."

"I'll admit that I wanted to see you last night, but I agree that we would have done a poor job of hiding it from Britt. Besides, I really did enjoy hanging out with Eric."

So he wasn't dumping her. Yet. "I need to talk to you about something else."

"I'm listening." He sounded guarded.

"I contacted a headhunter this morning."

"I thought your friend Aiden offered you a job."

"He did, but..." Her stomach twisted with nerves. "Randy says Britt really wants me to stay here, so I asked the headhunter to look for jobs specifically in Kansas City." She took a breath. "I know I told you I wouldn't look for a job here, but I need to do this for Britt. And me."

"Lanie. It's okay. I know you're nothing like Celesta or Nina. You need to find the best job that works for you, and if it happens to be in the Kansas City area, I know that has absolutely nothing to do with us. Don't worry about me."

"Thanks."

"You were really worried?" He sounded surprised.

"Well, I did tell you I wouldn't look here. I just don't want you to think I'm like..."

"The other women in my past? I know you're not. Relax." She smiled. "Thanks."

"Have you heard from your boss since you sent your resignation?"

"No, but she's on the West Coast. I know it's coming."

"Stay strong. Let me know how it goes."

"Thanks."

The call came two hours later, but it wasn't from Eve. It was from Eve's boss, the senior VP, Michael Hunt.

"Lanie," he said in a good-natured tone. "I was hoping we could chat about your e-mail to Eve."

"Sure."

"I have to say, I was surprised to read your letter."

Lanie steeled her back. "I meant every word I said."

"And that surprises me even more. You've been with us for ten years, and your performance had been exemplary."

"This is my fourth VP in five years, Mr. Hunt. Some have been good and some have been bad, and I've had to adjust and cater to them, and frankly, I'm done with it."

"I'm sorry you've felt neglected."

"*Neglected* isn't the word."

"Lanie, I'm going to be direct." He was silent for a moment. "We've been unhappy with Eve and how she's managed...some things. You've handled her amazingly well; in fact, you've handled all the other VPs amazingly well, not to mention all the construction crews you hire in every location you move to. Contrary to how it looks, I've been watching, and I've been impressed for some time, which is why I want to offer you a new position."

Lanie blinked. "Excuse me?"

"We'd like to make you a VP over the western region. You can set up an office anywhere you like, and while you'd have to travel every so often, you'd be able to establish a home base."

"Anywhere I want?"

"You'd have an office and a small staff, and you'd oversee existing stores as well as the stores we've got plans to open."

"Isn't that Eve's job?"

"Not anymore."

Oh. *Wow.*

"Obviously, you'll want to give this some consideration," he said. "So take some time to think about it. You can work out the remainder of your notice, then give me an answer the day of the grand opening. I'll even come to Kansas City and be a part of it."

"Thanks...I'll definitely consider it."

"Good. Good. Then I'll be seeing you in three weeks."

Chapter Twenty-Three

S omebody's in a good mood," Randy said, stopping in Tyler's office doorway and leaning his shoulder into the frame.

Tyler grinned, his heart feeling lighter than it had in months, maybe years. Lanie had not only called him, she'd told him she was looking for a position in Kansas City. Things were looking brighter. "Yeah. I am."

"You must have had a good day with your brother."

Tyler's eyes widened in surprise. "How did you know I saw Eric?"

"Lanie. She told Britt." When Randy saw Tyler's confusion, he took several steps into the room. "Britt was worried about you. You weren't yourself at the photo shoot on Sunday night and she—"

Tyler held up his hands. "Whoa. Back up a step. What do you mean, I wasn't myself?" *Crap.* He'd known Lanie wanted to keep them under wraps, and he should have been more careful. But this confirmed that he'd made the right decision in not going to the barbecue.

Randy tilted his head. "Before we started the photo shoot, you were anxious and pacing. And then you cancelled with us last night. So, since you drove Lanie home, and she was the last person we knew who had seen you in between, Britt quizzed her," he said. "She asked how you'd been during the drive. What you'd said."

Tyler grinned. If Britt only knew what had happened during the drive... "And Lanie said I told her I was going to see Eric."

"Yeah."

"And Britt's curiosity was met?"

Randy chuckled. "We both know she's always got questions, but Lanie convinced her there was nothing more going on with you two. Especially when Lanie told her about Aiden." He paused, his smile fading a bit. "You'll never guess who showed up—Victor."

"You're kidding." At the moment, he didn't give a damn about Victor. He was more interested in what Lanie had told Britt about Aiden. He suspected it wasn't about the job offer.

"Nope. I invited him like I always do, but this was the first time he made an appearance. He was bragging about his big case," Randy said, but his mouth was drawn, like something about Victor's presence had bothered him.

Tyler shifted in his chair. "You know Victor. He loves to talk himself up."

"He was talking about a sensitive case in a public setting."

That got Tyler's attention. He leaned forward and rested his forearms on his desk. "It was mostly just people from the law firm there, right?"

"And a few of Britt's friends. And Lanie."

"You have to tell one of the partners," Tyler said. "They need to know about this right away. This isn't the first time he's shot off his mouth off in a social setting. Talk to Roger Hughes. He'll be the most receptive."

"That was my thought as well. Which is why I already talked to him. He wants you to take over the case."

"What?"

"It could be a high-profile case. Lots of press. You're bound to piss off a lot of women."

"How the hell would I do that?" Tyler asked.

"It's one of those Margo Benson Boutiques, and once women find out you're trying to shut it down, you'll be public enemy number one with women in a hundred-mile radius."

Tyler forced a grin. "I think I can handle it." He sat back in his chair. Under any other circumstances, he'd jump at the chance, but all he could think about was all the time it would probably demand. Time he could otherwise spend with Lanie before she left.

Randy started to leave the office, but then stopped and turned around to face him again. "What do you think of Lanie?"

Tyler blinked, trying to figure out where that question had come from. He shrugged. "She seems nice. Britt is clearly happy that she's back." He was surprised his pulse had picked up and his palms were sweaty. "Why do you ask?" He reached for his bottle of water and took a swig.

Randy's face was expressionless. "Britt thinks there might be something going on with you two."

Tyler choked on his water and slammed his bottle on the desk, spraying water onto the papers strewn over the surface.

"Are you okay?" Randy asked, sounding alarmed.

"Yeah," he said through a cough as he tried to clear his airway. "Went down the wrong pipe."

"Does that mean there is or there's not?"

"I really can't believe we're having this conversation. You know I haven't dated since Nina."

"This is serious, Tyler. I need to know. Do you like her?"

Jesus. What was the right way to answer that question?

He shrugged. "She's all right. Seemed a little flighty on Saturday night at the art museum lawn, you know, with the drunken entrance and the shoe thing." Feeling like a traitor, he shrugged again and grabbed a couple of tissues.

Randy's eyes bugged out. "She was *drunk*?"

Shit. "No. I don't think she was drunk. I think maybe she'd come from having drinks with someone. I could smell alcohol on her breath. But she took an Uber, right? So it wasn't like she endangered anyone."

Randy grinned. "Except for you." He pointed to Tyler's forehead. "Since that happened over the weekend, you must have gotten a lot of questions today."

"Why do you think I'm hiding in my office?"

Randy turned serious again. "You're sure nothing's going on between you two?"

"You must be drinking Britt's Kool-Aid."

"That didn't answer my question."

This was more than idle curiosity. He hated to lie, but he'd promised Lanie. "No. Nothing's going on between us. Why are you so relentless about this?"

Randy stayed in the doorway, pausing as though he was considering his words carefully. "Britt's worried about her."

Tyler forced a grin. "Britt's worried about everyone."

Randy's mouth lifted into a small grin. "True, but she can't help worrying about the people she cares about."

"I feel lucky to be included in that camp." He started mopping up the water droplets, then, before he had time to think it through, he asked, "Why is Britt worried about her?" If Lanie was in trouble, he wanted to know.

Randy walked back into the room and lowered his voice. "Her job situation is shaky...But it's more than that. After Britt quizzed her about you, they had an argument."

Tyler's throat tightened. Lanie hadn't mentioned an argument with Brittany. She hadn't mentioned anything about the party at all. "What about?"

"Lanie's job." He hesitated. "She moves around a lot, and Britt hates it. She wants her to stay here. But then Britt dragged out a bunch of shit about Lanie's past relationships, and all in our backyard. During the party."

Dammit. Why hadn't Lanie told him? But then, why would she? They didn't really share their personal lives, but he wanted to change that. "That doesn't sound like Britt."

"It's not. The only thing I can attribute it to is wedding stress."

"She's not the first woman to be hit with a touch of Bridezilla. But it's Britt. She'll be fine."

"I hope so." Still, he hesitated.

Tyler stood and looked his friend in the eye. "Something's bothering you. What's going on?"

"I think I did something I shouldn't have." Then he turned and walked out the door.

What could Randy possibly have done? But after hearing about Lanie's argument with Britt, Tyler was more worried about her. He picked up his phone and texted.

Have lunch with me.

What would she think? Would she blow him off? He decided this would be a good gauge to what she was looking for in their relationship.

She answered seconds later.

Today?

Yes. I'm free until 2:00.

From the bubble in the text space, he could see she was typing, but thirty seconds later, she still hadn't sent a response. Finally, she sent:

I can't be gone very long.

He wondered why that had taken her so long and then he got it. She thought he wanted a nooner. But then, why wouldn't she? Up to this point, everything between them was built on sexual chemistry. He was sure there could be more. This was the first step in proving it.

Lunch. Capital Grill. Forty-five minutes. Tops.

12:30? she asked.

See you then.

Chapter Twenty-Four

Tyler was waiting for her when she walked in, not that she was surprised. He was sitting in the bar and stood when he saw her, moving straight for her with appreciation in his eyes.

When he reached her, he slipped an arm around her back and gave her a gentle kiss. "Thanks for meeting me."

"Thanks for asking."

"Since you only have forty-five minutes, I thought it'd be faster to eat in the bar. If that's okay with you."

"Sounds good."

He led her to a booth in the bar and gestured for her to sit on one side. She slid onto the leather seat and hid her shaking hands under the table.

Why was she so nervous?

"It's a good thing I dressed up today," she said. "It's not every day I eat at the Capital Grill." She'd always been a believer in "dress to impress" with her job. She wore a fitted, sleeveless black dress with a pencil skirt and a deep V neckline, along with three-inch black patent-leather pumps. Her hair was up in a twist, but a few wisps had escaped around her face.

"You look gorgeous." His gaze drifted to her cleavage then quickly returned to her face. "But you always look gorgeous."

She flushed, and he grinned, but it looked more boyish than rakish and she couldn't stop her own huge smile. It felt like they were on new ground.

"I've never eaten here," she confessed. "What's good?"

He named several items, keeping his eyes on her the entire time, never letting them leave her face until the waiter appeared a couple of minutes later, leaving menus and taking their drink orders.

"Water for me," Lanie said. "I need to head back to work."

"Same," Tyler told the waiter.

After he left, Tyler's gaze turned concerned. "Randy stopped in my office this morning."

She froze and tried badly to recover. Randy must have told him about the Aiden fiasco with Britt. "Oh?"

"He told me that you and Britt had an argument."

Her face flushed, but this time in utter embarrassment. "Oh, God. What did he tell you?"

He reached across the table and covered her hand with his own. "Lanie. It's okay. Nothing hurtful or embarrassing. He just said Britt went off the deep end and blasted you about your job and your past relationships."

"Did he give you details?" she asked in horror.

"No. And I would have stopped him if he had. That's for you to share with me, if and when you feel comfortable telling me. I don't want to hear it second- or thirdhand from Randy."

She nodded.

"But he *did* say she's worried about your job situation."

"I haven't told her I turned in my resignation and I'm not going to until I know what I'm going to do. Which is part of the reason I contacted the headhunter. To make Britt happy."

"The only person you need to make happy here is you."

"Thanks. But I wanted to do it too. It would be nice to be able to see her more often and hang out on random occasions."

The waiter came and took their order, and Tyler told her about his afternoon and evening with Eric, but none of the messy personal details, like why he hadn't spent much time with his brother in recent years.

"I'm taking him out to dinner on Wednesday night. I'd like to start seeing him weekly so he knows I'm not just blowing smoke up his ass."

She smiled. "I think that's a good idea." Wondering if she was sticking her nose where it didn't belong, she decided to ask—he could tell her to mind her own business if he didn't want to answer. "What spurred this decision to start spending time with him?"

"His principal called me last week. He couldn't get ahold of my dad. He said Eric was blowing off his classes and skipping school. Mr. Carter was concerned because he's been a good student until this year." His mouth twisted in amusement. "Unlike me. In any case, the principal's call made me realize I hardly knew the kid. Getting Royals tickets from my colleague was a good way to break the ice with Eric."

"So you could ask him why he was acting out?"

"No. Just to let him know he wasn't alone."

"Did he tell you why he was behaving out of character?"

"No."

"Has he improved?"

"I think he's just testing boundaries. All teens do it. I'm hoping he'll see that I'm here for him and really give a shit and he'll straighten his course."

"But you talked to him about it?"

She worried he'd get pissed, but he gave her a grin. "I did."

"Okay."

He looked confused. "You sound like you care about him. You don't even know him."

"He's your brother."

His expression suggested he didn't understand that, but he didn't ask any more questions. *Typical man.* She found it reassuring he wasn't perfect. He'd seemed too good to be true up to this point. "So..." she said with a slow smile. "Your Wednesday night is busy. But what about Thursday?"

His smile turned seductive. "I'm going to be very busy."

"That's too bad," she said in a sultry voice as her nerve endings sprang to life. "I had plans."

"What kind of plans?"

She raked her top teeth over her lower lip, and his gaze followed. "It might involve one of your ties."

She could see he was fighting to keep his breath even. "What are you doing tonight?" he asked.

"Seducing you."

He released a barely audible groan. "You've already begun."

She laughed. "I can cook dinner, but I don't have any food at my place."

He shook his head. "Come to mine. I have food. I'll cook." He paused. "Bring a change of clothes. I want you all night."

A wave of heat washed through her. *This man*, she wanted to tell Britt, *this man did crazy things to her body with only his voice*.

"Do you want me to pick you up?" he asked.

"No. Just send me the street address and let me know what time."

"Seven. I'll be home by then."

"It's a date," she said, surprised at how happy that made her.

They finished lunch, and Tyler paid the bill and walked her outside, his possessive hand on the small of her back until they were on the sidewalk. She turned to face him, and his hand remained in place on her back while his other hand cupped the side of her face.

He searched her eyes for something before he lowered his lips to hers, giving her a gentle kiss that quickly turned ravenous.

She wrapped her hand around the back of his neck and clung to him. How had this man gotten under skin in only a week? But sex with him was the best she'd ever had, and with the expiration date looming in the near future, she needed to make the most of it.

But she also realized she was making out with Tyler in broad daylight on a Tuesday afternoon.

She stepped back, but he still held his hand on her back.

"Sorry," he said. "I swore to myself I wouldn't touch you at lunch, but I find you so fucking irresistible."

Sucking in her breath, she dealt with a new wave of desire. Seven couldn't get here fast enough. "Maybe," she said softly, "we should stop pretending." She looked up into his eager eyes. "I think we should just give in and accept that we have crazy, off-the-charts chemistry and make the most of it. And then when the wedding comes, maybe we'll have worked it out of our systems so it will be easier to say good-bye." But even as she said the words, she knew how crazy it was. She was fairly certain she was only going to get more attached, yet she was powerless to stop the train wreck. Strangely enough, she didn't care.

He answered with his mouth, but not with words. "Clothes," he said, when he lifted his head. "Bring lots of clothes."

She grinned. "Because?"

"Because I might not let you leave."

She laughed, and her phone rang in her purse. She took several steps back, out of his reach. "I'm surprised I made it this long without a call. I'll see you tonight."

He turned serious. "Can I drop you off at your office? Or your store...? Where are you even going?"

She wanted to be done with the secrecy about her job. But although she might be leaving Margot Benson, she still had an NDA to consider. "My office is close by. It would take as much time to walk there as it would to your car in the parking garage."

He flashed her a sexy grin. "Are you sure?"

No. She wasn't sure at all. Telling him no took more willpower than she expected. Taking several more steps backward, she grinned. "I'll see you tonight."

Then she turned around and crossed the street before she changed her mind.

Chapter Twenty-Five

Lanie showed up at Tyler's apartment promptly at seven. He was eager to see her and resume where they had left off after lunch. She stood outside the door, still in her black dress and heels, carrying a leather duffel bag and a bottle of wine, but he could tell right away something was wrong.

He took the bag and the bottle and invited her in. "Is everything okay? If we're moving too fast, we can call this off."

She looked up at him with a forced smile. "No. That's not it. I've got a headache."

He tossed her bag on a chair in the living room and set the wine bottle on the counter, then pulled her into his arms, pressing her cheek to his chest. "Migraine?"

"No," she said, molding herself to him. "Good old-fashioned stress. I thought it might get better, but it seems to be getting worse. Maybe I should just go home."

She started to pull away, but he held her close. "Stay."

"But I'm terrible company tonight, and obviously I'm not in the mood to fool around."

"You have to eat, right? Maybe it will help."

"Tyler—"

"I've already started dinner. Stay. Then if you still feel bad, I'll take you home, and we can get your car back to you tomorrow."

"I don't have a car. I took an Uber."

He glanced down at her in surprise. "How did I not know that? How do you get around without one?"

"I don't own a car because it's too hard to move around, and since I put stores in urban areas—" Her body stiffened. "I try to get apartments close to where I work. I use Ubers, taxis, or rent a car for a day or so if I need one."

Something had just happened, but damned if he knew what. "That's pretty awesome. So you usually work at urban stores?"

She seemed to relax a little and buried her cheek into his chest. "It depends on the demographics of the city, but most are trying to upscale their downtowns. Those are my target areas."

That was the most he'd ever heard about her job. "Have you taken something for your headache?"

"No, not yet. But you holding me actually seems to be helping."

He looked down at the top of her head as he rubbed the back of her neck. She made a contented sound that reminded him of the sounds she made in bed, and the blood rushed to his groin. *Dammit.* He didn't want her to think he was trying to sleep with her. Not when she felt bad.

"Then let's have you sit." He tugged her to the sofa and had her sit the middle. Kneeling in front of her, he pulled off her heels and tossed them toward the window.

She'd closed her eyes, but now she pried one open and glared at him. "Don't lose those shoes, mister. They're my favorite black pumps. I'm still trying to get my bridesmaid's shoes replaced by Thursday night."

He grinned. "Yes, ma'am." He began to massage her left foot, and she leaned her head back and moaned. "Oh my God, that feels good."

He couldn't help laughing. "Had I only known rubbing your feet was foreplay." Then he massaged the other for several seconds. "You can't relax in that dress. Why don't you change? Do you have anything comfortable in that bag?"

She gave him a pointed look. "The idea was seduction, Tyler. Not Sunday morning yoga pants."

He pulled her off the sofa and down the hall to his room. He grabbed a T-shirt from his drawer and handed it to her. "This should be long enough to cover the important parts." Then he reached behind her and unzipped her dress before he returned to the kitchen. God only knew what she was wearing under that dress. He didn't plan to stick around and drive himself crazy.

He grabbed a corkscrew and opened the wine, then poured two glasses. As he was reaching for the ibuprofen, she padded down the hall wearing his oversized MU Tigers shirt. She was sexy in everything he'd seen her in, but for some reason, seeing her like this made her seem more real.

"Here," he said, handing her the tablets, then getting her a glass of water. "Take these." She swallowed them, and he traded the wineglass for the water.

"Are you hungry? We can just eat on the sofa if you like."

She made a face. "I've ruined our night."

"You haven't ruined anything. It's nothing fancy. Go sit down."

"Okay."

He scooped the fettucine alfredo he'd made into bowls and brought them into the living room, handing her one. "I have bread, too."

She took the bowl and sat up. "This looks delicious."

He grabbed his wine and the bread. He set them both on the coffee table, then picked up his bowl to eat.

She'd been fine at lunch, so he wondered if anything had happened after. "Did your boss give you grief about your resignation?"

"Actually, the opposite. The senior VP called and offered me a promotion."

For some reason he felt relieved that she didn't seem excited. "What did you say?"

"I said I'd think about it."

He couldn't get a read as to whether she was interested in staying or not. "Is Aiden upset you haven't given him an answer yet?"

Her head swung to face him with a questioning look.

"I figured if you're thinking about staying with your company, you wouldn't tell Aiden yes, but you wouldn't tell him no yet, either."

A weary smile crossed her face. "You're a very smart man." Lanie ate half her pasta, then pushed it away before she turned to face him. "Why are you being so nice to me?"

"My ogre-like tendencies are a myth I spread around to scare away women. Turns out I'm actually capable of being nice."

She leaned over and softly kissed his lips. "I knew it all along. It's not a very good secret. But my head's still pounding, so I think I should go home. I'm not much company tonight."

When she started to get up, he took her hand and gently pulled her back down. "I'll take you home if you like, but would you be more comfortable at home all alone or here where I can rub your feet?" He reached for her foot and began to rub.

She released a contented sigh. "You fight dirty."

"You have no idea." He reached behind him, grabbed a throw pillow, and stacked it onto the pillow on the other end of the sofa, then pushed her back so she was lying down. The T-shirt came to the very top of her thighs, and he could see the barest hint of her black panties.

God help him.

He stood and grabbed an afghan out of a chest behind the sofa and covered her legs.

She chuckled, then grimaced in pain. "When did we decide to become modest?"

"I'm trying to ignore that you're the sexiest woman alive, but you're a terrible distraction, Lanie Rogers. Do you want to watch something on TV?"

"Sure. I don't care what."

He decided to leave it off for now. This silence was probably better for her head. She lay back on the pillows and closed her eyes. He was relieved that her face looked less strained than when she'd first showed up.

He settled into the other end of the sofa and began to rub the ball of her foot. "What has you so stressed, Lanie?"

"Everything." With her eyes still closed, she reached up and began to rub her temple.

"Me?"

Her eyes opened and she smiled. "No. It's work. My contract says I get a very large bonus if I can finish out my three weeks and get a big project done on time. But there's a good chance I won't be able to get it done. It kills me because I've never missed a single deadline. *Ever.* It's driving me crazy to think it might end this way."

"It makes sense, though. You want to preserve your legacy."

Wonder filled her eyes. "Yes. That's exactly it."

"So stay with the company. You said your senior VP wants you."

She shook her head. "I can't bring myself to say yes because I think I'm ready for a change. But I have no idea what I want to do."

"If you get your bonus, maybe you could take some time to think about it. You don't have to rush into anything."

"I can't count on that bonus."

"So why don't you just take Aiden's job?"

She hesitated. "It's going to sound stupid."

"Coming from you? I doubt it."

Indecision filled her eyes. "Something about his offer just doesn't feel right."

Was she saying *Aiden* didn't feel right? He couldn't ignore that he was jealous of Aiden, even if they were really just friends.

But he waited so long to answer that she groaned and tried to pull her foot away. "See!" she said. "I told you."

He held on tight. "I was waiting for the stupid part."

"Tyler..."

"If the offer doesn't feel right, it doesn't feel right. Listen to your intuition. But some part of the job appeals to you, or you wouldn't be considering it."

"True. I like the idea of being a consultant. I wouldn't mind traveling from time to time, but I like the idea of growing some roots. Having a home. Family." Horror washed over her face and she shot up. "I didn't mean it like that. I meant Britt and—"

He pushed her back. "Relax. I knew what you meant. I would hate your job. I don't know about the time management stuff, but moving every few months? No, thanks. I like being close to my friends."

"And your brothers?"

He gave her a sad smile. "And my brothers."

Studying her face, he wavered before making his suggestion. How would she read it? "I think you should stay in Kansas City. You miss Britt, and we both know she misses you. I think deep down, that's what you really want. Surely you can find something here. And don't let the house stuff stress you either. Rent an apartment—unfurnished—and buy furniture. Or rent a house with a yard and plant a garden. Buy a car." He grinned. "Just do things one step at a time."

"How'd you get so wise?"

He laughed. "I am far from wise, but I like the idea that you think so. How's your headache?"

"Better. Thanks to you. Talking about all of this has helped."

"Who do you usually talk to?"

"It depends. Steph and I are close, but I can't confide some of these things to her. I'm her boss, so it's not always appropriate. And Britt's far from objective."

"So talk to *me*."

Her mouth pursed as she watched him. "And who do you talk to?"

"Randy. Britt. Matt and Kevin." He grinned. "You."

"I told you about my work woes, now you have to share something with me."

He picked up her other foot. "Like what?"

"What bothers you? What makes you anxious?"

Giving her a sideways glance, he began to massage her toes. "My brothers. My job." *You.*

"What makes you anxious about your brothers?"

"I told you at lunch."

"Why have you stayed away from your brothers, Tyler? You admitted you didn't see them very much and now you're seeing Eric three times in one week, which I think is wonderful. But there was some reason you stayed away."

Part of him wanted to tell her. But he worried he'd sound pathetic.

"You know," she said, pulling her foot free and sitting up. She crossed her legs, grabbed one of the throw pillows, and placed it on her lap. "Britt said some things to me yesterday that were hard to hear. But I've been thinking about them today."

"Lanie." He reached over and covered her hand with his own. "It sounds like Britt was out of line. Even Randy thinks so."

"But she said something that I think is true." She hesitated and searched his face. "She thinks I'm running from something, and I think she's right." Her gaze held his. "I think you stayed away from your brothers because you're running from something too."

She was right, but he knew what his demons were. "I know what I'm running from," he said. "And building this relationship with Eric is the first step. Believe it or not, you've helped with that too."

He sank back into the sofa. "I told you that my mother left us. What I didn't tell you was that she was mentally ill. She did some horrible things before she left, and she was definitely no mother in the end. My father wasn't much better. It's hard for me to trust people. I keep expecting them to let me down and leave."

And there it was. As much as he didn't want Lanie to leave, he knew having an expiration date on their relationship was a good thing. At least this way, he knew when it was going to end.

So why wasn't that as reassuring as he'd expected?

Chapter Twenty-Six

Late Thursday afternoon, Lanie rushed home to get ready for the photo shoot. Tonight's shoot was across from the Royals' stadium, and Britt and the photographer wanted the photos taken at night with the lights of the stadium behind them. But it meant they were meeting at eight.

Tyler had texted that he'd bring dinner to her apartment and they could change there and head to the stadium.

He showed up at six with his tux in a dry-cleaning bag and a takeout bag from Kona Grill.

When she opened the door, he greeted her with a huge grin and a kiss. "I wasn't sure what you'd want so I got sushi and salmon."

She wrapped an arm around his neck and pulled him closer. "Good choice. I love them both."

He grinned against her mouth. "Had I known sushi turned you on so much, I would have brought some to Britt's shower."

Laughter bubbled out of her, and she gave him one last

kiss before taking the bag from him. "You actually might have had a shot that night if you'd shown me a California roll."

He laughed. "I'm going to hang this in your closet."

"You got it cleaned," she said. "But it reminds me that Britt's going to kill me when I show up without my shoes. The bridal shop didn't get the replacement pair in yet."

"I'll use my charm to distract her," he called over his shoulder as he walked down the hall.

"And the fact that it will be dark," she called after him.

He came back and grabbed two plates out of her cabinet. "I'll admit that could help."

"We're talking about Britt. She'll figure it out the minute I get out of the car."

"No more talk about Britt. I want to hear about your day."

She sobered. Lying about her job was starting to eat at her, but she wasn't sure how to get around it. The only thing she knew to do was to focus on the future. "It was fine."

He looked up from cutting the salmon in half. "Did your headhunter come up with something here in Kansas City? Or anything at all, for that matter?"

"No, but there's something I didn't tell you about the VP job, and given what's going on with us, I feel like there needs to be full disclosure." Especially since she had to be so secretive about her current job situation. She waited until he glanced up at her. "I can set my office anywhere. I could set it here."

"But it hinges on finishing your big project?"

"Yeah."

"So if I understand correctly, there are two very different outcomes that depend on you completing your project. The first is you get a bonus if you leave, but if you stay, you'll get a promotion."

She grinned. "Who knew you were more than just a pretty face?"

He laughed as she divided the sushi onto plates. "I'm going to take that as a compliment."

"Brains and beauty. You're the whole package," she teased, but she realized it was true. *Dammit.* She'd finally found a guy she could see herself falling for, and not only was he a short-term-relationship kind of guy, but there was a chance she'd be moving away from him. But she wasn't gone yet, and she planned to enjoy every minute that she had. "So how was *your* day?"

Tyler set the takeout container on the counter. "I made progress on a tough case today."

She licked a piece of rice off her finger. "That's great."

"I'm close to making partner, and this case might be the deciding factor."

"No wonder you sound excited."

He smiled. "But the best part of today is seeing you."

She laughed, shaking her head as she handed him a pair of chopsticks.

They sat down to eat, and Tyler picked up one of the rolls on his plate. "Let's go out tomorrow night."

Lanie glanced up in surprise. "You mean a date?"

"Yeah, why not? I was thinking dinner and a movie."

"Sure. Sounds fun."

"But let's stay at my place tomorrow. Why don't you pack for the weekend?"

And this was where it had always started to unravel with her previous relationships. Men never understood her work schedule.

She lowered her chopsticks and glanced up at him. "I

won't have the weekend free. Steph and I have some interviews on both Saturday and Sunday, and I have plenty of other things to handle."

"So you can get your project done before your last day?"

"Yeah." Then she waited for the irritation, or frustration, or outright anger. But it didn't come.

He shrugged. "Okay. Then how about you just treat it like a workday and come home to my place when you're done?"

"You're not upset?" she asked in surprise.

He laughed. "I had a life before you, Lanie." Then he leaned closer and kissed her neck. "I have things to fill my time... until I fill you at night."

She sucked in a breath as her nerve endings lit on fire.

His arm slipped around her back to hold her still as his mouth slid up her jaw. "Is that a yes?"

"Yes..."

Tyler sat back up with a satisfied smile. "That's my girl."

His girl. He hadn't meant anything by his statement—in fact, he'd turned his focus on his sushi roll—but still the comment made her smile. She was surprised she liked the idea of being his.

They ate dinner, and Tyler told her about his dinner with his brother the night before. When they finished, they got dressed for the photo shoot, and Lanie searched her closet for a substitute pair of shoes.

"Britt's going to kill me, and I'll deserve it. We shouldn't have left that shoe in the hall."

He put his hands on her shoulders and grinned. "I'll take the responsibility for it."

She laughed. "What are you going to say? That you were so eager to get laid, I tripped on my dress, and we deserted my shoe in the hall?"

His eyebrows rose with mischief. "What? You don't think she'll buy it?"

"Maybe a little too well."

"How about you left it in my car, and I accidently threw it away?"

"That excuse only works if we were both extremely drunk, and in combination with your car, that sounds extremely irresponsible."

"Where's the shoe you *do* have?"

She grabbed it from the bottom of her closet and held it up. "Do you think one shoe is better than none? Am I supposed to hobble around on one foot? Or wear two different shoes?"

He laughed and pushed her onto the edge of the bed. "Oh ye of little faith. You underestimate my skills."

"Oh," she teased, "I'm well aware of some of your magnificent skills, but I suspect Randy might have a thing or two to say if you start seducing Britt."

"Lanie, when you're in the room, there is no one else but you."

"And when I leave the room?" she asked playfully.

His smile fell, and he turned surprisingly serious. "There's no one else then either."

His answer shocked her, but then he shocked her more when he turned around and left the room. "Where are you going?"

"Stay there."

"So our plan is for me to hide in my room?" she called after him.

Seconds later, he stood in the doorway with his hand behind his back and a cheesy grin on his face.

"What are you doing?" she asked, realizing how much she loved this playful side of him. She'd never had this in any of her previous relationships, and she'd had no idea she even wanted it until now.

He stepped into the room, placed a hand on his stomach and bowed at the waist, then stood. "Prince Charming would like to present you with this shoe." Then he pulled her missing shoe from behind his back and held out the purple pump.

"You found it."

"Someone turned it in to the property manager." Grinning, he knelt in front of her, then seductively lifted the hem of her bridesmaid's dress up to her knee.

"What are you doing?"

He looked up at her with his bad-boy eyes. "I have to try it on you, of course." He slipped it on, then slowly ran his hands up her calf to her thigh.

"I don't remember it happening this way," she pushed out in a breathless gasp as her body ignited. How did he turn her on so quickly?

"This is our own X-rated version," he said, leaning down to kiss her knee while his hand slid up to her panties.

"We'll be late," she said without protest as he pushed her back onto the bed. "What will we tell Britt?"

He pushed her dress up to her waist and tugged down her panties within seconds. A wicked smile crossed his face as he knelt between her bare legs. "That you met the Big Bad Wolf."

"Wrong fairy tale..." she gasped as he began to distract her.

He looked up at her and grinned. "My version's much better."

* * *

On Friday, Tyler showed up at Lanie's front door at seven thirty, surprised at how eager he was to see her. He'd dropped her off at her office that morning less than nine hours ago, but he was still blown away when she opened her door.

She was gorgeous.

They'd decided to go casual since they both dressed up for work, and thankfully, the weather had significantly cooled over the week. Lanie was wearing a fitted long-sleeved black T-shirt with a green scarf, and a pair of jeans that hugged her thighs and ass and were tucked into black boots. Her long dark hair was pulled into a wavy pony tail.

A wave of lust washed through him when he saw her, and he resisted the urge to drag her to her bed. This night was to prove there was more to them than just sex.

Still, he couldn't let her appearance go without comment. "How do you look more sexy every time I see you?"

"I was about to ask you the same," she said seductively, taking in his blue long-sleeved Henley and his jeans. Then her gaze lifted to his forehead. "Hey. You don't look like Dr. Frankenstein anymore."

He grinned. "Got my stitches out this afternoon. Now I won't scare small children and pets."

Her grin turned sexy. "You don't scare me."

He wanted to take her to her bed right now and—*no*. They were going to see this movie. Even if it was a romcom. "You're still good with seeing the movie first and then going to eat?"

"Then we can take our time at dinner."

"Where's your bag?"

He'd been worried she wouldn't stay, so he was relieved when she pointed to her leather duffel on the living room chair.

He picked up the bag and led her to his car. When they were inside, he asked, "Any offers today?"

She laughed. "No *job* offers, but the FedEx guy offered to deliver *his package.*"

Tyler jerked as bolt of jealousy shot through him. He gripped the steering wheel and turned to face her. "*Are you serious?*"

Surprise filled her eyes. "Relax. I was joking."

He started the car and backed out of the parking spot, trying to slow his pulse.

"I'm sorry," she said in confusion. "That really bothered you."

"I was just worried," he said. "That would have been totally inappropriate."

"You say things like that all the time."

"The difference is you and I are in a relationship."

"Is that what this is?" she asked quietly.

He stopped at a stop sign and turned to her. "We're deep in the middle of this arrangement or commitment or whatever you want to call it. I prefer to call it a relationship. This is real to me, even if it's going to end if you leave."

They drove the short distance in silence, and Tyler regretted his overreaction. When they got out of his car in the parking garage, he pulled her to a halt and searched her face. "Hey, I'm sorry."

"No worries." She glanced up at him with a guarded look.

"I shouldn't have made a big deal of any of it." He paused and decided to be honest. "I was jealous."

"Of the imaginary FedEx guy?"

"He wasn't imaginary in my head. And it was stupid, I know. I'm sorry."

She reached up and gave him a kiss. "I think it's cute."

"Oh my God," he groaned. "Not the 'cute' thing again. I'm going to call *you* cute."

He took her hand in his, and she looked at their clasped hands in shock but then relaxed as they walked to the theater. He understood her surprise. He was surprised himself.

She smiled at him as they waited in line to buy their tickets, and he was surprised at how happy he felt. Was this what it had been like for Randy with Britt, and Kevin with Holly?

After they bought their tickets, they were walking toward their theater when Tyler heard a male voice call his name.

If it was male, that meant it wasn't an ex-lover. Thank God.

The man moved closer, and Lanie stiffened slightly.

"Victor," Tyler said, putting his arm around her, confused by her reaction. "You on a date?"

"Nope, flying solo. But I see you are." Then his eyes widened. "*Lanie*. I'm surprised to see you here."

"Hi, Victor," she said with a smile, but Tyler could tell it was forced.

Unease washed over him. "You and Lanie have met?" But as soon as he asked the question he remembered where it had likely happened. Victor's answer confirmed it.

"At Randy's shindig. But I'm surprised she's out with *you*." He gave Lanie a skeptical look. "You said you had a boyfriend... Aiden, in Atlanta, right? The attorney."

Lanie cast a sideways glance at Tyler, then back to Victor. "Yeah, that's right. We're not together."

"So how do you know Tyler?" Victor asked.

Tyler's hand tightened on her hip and he tugged her closer. "We're both in Randy's wedding."

"I'm surprised you have time to date right now," Victor

said with a sneer. "I figured you'd be burning the midnight oil with your new case."

Oh, shit. Surely Victor wasn't stupid enough to mention the name Margo Benson. His carelessness had already cost him the case and earned him a five-day suspension for shooting off his mouth. Not that Tyler was worried about Victor jeopardizing his career. But with all the other complications of their relationship, Tyler didn't want Lanie to find out that all the extra hours he was putting in at the office was his attempt to shut down the new Margo Benson Boutique. She didn't seem like the type of woman to freak out over a clothing store, but he kept hearing that this wasn't just an ordinary boutique. Women had been known to send death threats to attorneys who had tried to stop a previous opening. He wasn't taking any chances. "You of all people know I work hard but find the time to enjoy myself."

"Yeah. The golden boy," Victor sneered. "You get it all. Including Lanie. Lucky you." Victor studied Lanie with an outright appraisal that had Tyler's hair on end.

The way Lanie's body stiffened clued him in that she didn't appreciate it either. Ignoring Victor, she took a step toward the theater. "Tyler, we better go or we might not get good seats."

"Yeah, you two go enjoy the movie," Victor said bitterly. "I'd hate to ruin your evening."

Tyler steered Lanie away from his colleague, muttering under his breath, "Stupid bastard."

"What was that about?"

"Victor's a screw-up who likes to blame everyone else for his issues. Me included."

Lanie looked up at him with a guarded expression. "It sounds like you know him pretty well."

Tyler tilted his head. "We work in the same firm, but

we're not really friends. Why the interest?" He couldn't ignore her reaction when she'd seen him.

"Just curious."

No. It was more than that. There was guilt in her eyes. Why? "What happened at the barbecue?"

"I met Victor," she said, looking nervous. "And I could tell he was interested in me. I didn't feel like dodging his advances, so I told him I had a boyfriend. Unfortunately, we women do it all the time, but given our current situation, I don't want you to get the wrong impression."

"So you told him that Aiden is your boyfriend? Is he an attorney?"

She pushed out a huge sigh and raked her teeth over her bottom lip. "I can't remember how the conversation went, but he asked if I liked attorneys, and I said yes and ended up telling him that my boyfriend was an attorney in Atlanta because he said he might know you." She shook her head. "I mean *him*. My boyfriend. I had to throw him off."

"Wait." He paused. "You were talking about me?"

She looked up with pleading eyes. "Please don't read too much into this. You and I just started seeing each other, and given the fact that I was at Randy and Britt's house and that you work with Victor, I couldn't very well tell him that I was seeing *you*. So I told him my boyfriend was in Atlanta. And then later Britt and I had our fight, and she was grilling me about my relationships, and Victor volunteered about my boyfriend in Atlanta. Britt put two and three together to make four and now Aiden's invited to the wedding." She ran a hand over her head. "It's such a mess."

The relief that washed through him was almost palpable, but damned if he knew why. "You were talking about *me*."

"Please don't think I'm another one of the crazies you've dated. I know exactly what this is."

He wished she'd tell him what this was, because he didn't have a clue. All he knew was that she was right—she was unlike any other woman he'd dated. "So you and Aiden...?"

"Are friends." She gave him an apologetic smile. "I told you that, and I won't lie. I'm not ashamed of my dating past, and I see no reason to lie about our current situation."

His lips twitched as he fought a grin. "Except to Britt and Randy."

Amusement filled her eyes. "Well...they're the exception to the rule." Her smile faded. "You agree with me, don't you? About not telling them?"

"I agree." Especially after Randy had acted so weird when he thought Tyler might be interested in Lanie. For whatever reason, Randy didn't approve. It hurt more than Tyler cared to acknowledge, but it only confirmed that Lanie was right. With all the wedding activities over the next few weeks, it was better to hide that they were seeing each other and then reevaluate their plan after the wedding.

Then a new horror hit him—what if this was much more casual for her than it felt for him? He had to know.

"Britt said you've called every man you've dated a friend." He suspected he was going to regret this question. "And how do you classify me?"

She gave him a teasing grin and tugged on his arm. "My leased lover. Now, let's go find our seats."

He reluctantly conceded, and the movie started soon after they sat down, but Tyler kept running their encounter with Victor in his head. Had Lanie acted guilty because she'd let everyone think Aiden was her boyfriend and now he was invited to the wedding?

Or because she was hiding something else?

No. That was his past leaching in, trying to undermine

what he had with her. She'd hit the nail on the head when she called out his insecurities. Temporary or not, he didn't want what he had with her marred by them.

He felt better when the movie ended and they walked outside into the cool evening. "Do you have a preference where we go for dinner?"

She didn't answer; instead she searched his face. "Are you okay?"

"Why wouldn't I be?"

"Before the movie..."

"I was an idiot. If you hang around me long enough, you'll see more of it. I'm sorry."

Shaking her head, she wrapped her arms around his neck and hugged him.

He involuntarily slipped his arms around her back and pulled her close, realizing she felt right. Like there'd been a huge hole and she filled it perfectly. But what did he do with *that* realization? Especially when he only had three weeks left with her?

But what if she accepted the VP position and stayed in Kansas City? He was surprised how excited he was at the prospect.

"Now, about dinner?" he asked.

She stretched up and kissed his cheek. "I'm open to *anything*." The innuendo was blatant.

He sucked in a breath to dampen his rising libido.

But Lanie had other ideas, brushing her lips against his and biting his lower lip.

"Maybe we should get takeout," he grunted.

She laughed and ran her hands over his chest, moving downward to his waistline. "I knew you were brilliant."

The buzzing in his pocket broke the silence.

"Aren't you going to get that?" she asked.

"It can wait." But something in the back of his head said it couldn't. He pulled out the mobile, surprised to see his brother's name on the screen.

"Eric?" he asked as soon as he answered. "Can I call you back later?"

"Tyler, I need your help."

Adrenaline raced through him. "What's wrong?"

"I'm with these guys, and we've been drinking, and now they're about to drive. I need a ride home."

Tyler glanced over to an alarmed-looking Lanie. "There's no one else to get you?"

"I knew I shouldn't have called you! Fuck you!" Eric shouted and his words sounded slurred.

"Eric. Wait. Don't hang up. It's just that I'm at the Plaza. It's going to take me a good twenty-five minutes to get there. If you're in danger and someone's closer—"

"I'm not in danger," he said, sounding calmer. "I'm just about to get stranded."

"Then text me your address. I'm on my way."

"Tyler . . . thanks."

"You did good calling me, kid. I'll be right there."

Tyler hung up, feeling guilty over the disappointment he felt that his evening with Lanie had been interrupted.

"You need to pick up Eric?" she asked with worry in her eyes.

He ran a hand over his head. "Yeah, he and his friends have been drinking. He's okay, but he doesn't want to get in the car with them. Gotta give him credit for that."

She cracked a small grin. "It's just after ten. They must have gotten an early start."

"Yeah. I guess so."

"What are we doing standing here? We need to go."

He blinked in surprise. "You want to go with me?"

She put a hand on her hip. "I thought we were spending the weekend together."

"We are, but—"

"You can't ditch me that easily." She snagged his hand and dragged him a few steps. "I see how it is. You get your stitches out and now you think you can do better than me. You planning on trading up?"

She was teasing and they both knew it, but he couldn't handle her suggesting she wasn't good enough.

He pulled her to a halt. "Just you, Lanie. Only you."

Emotion filled her eyes, but then she forced a smile. "Me too. Only you."

Chapter Twenty-Seven

They found Eric sitting alone on a picnic table at Lake Jacomo.

The twenty-five-minute drive had been understandably tense, but Lanie saw the tension fall from Tyler's shoulders the moment he saw his brother was okay.

Eric hopped off the table and walked toward them in a slightly wavy path.

"How much do you think he's had to drink?" Lanie asked.

"Enough."

It took Eric three tries to get the back passenger door open, then he fell into the car, reeking of beer and cigarettes.

Tyler leaned over the back of the seat to look him. "You okay?"

"Yeah." The boy sounded embarrassed, then he glanced up at Lanie with interest. "Hey, you're Lanie." He turned to Tyler while pointing at her. "She's Lanie, isn't she?"

Tyler shot Lanie an annoyed look. "I change my answer to 'Too much.'" He backed up and headed out of the parking lot.

But she laughed and turned around in her seat to face Eric. He looked a lot like his brother, only leaner and not as tall. She suspected he'd catch up. "So you know me?" she asked.

"Oh, yeah…"

"How?" she asked. "I'm curious."

Eric flopped back in the seat and held up a finger to count with. "First, when I saw you at the baseball game."

"You saw me?"

He nodded. "Tyler kept making goo-goo eyes at you. During the seventh inning, he didn't even know the score."

"Is that so?" she asked.

"Blatant lies," Tyler mumbled.

"I thought he was gonna beat up that guy you were with. Adam or Alvin or something like that."

"Aiden?"

"Nah," he said, he face scrunching up as he tried to concentrate. "That's not it."

"So when else did you hear about me?"

"On Monday. He was mopin' around without you."

"I object!" Tyler shouted.

Lanie shot him a grin. "Overruled." She turned to Eric. "What did he say?"

"He was sad that you didn't want him at that party. So he picked me as second choice. I'm always second choice. Always."

Did Tyler really think she didn't want him to go to the party? Guilt and sadness seeped into her blood, and she wasn't sure who to deal with first. But Eric seemed the most distressed. "Eric, are you hungry?"

His eyes narrowed "Why?"

"Because I'm starving and I'd like for you to come eat something with me."

"What about Tyler?" he asked with heavy eyelids.

"He can come too, if you want. Or not." She grinned at Tyler then turned her attention to his brother. "It's up to you."

"Yeah. He can come."

Tyler's glare suggested he thought this was a terrible idea. Was it because Eric was divulging his secrets? Or because Eric had a fifty-fifty chance of barfing?

"Let's go to IHOP," Lanie suggested.

"Yeah," Eric mumbled as he closed his eyes. "IHOP sounds..."

She turned back around, and it was apparent Tyler wasn't happy. "He needs to sleep it off."

"Where he'll either wake up alone with a massive hangover, or we'll sober him up and take him home, and he'll wake up knowing two people gave a damn about him."

His mouth parted.

She grinned. "You're good with helping me work through big decisions. I'm good with the touchy-feely stuff. We make a good team."

He reached over and grabbed her hand, lacing their fingers and squeezing. "We do." He looked at her. "But have you given any consideration to what we're going to do when he throws up his guts?"

"One problem at a time."

That problem was solved when they parked in the IHOP lot. Tyler opened the passenger door, and Eric leaned out of the car and threw up all over Tyler's shoes.

Lanie alternated between giggling and gagging on her own urge to vomit.

"It's not funny, Lanie," Tyler said as he shook off his foot.

"Sorry, man," Eric said. Then he threw up again.

Tyler looked at Lanie over the top of the car. "We need to call this."

"No. Let him get it out of his system, then he needs to drink water. I'm sure you've had plenty of drinking binges. You know the drill."

Tyler helped Eric out of the car and walked him around the parking lot, and when they met Lanie on the sidewalk outside the restaurant, Eric didn't look as pale and sweaty.

"Ready to get some pancakes?" Lanie asked.

Eric nodded, then threw up in the bushes.

"*Lanie.*"

"Fine," she said. "I'll walk him."

But Tyler grimaced, then hauled him around again. Eric was ready to go in when they returned, but when the waitress led them to their table, she scrunched up her nose at the smell on Tyler's shoes.

"Can we get our waters right away?" Lanie asked as she sat down.

"Yeah." The hostess seemed in a hurry when she walked away.

Tyler still stood next to the table and thumbed toward the restrooms. "I'm going to perform an act of public service and wash off my shoes."

A sheepish look washed over Eric's face. "Sorry."

"No harm, no foul." Tyler cracked a grin. "At least they weren't my new shoes."

He took off, leaving Eric and Lanie alone.

Eric folded in on himself, hanging his head in embarrassment "You must think I'm an idiot."

"*Please.* Everyone gets drunk and pukes at some point in their life." She smiled. "Hopefully this is your one and only." She knew that was unlikely. He was a seventeen-year-old boy. He had lots of drinking in his future. But the difference was that most teens and college students drank with their friends. They didn't end up alone.

What was the story there?

"Once, when I was in college, I got drunk off this Kool-Aid punch my friends had made after I'd eaten several pizza slices. Let's just say I've never had drinks with red dye since."

He grinned.

"I can assure you that even your cool drinking friends puke their guts out when they drink too much, but they must not be very cool if they're driving. They could kill themselves or innocent people. At least you had the good sense to be responsible."

"They don't see it that way."

She shrugged. "Obviously, they're idiots. But you're not. Tyler told me you've been an A student until this year."

His gaze jerked up. "He's talked about me?"

"He's proud of you. How smart you are. How you have your head screwed on straight."

"He probably doesn't think so now."

"Hey, everyone screws up. Even me. Even Tyler. But too many people don't learn from their screw-ups. They just keep repeating them." She looked him in the eye. "But you're smarter than that. I can see it in your eyes." She hesitated, worried she was about to push him too far. "Why are you hanging out with the guys you were with tonight?"

"Kids think they're cool. I need to up my status at school."

"Why?"

"I did something . . . embarrassing this summer."

"Everybody does stupid things," Lanie said in a soft voice. "When I was in high school, I walked into homeroom with my dress tucked into my underwear. It doesn't get much worse than that."

He hesitated then said, "I wrote a poem. To a girl I liked. She showed it to everyone and now I'm a huge joke."

"Wow." Lanie was being generous. She wanted to say *that bitch*, but it didn't seem appropriate.

"And now...I just want people to like me again." He closed up, and Lanie could see he was done talking. But at least it was a start. Hopefully, Tyler could get him to open up more.

When Tyler came back, Lanie and Eric were discussing their favorite music artists, and Lanie promised she'd check out a group called Hands Like Houses.

Eric recovered enough to eat a giant stack of pancakes, and even though he refused to talk about what had happened with his so-called friends, he talked about his classes and his favorite teachers. Tyler kept sneaking glances at Lanie, and the look in his eyes—a mixture of contentment and happiness—confused her.

It was nearly midnight by the time they dropped Eric off at his house, and Lanie felt better that he'd sobered up.

"I hope I see you again, Lanie," he said as he got out of the car.

"Yeah," she said feeling guilty. With three weeks left, it didn't seem likely. But then again, if she took the VP job, maybe she would. She smiled. "Yeah, me too."

Tyler waited until Eric was in the house before he pulled away from the curb, then he reached over and squeezed her hand. "I'm sorry."

"Why? I love your brother."

"Eric likes you too."

"He talked to me while you were in the bathroom. Something embarrassed him this summer—he wrote a poem for a girl and she showed it to everyone. I think kids are giving him a hard time. He said he was hanging out with those kids tonight so people will like him again. I suspect he's so upset by it he's not doing his work."

"Dammit." He turned to her. "How'd you get that out of him?"

She shrugged. "I just talked to him. Maybe he felt comfortable talking to me since I'm just a friend."

She thought about Tyler's life—his friends and his family and how lucky he was to have them. She barely spoke to her parents. The only family she had was Britt, and she wanted what Tyler had. The thought of moving to Atlanta brought tears to her eyes.

"Lanie?" Tyler asked. "Are you okay?"

"I'm going to turn down Aiden's offer. I'm going to stay here."

"Really?"

"Yeah. As long as I meet my deadline, I can stay with my company and open an office here in KC."

He pulled into a parking lot and put the car in park, then turned to face her. "You're going to stay in Kansas City?"

"If I get my project done, then...yeah." The stunned expression on his face made her stomach sink. "Look, Tyler. You don't have to worry. I'm not staying for you. Hanging out with your brother made me realize I don't want to miss out on any more time with Britt."

A grin lifted the corners of his mouth. "And am I a fringe benefit of staying?"

She smiled. "It's like you're my own special benefit package."

He laughed. "If you come back to my condo, I'll be more than happy to share the details with you."

Lanie was falling for him and, for once, she wasn't tempted to run.

Chapter Twenty-Eight

As Tyler drove to Union Station where he and Lanie would meet the wedding party for their final photo shoot, he couldn't help but see the worry coming off of Lanie in waves. She was convinced Britt would finally figure out they were a couple.

They'd been together for several weeks, and Tyler had expected his feelings for Lanie to have cooled off by now, but they'd only heated up even more. He and Lanie had used their erratic schedules to take turns begging off wedding activities so that Britt wouldn't see them together, but there was no way either one of them could get out of this one.

"You have to promise to try to keep your hands off me as much as possible," she said. "Otherwise Britt is sure to figure it out."

"So let her."

"Tyler. We've discussed this."

"No," he muttered in frustration. "*You've* talked about this. I've been ready to tell her for over a week. She's an intelligent woman, and she realizes that we've been taking turns skipping her forced wedding fun. She's bound to have figured out something is up."

"You had a legitimate excuse last time," Lanie said. "Even Randy backed you up at the wine-tasting party. He said you were working on your big case. And besides, I had lunch with her a couple of days ago, and she never mentioned you at all."

"Nevertheless," he said, "this is your last week at your current position. Have you heard anything more about your promotion?"

"You know I won't know until after the wedding."

He turned to look at her. "I've never heard of a corporation holding off a promotion until after an employee quits." His brow furrowed. "You have a contract, right? Why don't you let me look at it?"

"What?" she asked. "Why?"

Why was her reaction so strong? "I specialize in contract law, Lanie. I can see if what they're doing is covered in your contract."

"No. That's okay..."

He gave her a sly grin. "Besides, if I'm your attorney, you can break your NDA with my client privilege." He shook his head. "I don't know why I didn't think of it sooner. My only excuse is that you've driven me to temporary insanity."

She turned to look out the window. "No. I think it's better this way."

His smile fell. "Are you serious?"

"Tyler."

He turned into the Union Station parking lot. "Why won't you let me review it? Don't you trust me?"

She turned to him with a pleading look. "Of course I do."

"Then why won't you let me see it?"

"I just can't."

Her refusal hurt more than he'd expected. "What are you hiding from me?"

"You know I have an NDA. I've never made that a secret."

He pulled into a parking spot and threw the car into park. "I'm giving you an opportunity to get rid of that secret. Why won't you take it?"

Tears filled her eyes. "I can't."

Disappointment made his shoulders sag. "You mean you won't. There's a difference." He gripped the steering wheel and shook his head. "Are you even planning on staying? Because I have to tell you that this promotion story is beginning to sound dubious."

"I want to stay," she said, her voice quavering. "But I won't know until next week."

He took a breath, asking himself if he was being fair to her. He didn't understand why she wouldn't show him her contract, but he needed to respect her boundaries. "Okay, if there's a chance you're staying, then let's start making plans with that in mind. You don't even know where you're going to be living in two weeks. You mentioned looking for an apartment. Why don't you just move in with me?"

She shook her head, staring at the dashboard. "No. We'll discuss this once I know I have the promotion."

"Fine," he said, starting to get pissed. "So then let's discuss what happens if it *doesn't* come through. Will you go work for Aiden?"

"If he'll still take me."

"You won't look for something here?" he asked in dismay.

"There's nothing here, Tyler," she said, finally turning to look at him. "I checked in with my headhunter on Friday, and there's nothing."

"Okay," he said. "Then we can—"

"I can't talk about this now," she said, her voice full of emotion. She opened the car door and practically fell out onto the pavement in her haste to get away from him.

He intercepted her about ten feet from the car, in full view of the wedding party. "Lanie, stop."

"What are you doing?" she asked, with tears in her eyes. "Britt's going to wonder what in the hell's going on."

"Then let her!" he shouted.

Her mouth dropped, and she took a step back as fear washed over her face. "I'm not ready to tell her."

He took several breaths as he turned his gaze to the now gawking Britt and Randy. "Why do I think you never will?"

She looked down at the ground.

"I love you, Lanie." His voice broke as the truth hit him. But the next part broke his heart. "But I don't think this is going to work."

Her gaze jerked up, and she stared at him with tears threatening to spill down her cheeks. "*Tyler…*"

"I'm all in, Lanie. I've been all in since the minute I saw you in the garage, but you're holding back, and I don't understand it. The only thing I can come up with is that you don't feel the same."

* * *

Lanie watched Tyler stomp off toward the wedding party, her mouth still open in shock.

Tyler loved her. *He loved her.*

But he'd also just broken up with her.

Oh, God.

Did she love him too?

Britt's gaze went back and forth between the two of them, her confusion evident.

What was Lanie going to tell her? What was she going to say to Tyler?

Maybe she should start looking past the opening. Her life went on whether the store opened or not. Especially since things were looking good with the store. Weeks had passed since she'd overheard Victor at the barbecue, and nothing had happened. The store would open a week from tomorrow, and she'd be able to take the vice president promotion and set up an office in Kansas City.

Maybe she *could* start thinking about the future.

She *really* needed to talk to Tyler.

He'd bypassed Britt and headed straight for Kevin. And Britt was headed straight for her.

"What's going on with you and Tyler?" Britt asked, blocking her path.

"Nothing," she said, darting to the left, but Britt blocked her again.

"That didn't look like nothing. And if it was nothing, then why are you trying so desperately to get to him?"

Lanie stopped. She was getting damn tired of all the lies, but she needed to speak with Tyler before confessing all to Britt. "We had a fight in the car. I got pissed because he had the air too cold and wouldn't turn it up. Now I really need to go apologize."

"It looked like more than that."

Lanie lifted her shoulder into a half-shrug, fresh out of cover stories.

"I knew we should have picked you up. Something happened the night Tyler took you home from Loose Park. The two of you have been avoiding each other ever since."

Remembering when he'd brought her home that night

brought fresh tears to her eyes. What was she doing? Was she really letting him slip away?

But her hesitation and her tears gave Britt the wrong message. "What did he do?"

"Nothing, Britt. He didn't do anything wrong." No. He'd been perfect.

She was an idiot.

"Then why are you so upset?"

Because he loved her, and somehow she'd broken his heart.

"Fine, don't tell me. I'll find out myself." Britt spun around and stomped off toward Tyler.

"Britt!"

Lanie started to run after her, but her left heel snapped off and she stumbled, nearly falling on her face. She didn't have to worry about witnesses this time, because everyone was gaping at the furious bride who was storming the clueless groomsman. She bent down and slipped off her shoe, but the heel was caught on her hem.

"What happened with Lanie?"

Tyler turned to Britt, his eyes wide.

"Well?" Britt demanded, both hands on her hips. "What happened?"

His face became an expressionless mask. "You need to ask Lanie."

"She won't tell me, so I'm asking *you*."

Celesta hurried to Tyler's side, clinging to his arm. "I have no idea what your cousin has done, but I'm sure Tyler's the innocent party."

Britt turned her glare to Randy's cousin. "Stay out of this, Celesta. It doesn't concern you."

"No. I won't let you attack him when it's so obvious that Lanie's the one to blame."

"Celesta," Tyler said in a warning tone as he brushed her hand off his arm. "Let it go."

"No!" Celesta said. "This is so unfair. Why are you blaming him when he's the one who's obviously upset?" She pointed toward Lanie. "And she's obviously drunk again, weaving around like that."

Everyone turned to face Lanie, and their scowls suggested they believed Celesta. Not that she blamed them. She was bent over, still working on her heel, bobbing around like a boxer in a prizefight.

"I'm not drunk," Lanie shouted, then blew out a puff of air to move the strand of hair hanging in front of her eye.

No one looked convinced.

Kevin grabbed Tyler's arm and pulled him about six feet away in front of the fountain. "We're burning daylight, and some of us actually want to go home. Let's do this."

Since this was their fourth photo shoot, everyone seemed to know where their places were, so they were all ready and waiting for Lanie as she hobbled to her spot and balanced on one foot, thankful her dress mostly hid her feet.

Tyler didn't look at her, keeping his gaze turned instead on the street behind Holly and the photographer.

"Tyler," she whispered.

He gave his head a slight shake. "Don't."

By the time they'd made it through several poses, Lanie began to panic. Tyler was stiff and silent, and she wasn't sure how to fix this. She couldn't let him see her contract. She had to protect him from conflict of interest. But what could she do?

"We're going to try something else," Holly said, moving toward them. "I want the bridesmaids to stand on the edge of the fountain and the groomsmen to stand in front."

Lanie was struggling to stand on the concrete with one heel, let alone on a one-foot-wide ledge next to a fountain.

She started to climb up, leaning sideways, when Tyler grabbed her elbow and steadied her.

"Thank you."

He looked into her eyes. "I can't let you fall in." A half hour ago, that statement would be filled with innuendo, but now it was cold and aloof.

"Tyler."

"Will you just leave him alone?" Celesta snapped from her position on the ledge next to Lanie.

"This is none of your business, Celesta," Lanie said, trying to get her balance.

"You're obviously drunk." Celesta turned to Tyler. "Don't worry. I'll make sure she doesn't hurt you when your back is to her."

"I'm not going to hurt him!" Lanie exclaimed.

"The scar on his forehead is proof that you're capable of it."

"Celesta," Tyler growled. "Lay off."

"I don't even know why you're interested in her. She is *so* not your type."

"And you are?" Rowdy asked.

Celesta lifted her chin. "As a matter of fact, I was."

Britt spun around. "Wait. *Was?*" Her eyes widened. "Oh my God. *You slept with Celesta?*"

"Why do you say it like it's a bad thing?" Celesta huffed.

But Britt had turned her attention to Tyler. "I can't believe you! I thought you'd changed!"

"I slept with her years ago!" Tyler shouted. "Before I even knew you! Not that it's any business of yours."

Randy's face turned red. "Don't shout at my fiancée, Norris."

Tyler ran his hand over his head in frustration. "I'm sorry, but I'm not going to stand here and let her insult me for some mistake I made four years ago. We all know I was a total fuck-up back then."

"Mistake!" Celesta shrieked.

Tyler cringed and looked up at her. "I'm sorry. I shouldn't have said 'mistake.'"

"Your only mistake was letting me go! I'm your type, not Lanie."

"Lanie?" Britt said in confusion.

Celesta tried to ease past Lanie to get closer to Tyler, and Lanie lost balance on her one foot, falling backward into the fountain and landing flat on her back in the water.

"Lanie!" a chorus of voices shouted.

Lanie sat up and realized that she wasn't alone—Celesta had fallen in too and she looked furious.

"You pulled me in!" Celesta shouted.

"Have you lost your mind?" Lanie asked as she tried to get to her feet. "You're the one who pushed *me* in."

Tyler stood at the edge of the fountain. "Lanie, are you okay?"

"I'm fine. My pride is bruised more than my butt."

"Why are you asking about her?" Celesta shouted. "Why aren't you asking about *me*?" She got to her feet, making a production of her wet skirt clinging to her legs.

Tyler reached out a hand to help Lanie out of the water, but Celesta shoved Lanie's hand out of the way and grabbed Tyler's hand instead.

"Celesta, what are you doing?" Britt asked in shock.

A look of determination covered Celesta's face. "I'm claiming what's mine."

Tyler tried to pull his hand free, but Celesta held tight and jerked, causing Tyler to lose his balance. As he fell forward, he lifted one foot to the ledge to gain some balance. While he tried to right himself, Celesta refused to release his hand, and he fell into the fountain, landing on top of her.

Suddenly, the entire group was shouting and moving in to help. Lanie sloshed over to Tyler and reached him first. He'd landed face-forward, with his face buried in Celesta's chest.

"Tyler!"

He jerked up and turned to Lanie in horror. "That was an accident. I didn't mean to do that."

Celesta had released his hand, so Lanie helped him to his feet while Celesta floundered around in the two-foot-deep water as though she were drowning.

"Are you okay?" Lanie asked. She was relieved he hadn't pulled away from her.

He grinned. "My pride hurts more than my shins."

The sight of him smiling at her brought tears to her eyes.

"Are you hurt?" he asked, worry replacing his amusement.

"No. I was just scared," she whispered. "You said..."

"I was an idiot," he said, dropping her hand.

She missed him, even though he was standing a foot away. She didn't want to hide this anymore. She wanted to touch him anytime she wanted. She turned to the group.

"Tyler and I are together," Lanie said. "We've been sleeping together since the night I tried to kill him."

Brittany's mouth dropped. "*What*? I thought you were with Aiden?"

"Two men!" Celesta shouted. "She has no shame!"

Brittany started shouting that it wasn't any of Celesta's business how many men Lanie slept with at one time, then Celesta started shouting at Randy for marrying a bitch.

Tyler stared down at Lanie in amazement. "I can't believe you did that."

She grinned and lifted her shoulder in a nonchalant shrug. "I was tired of Celesta trying to take my man."

He laughed. "Your man?"

She scrunched up her nose. "That sounds so wrong. I hope you enjoyed that, because I doubt I'll ever call you '*my man*' again."

He laughed. "I can live with that, I think."

She rested her hands on his shoulders while the shouting continued behind her. "I'm sorry I've been so stubborn. I love you. I was just too stupid to admit it."

"Say it again," he said.

She laughed. "The stupid part or the 'I love you' part?"

His face lit up with a grin. "Take your pick."

"I love you." She reached up on her tiptoes and kissed him.

He slid his arm around her back and pulled in close. She shivered.

"You're wet and cold. Let's go home," he said against her lips.

Home. Yes. Tyler felt exactly like home.

He lifted his head, and when he smiled at her, she nearly melted with happiness. She'd been looking her entire life for him, and now that she'd found him, she was never letting go.

Things turned to chaos. Celesta stomped off, threatening to boycott the wedding. Holly threatened everyone with torture if they upstaged the wedding. Britt was shocked, then happy about Lanie's announcement, but Randy looked worried.

He found a way to pull Lanie to the side and said, "You can't tell Tyler that you know anything about the Margo Benson case."

"That fight we were having when we got here?" she asked. "He'd asked to see my contract."

"You told him who you work for?" he whisper-shouted.

"Why are you so freaked out, Randy?" she asked. "Of course not. I told him no. Why do you think we were fighting? But I promised to keep your involvement a secret and I meant it. I take my promises seriously."

"You have to promise not tell him *anything* that links you to . . . *you know what* until after the opening."

She shot him a glare. "I also take my NDA seriously. And Tyler realizes that. That's part of the reason he suggested looking over my contract—so he could claim client-attorney privilege, and I wouldn't have to break my nondisclosure."

"You can't show him, Lanie."

"Good Lord. We've already established that ten times over. But I'm tired of keeping secrets from him."

Randy held her gaze. "Then maybe you should take a break from him until after the opening."

Her mouth dropped open. "Are you serious?"

"It's not a bad idea."

She put a hand on her hip. "If it makes you feel any better, I'm going to be working long hours this week, and Tyler has some big case he's getting tons of pressure about, so we'll hardly see each other until the wedding."

Guilt filled his eyes. "Lanie, there's something you need to know."

"What?"

"Tyler—"

Britt snuck between them and pulled Lanie into a hug. "I'm so happy for you, Lanie! I wish you'd told me sooner, but I kind of understand why you didn't."

"Thanks. It's been hard to keep this from you."

A breeze blew over them, and Lanie shivered. Tyler noticed, wrapping an arm around her back. "I need to get her home and into dry clothes."

"Yeah," Kevin said. "*Into* clothes."

Tyler pointed at him. "Watch it."

Kevin turned to his wife. "I told you. He's a goner."

Chapter Twenty-Nine

On Thursday afternoon, Lanie was happier than she'd ever been. They were opening in four days, and things were right on track. The construction was complete. Almost all the clothing had been delivered. The employees had been hired and were almost finished with their training.

For the first time, Lanie believed not only that the store would open without a hitch, but that she and Tyler could have a future together.

Lanie had been right about barely seeing Tyler this week, but she hadn't felt panicked about it since she knew she'd be there next week to spend time with him.

Part of her increased workload was because Stephanie had flown to Phoenix for a couple of days to check on the retail space for the next Margo Benson Boutique, but she was due back this afternoon. Lanie had missed her more than she'd expected. It wasn't unusual for Steph to take off for a few days, and Lanie was used to her absences, but this one felt different—maybe because after the opening, Stephanie was moving on without her. The thought made Lanie pause and worry that she'd made the wrong decision when she'd turned in her resignation, but deep down, she knew it had been the right move. Still, she felt like she was losing her best friend.

She was about to head back to the office and wait for Stephanie. But as she grabbed her purse, she heard a persistent rapping at the front of the store. She considered ignoring it—they were used to curious passersby trying to get a look inside—but this sounded different than usual. Scowling, she walked to the front and opened the door, shouting through the tarp, "I'm sorry, but we're closed."

"Ma'am," a deep voice said, "this is official business of the Jackson County courts."

Lanie's heart lodged in her throat. She quickly unlaced the cords holding the tarp shut and pushed it aside to face a man in a dress shirt and tie who shoved a folded stack of papers at her. "Have a nice day," he said in an apologetic tone.

Not anymore.

She locked the door, then slowly walked to the sales counter and opened the packet.

Dinah Pettier, owner of Dinah Fashions, had filed a lawsuit to block the opening of the retail store owned by Montgomery Enterprises, and an injunction had been ordered to keep the store from opening until the matter had been resolved.

This was bad. It wasn't the temporary stay that Victor had filed weeks ago. She was no attorney, but it didn't take a genius to figure out that her opening was destroyed.

She walked the block to her office and scanned the pages. After she sent the document to the corporate attorney, she waited for the call that came ten minutes later, confirming what she already knew. This injunction was more serious and would likely keep them from opening.

No opening. No promotion. No job in Kansas City.

No Tyler.

No, she couldn't think about Tyler right now.

She sat in her chair, staring at the papers on her desk. She needed to figure out what to do about her career. She'd called Aiden a couple of weeks ago and turned down his offer. Would he let her change her mind? Or maybe she could—

What was she going to do about Tyler?

Tyler had deep roots here in Kansas City—a successful career, his brothers, and his best friends. He couldn't move somewhere else, and she couldn't handle a long-distance relationship.

When Lanie was little, her father had taken sporadic trips for work, but a year after her mother started working again, her father was offered a job in Dallas. He'd begged her mother to move, but she'd taken a job she loved and refused to give it up. Her father had taken the job, commuting back and forth on the weekends, but when he was home, he was angry and bitter at her mother for separating their family. Two years later, he gave it up and moved back home, but the damage had been done— her parents' marriage had been irreparably broken.

If Lanie moved to Atlanta, she'd rather leave with warm memories of her time with Tyler than have their relationship disintegrate into something ugly and bitter.

She should have been prepared for this new legal development. Since nothing legal had happened immediately after the barbecue, Lanie had mistakenly believed that they were in the clear. She'd trusted it so much that she'd planned to start moving her few belongings to Tyler's condo the day after the wedding.

What was she going to do now?

The door opened and Stephanie walked into the office, rolling her carry-on suitcase behind her. She dropped her purse on her desk, and her eyes widened when she glanced at Lanie. "What happened?"

"It's over."

Stephanie froze. "Did something happen with Tyler?"

Tears burned her eyes. She'd deal with the Tyler issue later. She needed to focus on her job. Lanie picked up the legal papers and handed them to Steph. "It's a new injunction. And legal thinks this one will stick."

Stephanie sat in her chair and quickly flipped through the papers. "But they're going to fight it, right?"

"Of course, but we have to prepare for the worst."

Stephanie leaned her head back into her seat. "We won't be able open," she said in defeat. "This has never happened before. How does this work? We stay here and open at a different location? Or we give up and move on to Phoenix?"

"I don't know, but I know I won't be part of it."

Stephanie looked confused. "But won't you be part of that decision if you're the new VP?"

A lump filled Lanie's throat, and she took a second to clear it. "No. I won't be the new VP. I won't get the promotion if we don't open."

Horror filled Stephanie's eyes. "You didn't tell me that part."

Lanie shrugged, trying to play off the omission. "You didn't need the pressure. Just getting the store open after all the delays was pressure enough. Besides, it's my issue to worry about, not yours, Steph."

"We're friends, Lanie. Of course it's my concern." She was quiet for a moment. "What are you going to do?"

Lanie forced a smile. "I guess I'll see if Aiden will still take me."

"But you wanted to stay in Kansas City. What about the headhunter?"

Lanie shook her head. "There's nothing here. I told her to let me know if she found something, and I haven't heard a thing."

"There's an option you haven't considered," Stephanie said. "You can still come to Phoenix with me."

A sad smile crossed Lanie's face. "No. Even if I wanted to go to Phoenix—and I don't—corporate would never let me. If we don't open, my career with Margo Benson and Montgomery Enterprises will be over."

"It was hard enough knowing you weren't coming with me to Phoenix," Stephanie said. "But at least I knew you'd still be my boss."

The lump was back in Lanie's throat. "But I'll still be your friend."

Stephanie bit her bottom lip and she offered a quavering smile. "I hope so."

Lanie vowed to make sure their relationship didn't die like all her others. "Hey," she said cheerfully. "Let's not plan the funeral yet. Legal is working on it, and in the meantime, we're going to keep working as though nothing has changed. Then, when legal works their magic, we'll be ready to open. In the meantime, I need to make a call to Aiden." She paused. "Just in case."

"What about Tyler?"

She shook her head. "I don't know."

Stephanie sensed her hesitation. "We'll be ready. We *will* open on Monday morning. The attorneys still have a few days to figure something out."

Lanie wished she was as certain. "Everything's ready for our training session tomorrow, so I think I'm going home. I have a massive headache, and a warm bath might help." She grabbed her purse. "But I'll see you bright and early tomorrow morning.

Stephanie picked up her phone. "Let me call you an Uber."

"No. I need the walk." Maybe it would help her to clear her head and figure out what to do next. She started to open the door, but an overwhelming sense of doom washed over her, and she stopped with her hand on the doorknob.

"Lanie?" Stephanie asked, sounding worried. "Did you want me to call you a car after all?"

"I'm going to lose him, Steph."

"What?"

She turned to face Stephanie. "I'm going to lose Tyler."

Stephanie stood and pulled Lanie into a hug. "You don't have to. You can make it work just like you and I will."

Oh, God. She was right, but the suggestion had the opposite effect of comforting. She'd tried to maintain friendships with a few high school friends during college, and a few college friends after graduation, but with the exception of Aiden, every single one had failed because of distance. The only reason her friendship with Aiden hadn't died was because the business world kept throwing them together, and he was too stubborn to let it go.

But it reinforced her belief about long-distance relationships. It wasn't just her parents' marriage that died because of distance. So had all her friendships. No wonder she'd walled herself off during the last nomadic five years. She'd been protecting herself from the inevitable heartbreak. Nothing lasted.

But she couldn't tell Steph any of that. Steph still believed they could make it work, and Lanie wasn't going to take that belief from her. "Yeah," Lanie said with a tight smile. "Thanks."

When she got to her apartment, she decided to skip the bath and, instead, changed into yoga pants and a T-shirt. No matter the outcome of the opening, she was moving out of this apartment within two weeks and she needed to pack up her meager belongings. Tyler had promised to help her on Sunday, but now she felt the urge to put as much distance between her and Tyler as possible.

She couldn't count on legal to come through this time, which meant she would soon be unemployed and homeless. She needed to be proactive, not reactive. She needed to take charge and make a plan. She found her phone and called Aiden.

"Hey, Lane. Calling me late on a Thursday afternoon—is everything okay?"

She didn't blame him for his confusion. She rarely called him first. "Actually, no. The store just received a new injunction this afternoon, and unless legal comes up with something quick, there won't be an opening on Monday."

"Shit."

She chuckled. "My feelings exactly."

"At least you still have your sense of humor."

"If I don't laugh about it . . ." Her voice trailed off, leaving off the "*I might cry.*"

"I'm sorry," he said. "So that means no VP promotion, right?"

"Yeah."

"My offer's still on the table. You turned *me* down, not the other way around."

Lanie nearly choked on tears of relief. "Thanks, Aiden. You have no idea how much I appreciate that. Are we still working with the same timetable of when you need me to start?"

"That doesn't seem fair," Aiden said. "That gives you less than a week."

"The sooner, the better," she said. It was better to rip off the Band-Aid than draw out the agony.

"Is your cousin disappointed?"

"I never told her I was staying." She took a breath, fighting the urge to cry. "I was going to tell her after the wedding. As a gift."

"You'd better have gotten her something else," he said wryly.

"Tyler and I bought them a gift last weekend."

Aiden was quiet for a moment. "And what does Tyler say about all of this?"

"He doesn't know yet either." She paused, then said, "But I can't stay here without a job. I have to go where the job is."

"Thanks for all the enthusiasm," Aiden teased.

"Aiden, you know it's not like that." Her voice broke.

"Are you crying?" he asked in surprise.

"No. Maybe."

"You must really like this guy."

"I love him," she said with a sniffle.

"Wow. I've never heard you say that before."

"Because I've never loved a guy before."

"That sucks, Lane. I'm sorry."

"Thanks."

They said their good-byes, and Lanie hung up the phone

pondering the million-dollar question: How was she going to tell Tyler?

Taking a deep breath, she texted Tyler that she'd meet him at his apartment later and bring dinner. She had to tell him. Tonight.

Chapter Thirty

⟜

Tyler was at a bar celebrating his win with Randy and several other colleagues over drinks when he saw Lanie's text.

He picked up his phone and called her. "Hey, don't cook," he said. "Let me take you out."

"Aren't you working late?"

"Not tonight. I can pick you up around six thirty. How about we go to Capital Grille, but sit in the actual dining room this time?"

"Wow," she said, but her voice lacked enthusiasm. "Are we celebrating something? Where are you? It sounds noisy."

He slid off the bar stool and moved to the hallway by the restrooms. "Lanie, is everything okay?"

"Yeah, I'm fine."

She didn't sound fine. "Do you have a headache? We can stay in."

"No, if you're suggesting Capital Grille, it sounds like a special occasion. I'll be ready."

A month ago, he would have bought that nothing was wrong, but he knew her now. He knew that something was off.

"You know what I'd really like? A quiet candlelight dinner at my apartment with you. How about you head over to my apartment and set the table, then open a bottle of wine and take a bath in my tub? That sounds relaxing, doesn't it?"

"Tyler."

Her voice broke, and now he was really worried. "Lanie, what's wrong?"

"You were right. I have a headache. If you don't mind staying home, that sounds great."

"Head over to my apartment early so you can have a long soak. Don't worry about setting the table. I'll take care of everything."

"I love you, Tyler." Her voice broke again.

"Now you're scaring me, Lanie. I think I should come home now."

"I'm fine. I promise. I'm just stressed. Go hang out with your friends, and I'll see you when you get home."

Could she be any more perfect? "I love you, Lanie. I'll be home soon."

She'd told him to stay, but he decided he'd tell his friends he was leaving early.

"No!" one of the associates protested. "We're celebrating! You can't go!"

"I need to get home to Lanie. She's not feeling well."

"That's what they all say, dude," another guy said. "Who would have guessed that Tyler Norris could be pussy-whipped."

Tyler felt uncomfortable, not because he thought he was being controlled by Lanie, but because several months ago, he would have been on the other side, calling some other poor bastard the same name.

Jesus. Had he grown up?

"If you believe that, then you've chosen the wrong woman," Tyler said, pulling out his wallet.

Randy stared at him with a strange expression but he stood and pushed Tyler's hand away. "I'll take care of your drinks, but let me walk you to the door."

"I'm safe to drive, Randy. I've only had one beer."

"That's not why I'm walking with you."

"Okay." Now two people close to him were acting strange. What the hell was going on?

When they were out of earshot of the other guys, Randy asked, "Do you think the injunction's going to hold?"

The injunction was solid, and he'd resisted the urge to tell the partners "*I told you so.*" Sure, he could have filed one earlier—and they had pushed hard for him to do just that— but that precedent had been shakier. He'd begged for more time to come up with something more ironclad, and he'd come through.

His partnership was in the bag.

But Randy rarely asked about his cases, so this was odd. "Why the interest?"

He shrugged but looked uncomfortable. "Just curiosity. Britt would kill to have a Margo Benson store open here."

"Her and every other woman," he grumbled.

"Say . . . how serious is it with you and Lanie?"

"Pretty serious."

"That was fast."

"I know." Tyler grinned like a fool. "No one's more surprised than I am."

"What do you know about Lanie's job?" Randy asked, looking concerned.

Tyler tensed. "Why are you asking?"

"If things are serious between you two, then you really need to know."

"She's signed an NDA, and says she can't tell me anything." Then a new thought hit him. Why hadn't he thought of it before? "What about Britt? Does she know?"

Randy's gaze held his. "You need to talk to Lanie."

"Dammit, Randy. Does Britt know? Wait, do *you* know?" When Randy didn't answer, he said, "You do."

"I can't tell you. I'm sworn by attorney-client privilege."

Tyler shook his head. "*Wait*. Lanie hired you to be her attorney?"

Randy leaned closer. "It was strictly off the books; I was doing Britt's cousin a favor and looked over her contract. No one else knows, and I'd really like to keep it that way."

The firm frowned on pro bono work for extended family and friends, but something still seemed off.

"You need to talk to her, okay?" Randy said. "Especially if things are serious with you two."

Tyler rubbed his temple. "Yeah. Thanks."

"She's an amazing person, and Britt thinks the world of her," Randy said as he walked out the door onto the sidewalk. "Don't hurt her, okay?"

"I love her. The last thing I'd ever do is hurt her."

Randy nodded but he didn't look convinced as he walked back inside the bar.

* * *

Tyler let himself into his apartment, relieved when he saw the table set and the sound of running water in the bathroom. Between Randy's chat and Lanie's tears, Tyler was paranoid and freaked out, and nearly convinced himself that Lanie was about to break up with him, although he couldn't figure out why she would. Sure, they'd both worked long hours the last week, but when they were together, it was amazing.

He walked down the hall and stopped in the partially open doorway and peered inside. Lanie was in a tub full of bubbles with her hair up in a messy bun. Her eyes were closed, but her jaw still looked tense.

Her eyes opened and she gave him a hesitant smile. "Hey, what are you doing home already?"

He walked toward her, loosening his tie. "I was worried about you."

She sat up, the water and bubbles dripping down her breasts, completely oblivious to the effect she was having on him. "I told you to stay with your friends."

He sat down on the edge of the tub and cupped the back of her head as he leaned over to kiss her. "Funny thing. When I asked myself if I'd rather be with a group of drunken attorneys or you, it was a shockingly easy choice."

"They were drunk already?"

"Well on their way."

She frowned. "I don't want to be that girlfriend, Tyler."

"Which girlfriend?" His hand trailed down her cleavage. "The gorgeous, sexy girlfriend? Because, sorry, babe, you're that girlfriend."

"No, the clingy girlfriend. The one you think expects you to spend every spare moment with her and never lets you hang out with your friends."

He sat up and unbuttoned the top button of his dress shirt. "Lanie, you are so not that woman, and if you became that woman, I'd wonder if you'd been replaced by your evil twin. Now tell me what's going on."

She gave him a sad smile. "I'm just tired and I have a headache. I'm sorry you rushed home for nothing."

While she did look tired, he knew there was more she wasn't saying. Nevertheless, he wanted her to tell him on her own. "Why don't you stay in here a little while longer and relax?" He glanced around. "Do you want a glass of wine?"

"No. I'm good."

She emerged fifteen minutes later, dressed in pajama shorts, a spaghetti-strap cami, and no bra. Her hair was still piled on top of her head, and she'd taken off her makeup. "Sorry," she said with a warm smile. "I know it's a little early in our relationship for me to be slacking like this, but this is what you get."

He'd been sitting at the island working on his laptop. He closed the lid and walked toward her, pulling her into his arms. "You're absolutely perfect. You must feel better from your bath."

"Much better. Now let's eat."

* * *

Lanie overslept the next morning, so she took a quick shower, finding it difficult to brush off Tyler's attempts to make it more leisurely.

"You know, it's next to impossible to tell you no," she said, as he pretended to wash her breast for the fifth time.

He lowered his mouth to her neck. "That's what I'm counting on."

The night before, she'd decided she was done with secrets. She was going to talk about her work, NDA be damned. She was getting fired anyway. What did it matter? "I have to get to work. We have our first run-through today, and I can't be late."

He lifted his head. "Run-through?"

She turned around to face him. "I want to tell you everything, but I know you'll have questions, and I don't have time to answer right now. Tonight, okay?"

He smiled. "I've waited this long for you to tell me about your job, I can wait until tonight."

"No more secrets after this," she said, then grabbed a towel and stepped out of the shower.

"Secrets?"

She didn't miss the momentary fear that flickered in his eyes. Of course he'd be worried about secrets after the crap his mother had pulled. Would he be upset when he found out his firm's connection to the store? Would he be even more upset that she'd known and hadn't told him? She leaned over to kiss him. "Nothing to worry about. Just my NDA stuff. I'll tell you tonight."

She hurried to his bedroom and grabbed a dress out of his closet, thankful he'd insisted she keep several outfits at his place in case of mornings like this.

He usually dropped her off at her office but she needed to go to the store, so as they drove toward the boutique, she decided to skip the usual routine. "Don't drop me off at the office. My store's just down the street."

Tyler shot her a surprised glance. "One of the stores you work at?"

"The *only* store I work at."

He'd rounded the corner, and the store was in view halfway down the street.

"Here at this corner is good," she said.

"Lanie, where do you work?" Tyler asked in a quiet voice as he pulled up to the curb.

She could see he was putting things together. Was he worried about the conflict of interest with his firm?

"Tyler, I know you must have a lot of questions, but..."

He put the car in park and turned to face her with worry in his eyes. "You're not a time management consultant, are you?"

"No. It's my cover," she said. She gripped her hands in her lap to keep them from shaking. "I'm in charge of opening a new store for Montgomery Enterprises. My project is the opening."

His eyes widened. "Yesterday...you were upset... Randy...he knew."

"I know your firm represents the store trying to keep us closed. Randy had looked over my contract and asked me to keep it quiet. He didn't know about your firm's involvement when he reviewed it. But that night at Loose Park, when I talked to him after the shoot, he assured me you had nothing to do with the case."

"Lanie." He sounded like he was strangling.

She grabbed his hand. "I know you think I lied to you, but I couldn't tell you. But now..."

"Lanie. It was me. I'm the one."

She shook her head. "You're the one what?"

"It was me, Lanie. I'm the one who shut you down."

Chapter Thirty-One

$\backsim$

She dropped his hand and sat back in the seat, feeling like the air was being sucked out of the car. "What? But Randy...he said you weren't on the case. Victor was."

"He was right. I wasn't involved that night. After the barbecue, they removed Victor from the case and they put me on instead." He slammed his palm into the steering wheel. "That's the big case I've been working on. I've been working my ass off to shut you down." He shook his head. "I didn't know. I swear, I didn't know."

"I know," Lanie whispered. "I believe you." But it didn't change the fact that he'd destroyed her.

Oh, God. He'd destroyed them.

He sucked in a deep breath, then turned to her with pleading eyes. "What are you going to do?"

She smiled, but her chin quivered. "You're very good at what you do. My attorneys aren't sure they can overturn it."

"Lanie." His voice broke. "I didn't know."

Her eyes burned, and she started to cry. "I know."

He turned away and ran his hand over his head. "You lost your promotion."

"Tyler..."

"The headhunter? Is there anything here?"

"No."

"What are you going to do?"

She sat back in the seat again. "I'm moving to Atlanta. I called Aiden yesterday afternoon."

"What? You can't go."

"I *have* to. Next week I'll be homeless and I won't have a job."

"You could take some time to figure out something else. You could stay with me."

She turned to look at him, her heart breaking into pieces. "I can't," she said, her voice cracking. "It's not in me to not work, and I can't freeload off you."

"Lanie, for God sakes, I fucking got you fired. You wouldn't be freeloading!"

She reached for the door handle. "I can't do this right now. I have to think."

"I'm sorry, Lanie. I'm so fucking sorry."

"I know." She knew that he was losing just as much as she was, but it didn't make her feel any better. It only made her feel worse.

* * *

Tyler felt like he was going to throw up. In a matter of moments, he had lost the only woman he had ever loved. But he'd also lost the case. Now he had to go in and tell the partners that he'd been sleeping with the woman who was in charge of opening the Margo Benson Boutique.

Son of a bitch.

What the fuck had Randy been thinking, keeping this a secret?

He drove to his office on autopilot and told himself over and over that he wasn't going to beat the shit out of his friend.

His partners weren't happy that he was in a relationship with Lanie, but he was relieved they didn't bring any disciplinary action against him. When they finished with him, he headed straight for Randy's office.

Randy was sitting at his desk, but he stood as soon as he saw Tyler in his doorway.

Tyler slammed the door shut behind him, but Randy didn't flinch. "You found out."

"You son of a bitch."

"I couldn't tell you, Tyler."

That was the shittiest part of it. Randy was right. He couldn't warn Lanie, and by the time Tyler had come on board on the case, Randy had no idea he was involved with Lanie.

"I don't know what I'm going to do," Tyler said.

"How's Lanie doing?"

"Not good." He wanted to comfort her, but why would she want his comfort when he was the one who had caused her pain?

"Maybe I should call Britt."

"That's a good idea. Lanie needs someone to talk to." Tyler started to pace. "She's going to hate me when this is all over."

"I think she just needs time."

"I don't have time. She's moving to Atlanta next week."

"What? She took the job with her friend?" he mused.

"Yeah." Tyler headed for the door.

"Where are you going?" Randy asked.

"To win Lanie back."

* * *

A few hours later, Tyler sat in a restaurant, waiting. He'd texted Lanie and told her he needed to talk to her so he could explain his side. She'd waited so long to respond that he was sure she was blowing him off, but she finally texted that she could meet him for lunch. When he offered to pick her up, she said she'd meet him at Houston's at noon.

He'd gotten there first, so he saw her when she walked in. His heart leapt into his throat, and he stood as she approached. He wasn't sure what to expect when she saw him, but he hadn't expected her to wrap her arms around the back of his neck and bury her face in his chest.

He held her close, laying his cheek on the top of her head. He couldn't lose her.

She looked up at him with sad eyes, and all he could think was that he was the one who had hurt her. "Lanie."

"Shh." She lightly kissed him on the lips. "Let's sit down."

She slid into the booth across from him. "Thanks for meeting me," he said as he sat down. "I didn't know if you would."

"Tyler, I love you. Of course I wanted to see you."

"You don't hate me?"

"Did you set out to purposely hurt me?"

"Of course not."

"Then why would I hate you? It could be argued that you have a reason to be upset with me, since I knew your firm was involved and I didn't tell you."

"No. You're the innocent party here."

The waitress walked over and took their drink order. Tyler was tempted to order wine, but he wanted a clear head, and he noticed that Lanie skipped the wine as well.

"You called Aiden?" he asked as soon as the waitress left.

Lanie glanced down at her clasped hands on the table. "Yeah."

"And you leave next week?"

"Next Wednesday."

His chest hurt. He didn't want to lose her, but he didn't know how to stop it. "Do you need help moving your things? I can go to Atlanta with you and look for an apartment."

She glanced up at him with tear-filled eyes. "I think it's better if we end it before I go on Wednesday."

He blinked, sure he'd heard her wrong. "*End it?* You're going to end this because of what I did?"

"No. I'm upset, but I'll eventually get over it."

"Then why do you want to end it?"

"I don't *want* to end it, Tyler, but I'm moving to Atlanta."

"So? There are plenty of direct flights to Atlanta. I can come see you. You can come see me."

"No." She shook her head. "Long-distance relationships don't work. I'd hate to see us die a slow death of resentment or, God forbid, lack of interest."

"Then work there until you can find something in Kansas City."

"I can't do that," she said in dismay. "Aiden's counting on me. If I work for him, I'm committing to his business."

"For how long?"

"I don't know. Three years? Ten? Maybe forever." She gave him a sad smile. "So you see why this won't work. If I move to Atlanta, I'm committing to it, which means I have no intention of leaving. And since you're settled in Kansas City, a relationship is impossible, because I don't want to only see you a few days every month or so for the rest of my life."

"Who says I'm settled in Kansas City?" he asked.

"You're the most settled person I know. You can't move. You're needed here, and I see no reason to draw out the pain of an inevitable break-up. Better to get it over with as soon as possible."

"No," he said, shaking his head. "I'm not a partner in my firm. I can move."

"What about your friends? Your brothers?"

He shrugged, but deep down, he didn't want to leave Eric. His brother needed him.

"See?"

He reached across the table and covered her hand with his. "Don't end us yet. Give us some time to figure it out and make it work."'

She remained silent but nodded. He was taking that as a yes.

"You're the first woman I've ever loved, Lanie. I don't want to lose you."

"I don't want to lose you either."

Chapter Thirty-Two

Lanie went back to the store after her lunch with Tyler, if for no other reason so that she could come up with a plan for how to handle the employees. She still hadn't told Stephanie about Tyler's involvement in the shutdown. She couldn't tell her in front of their employees.

Their training was going well, and a couple of hours after lunch, Lanie sent them home. When they were gone, she grabbed her purse. "Let's go get a drink."

"We still need to work on paperwork," Stephanie said.

"No," Lanie said, pulling out Stephanie's purse and handing it to her. "No more work today."

They locked up and walked down the street to the Irish bar. After they got their drinks, Lanie took a deep breath. "Tyler was the one who shut us down."

"What? When did you find that out?"

She rubbed her forehead. "I knew his firm was behind it, but Randy had assured me that Tyler wasn't involved, which was true until after Britt's barbecue. And Tyler had bought my cover story so well, he'd never thought we were any part of it. He didn't find out until this morning, when I had him drop me off at the store."

"Oh, Lanie. Are you furious with him?"

"He had no idea I was involved. How can I be angry with him for being so good at his job?"

"Yeah, I guess you're right."

"I talked to corporate," Lanie said. "They want you in Phoenix a week from Monday whether our store opens or not."

"And you're going to Atlanta?" Stephanie asked.

"Yeah, I'm leaving next Wednesday."

"I wish I was going with you," Steph said, then grinned. "Maybe you could put in a good word for me with Aiden."

"Are you serious?" Lanie asked in surprise. "You never hinted that you wanted to move on from Montgomery Enterprises."

"It won't be the same without you, so promise me that you'll ask him."

Lanie was surprised at the desperation in her eyes. "Of course, Steph. You and I are a great team. Aiden would be lucky to get us both."

"So what are you going to do about Tyler?" Stephanie asked.

Lanie sighed. "One problem at a time."

* * *

Several hours later, Lanie opened her apartment door. Tyler stood in the hall, holding a bag of sushi and a bottle of wine.

"I brought packing sustenance."

She grinned, even though she felt like crying.

Tyler walked into her apartment and kissed her. "I love you, Lanie," he said when he lifted his head.

"I love you too."

He set the bag on the counter. "Let's eat first and pack later." He pulled out a container as he looked around the apartment. "For someone who doesn't have much stuff, you have a lot packed."

"I got a start on it the other day. And no, there's not much left."

"So you lured me here under false pretenses," he teased, but his eyes were sad.

She grinned. "You must be the first person in the history of the world to complain about not packing."

They ate in a heavy silence, and when they finished, Tyler followed her to her room and helped her fold and pack most of her clothing into two boxes. He stacked them in the living room with the other boxes. "How are you going to get them to Atlanta?"

"I'll hire a moving company."

"To relocate a dozen boxes?" he asked. "I'll borrow Matt's truck and haul them down for you."

Lanie shook her head. "No, Tyler. I'll handle it."

He turned to her and lifted his hand to her cheek. "I know you're new to the whole boyfriend-perks thing, but moving falls in the top ten duties."

She grinned, but tears filled her eyes. How could she leave him?

He pressed his forehead to hers and closed his eyes. "Oh, Lanie. Don't cry."

"Yesterday I thought I was going to get to be with you forever," she said.

"We can still have forever."

"But it's not the same."

He kissed the tear on her cheek, then softly brushed his lips down to her mouth.

She looped her hands around the back of his neck and held him close. She needed him. She needed him to make love to her, to reassure her that everything would work out. She needed the strength he gave her.

And that scared her.

His mouth moved to her jaw, his lips brushing the sensitive skin of her neck, and she shivered. He pushed her shirt off the edge of her shoulder as his tongue make a lazy path along her collarbone. Then he returned to her mouth, his tongue leisurely coaxing hers.

She melted into him, her chest pressing into his.

"I want you, Lanie," he whispered against her lips. Then he bent and scooped her into his arms, kissing her as he carried her down the hall to her bedroom.

He lowered her to the bed, lying down next to her as he continued to kiss her. His hand rested lightly on her stomach, then slid under her T-shirt, skimming over the skin of her abdomen and up to her breast. His thumb brushed her nipple over the thin fabric of her bra. She moaned into his mouth as he continued his torture.

She reached for the button of his shirt, but he grabbed her hand and held it still. His mouth moved lower again, down her neck and to her chest, stopping at the neckline of her T-shirt.

"Tyler."

He sat up and pulled her to a sitting position, tugging her T-shirt over her head and unclasping her bra, then tossing them both to the floor. He cupped her breast, his thumb circling her nipple as he watched her face. His eyes held hers, and she expected him to smile, but instead he studied her as though he were committing her face to memory.

"I love you, Lanie."

"I love you too," she whispered.

He pushed her back on the bed then unfastened her jeans and tugged them off, along with her panties. She was completely naked, and he was completely clothed, but when she reached for the button of his shirt again, he grabbed her hand and placed it on the bed over her head.

He lowered his mouth to her chest, taking his time kissing both breasts, while his hand made lazy circles on her abdomen. But then it slid lower, between her legs, slipping between her soft folds. She released a gasp as his hand and his mouth made her ache for him.

"Tyler, I want you."

He continued his path of kisses down her stomach then between her legs while his hand stroked her breasts.

He was unhurried, taking his time. She felt worshipped.

He brought her to the edge of a climax, easing off then and leaving her whimpering for more.

He knelt on the bed between her legs and watched her as he unbuttoned his shirt and pulled it off, then unfastened his pants. He never took his eyes off her while he stood at the foot of her bed and let his pants drop to the floor.

His gaze held hers as he lowered himself to the bed, between her legs, as his lips covered hers, his tongue exploring her mouth. Then he lifted on one elbow and watched her face as he entered her in one deep stroke.

She arched her back, lifting her hips to take him deeper.

He began to move in long, slow strokes, while he slipped his hand between her legs, bringing her closer.

"Tyler."

He increased his speed, driving deeper and pushing her higher and higher until she cried out his name, clinging to him while she toppled over the edge. He thrust one last time, then collapsed next to her. He wrapped an arm around her back and rolled her to her side so she faced him.

"I love you, Lanie. We'll make this work."

She offered him a smile, even though she wasn't so sure.

Chapter Thirty-Three

Tyler stood at the altar while Britt and Randy exchanged their wedding vows. All eyes were on the happy couple, but Tyler's were on Lanie. And her eyes were on him.

After what seemed an eternity, the minister announced that Randy could kiss the bride. The church erupted in applause when they kissed, and all Tyler could think was he hadn't touched or talked to Lanie in nearly two hours, and that was not acceptable. Not when she was leaving in three days.

The processional music began, and Randy escorted his new bride down the aisle, and Tyler suddenly wanted that too. He wanted to be married to Lanie.

The rest of the wedding party moved to follow Britt and Randy out of the church, and Tyler met Lanie at the middle of the altar, taking her hand and squeezing.

She smiled up at him, and he was relieved that the sadness he'd seen the last few days was missing, as though it was impossible to be sad at Britt and Randy's wedding.

As soon as they were in the foyer, Tyler pulled Lanie to the side and gave her a deep, soulful kiss. When he lifted his head, he was pleased to see she was as affected as he was.

"Are you ready to dance?" she teased.

"Only with you, Killer. And only if you take off your shoes."

She laughed. "I think that can be arranged. It was a good thing I ordered the extra pair of shoes after you lost the one. Who knew I'd break a heel?"

"Those things are cursed," he said with a smile. "I plan to bury them in a graveyard at midnight, and save humanity."

She laughed again, and it filled his heart with joy. He was going to miss her laugh when she was gone.

They drove to the reception, and although they were supposed to sit at the table with the wedding party, Lanie suggested they sit with Matt and Kevin.

"It will give me a chance to get to know them better," she said.

They found Matt and Kevin's table, and Lanie grinned when she saw the couple sitting next to Matt.

"Aiden," Tyler said in surprise, trying to keep his voice light and friendly, but it was hard. The woman he loved was moving to work with the bastard, and while he knew Lanie didn't have romantic feelings for Aiden, he wasn't sure if Aiden could say the same.

Aiden stood and leaned across the table, and shook Tyler's hand. "So you're the man who finally captured Lanie's heart."

Tyler locked his gaze with Aiden's. *Son of a bitch.* He was jealous. And Lanie was going off to live with the guy—literally, since Aiden had offered to let her stay with him until she found a place to live.

The glance Matt shot Tyler confirmed he'd noticed.

But Lanie walked around the table to give Aiden a hug. "What in the world are you doing here?"

He held his hands out at his sides. "Thanks to you, I was invited."

"But you don't even know the bride or groom."

"But I know one of the most beautiful bridesmaids in the world."

Lanie laughed. "Save it for the clients, Aiden." She glanced at her assistant in the chair next to him. "Stephanie, I see you two found each other."

"It wasn't hard," Stephanie said with a grin. "He was the only guy asking for a folding chair to sit in the aisle, since he wasn't a friend of the bride *or* the groom."

"You didn't!" Lanie said

Aiden smirked.

After they ate dinner, the bride and groom had their first dance, then the wedding party joined them on the dance floor.

Tyler took Lanie into his arms and held her close as they swayed to the music. He looked over at the bride and groom, who were smiling at each other. "They look happy."

Lanie turned to watch them. "Being in love will do that."

"I told you I loved you and four days later, I had to fucking ruin it," Tyler said.

"Hey," she said, placing her index finger lightly on his lips. "None of that."

"Lanie, closing your store is the single biggest greatest regret of my life, and that's saying something, after some of the stunts I've pulled."

She gave him a soft kiss, and he felt that the sadness he'd seen for the past several days had returned. "I know."

"Why aren't you beating me up for doing this?"

"Because you're already beating yourself up enough for both of us."

* * *

"Can I cut in?" a male voice asked behind her.

She glanced back to see Kevin, wearing a big grin.

Tyler mock-scowled. "I don't think so. Who knows what you'll tell her."

Kevin moved closer. "Come on. I promise to be on my best behavior."

"Tyler," Lanie said. "It's okay."

Tyler dropped his hold, and Kevin took his place.

Lanie let him lead her around several measures before she said, "I'm kind of surprised you cut in."

"Because I risked losing a limb with Tyler?" he teased. "I can take him."

"No, because I kind of got the impression you don't like me."

"Really? Why?"

"Maybe because you're worried I'm going to hurt your best friend."

Kevin's grin faded. "Yeah. That's what I wanted to talk to you about. I know you've been talking about ending things with him when you leave next week."

"Kevin, I'm sorry. You have to know this is killing me."

"I know. I guess I don't understand why you have to end it. Can't you at least try it and break it off later if it doesn't work?"

She shook her head. "I'm trying to be optimistic. But honestly, I just don't think it's going to work."

"He loves you, Lanie, and losing you is going to kill him." He paused. "Are you punishing him for shutting down your store?"

"What? No." She glanced over at her table and spotted Tyler. He looked like he was ready to cut back in at any moment. "I don't want to leave, but I don't have a job here, and there's a great one in Atlanta. And as far as trying a long-distance relationship, I've seen too many fail to do that to him."

"Lanie, please don't just leave him like this."

Tears filled her eyes. "I don't want to, Kevin."

Tyler broke in moments later, and Kevin took off, while Tyler pulled her back into his arms. "Lanie? Are you crying?"

"No. I'm fine."

She forced a smile, then, when the song was finished, she suggested they go sit with his friends. But as they left the dance floor Britt stood by another table and motioned Lanie over.

Tyler gave Lanie a quick kiss. "You go see what she wants, and I'll get us something to drink."

"Thanks." She closed the distance between her and her cousin, sad all over again. It wasn't just Tyler whom she was leaving.

"You look beautiful, Britt," she said. "You look happy."

"I am," Britt said. "What's this I hear about you leaving?" When Lanie didn't respond, Britt pressed on. "How can you leave after falling in love with Tyler? Do you know what a great guy he is?"

"I lost my job, Britt, but I'm lucky to have found a new one. I tried to find a way to stay here in Kansas City, but it didn't work out." Her voice broke. "You have no idea how badly I wanted it to work out."

Britt pulled her into a hug. "I know, Randy told me about Tyler and the injunctions. I'm sorry."

Lanie kissed her cheek, then headed for the front door. She needed a moment to clear her head.

She stood outside, looking up into the stars for a couple

of minutes, when she heard the door open behind her. "I'm sorry I didn't tell you I was coming outside," she said. "But I just needed a moment."

"Then maybe I should go back in," Aiden said.

Lanie turned around in surprise. "Aiden. I thought you were Tyler."

"You needed a moment from Tyler?"

"No, I needed a moment from all the people trying to tell me that moving to Atlanta is a bad idea."

His eyebrows rose. "People think you shouldn't move?"

"Not because of the job. Because I'm leaving Tyler."

"Why are you leaving Tyler?"

"Come on, Aiden," she said. "You know why. I need a job." She pushed out a sigh and rubbed her temple. "That sounded bad. I'm really excited about working for you and with you. I believe in what you're doing." She gave him a sad smile. "If only I could pick up your business and move it to Kansas City, it would be perfect."

"Lane, I'm so sorry you're facing this choice. I'm not going to lie—I'm excited you're coming—but I hate to see you so torn."

"It's part of growing up, right? You have to make the hard choices." She wiped a tear from her cheek.

"Yeah. I guess so." He motioned to the door. "Now, let's get you inside before Tyler comes out here and kicks my ass for keeping you away from him in the short time he has left."

Lanie gave him a hug. "Thanks, Aiden. You've been a godsend."

He laughed. "I like the sound of 'godsend.'"

She shook her head with a grin. "Don't let it go to your head."

Chapter Thirty-Four

Lanie stayed over at Tyler's condo after the wedding. When she told him she needed to go in on Sunday to take care of some final paperwork that had to be done before her last day, he almost told her to tell them to screw it. But this was her fifteenth store opening, and he was the cause of it being an epic failure. So he convinced her to stay in bed an hour longer while he showed her how much he loved her, then he took her to a local coffee shop for coffee and a pastry before he dropped her off at her office around eleven.

"This is going to take me all day," she said as she opened the car door. "So why don't you call Eric? You missed your standing Wednesday-night dinner, so why don't you hang out with him today while I'm working?"

He had to admit it was a good idea. It would take his mind off the fact that Lanie was leaving in a few days. He called Eric on the way home and invited him to his condo for pizza and to watch the Chiefs game.

While he waited for his brother to show up, he started

gathering Lanie's things to make it easier for her on Tuesday, then set them on the kitchen table. He'd just laid a couple of dresses over the back of one of his dining room chairs when he heard a knock at the door.

Eric looked worried when Tyler opened the front door. "Dude, you look like shit."

"Didn't you ever hear, if you don't have something nice to say, don't say anything at all?"

"Yeah," Eric grinned. "You should hear the *mean* comment."

Tyler laughed in spite of himself and let his brother in.

"I take back all the shit I ever said about your condo," Eric said, walking around the living area.

Tyler felt like an ass for never inviting him over before. Just one more thing to add to his pile of shit-head moves. "Wait. You never talked shit about my condo."

Eric gave him a knowing grin, and Tyler laughed. Who knew his kid brother was exactly what he needed to feel better? He never would have even considered it a month ago. But since that night at IHOP, he had a connection to his brother he hadn't felt before.

He owed that to Lanie.

He couldn't believe he was losing her. And it was his own damn fault. Why hadn't he put things together sooner?

His eyes burned, and he walked into the kitchen to buy time to get himself together. "Want a drink?" He opened the fridge. "I've got beer and...Diet Coke."

Eric laughed. "You drink Diet Coke?"

"No. Those were Lanie's."

"Were?" Eric noticed the dresses hanging over the chair and the partially filled box on the table. "You dumped her." He sounded disappointed.

"The person responsible for the dumping is in question."

"How did you screw it up?"

"Who said *I* screwed it up?" Tyler asked. It burned even more that he had, but dammit, he'd just been doing his job.

"Please, you're a Norris. It's what we do best."

Tyler grabbed a beer and handed his brother a Diet Coke. To his surprise, the boy popped it open and took a drink. Tyler took his own generous gulp.

"So tell me how you came up with your theory," Tyler said as he sat down.

"That Norris men screw up?" Eric plopped down next to him. "Look at me and the mess I was in at school. Alex has his own girlfriend issues. Dad...he's practically a lost cause. Then there's you. Never had a girlfriend until Lanie. That's pretty sad for an old dude."

"I object," Tyler said. "I'm not an old dude."

A grin spread over Eric's face. "I knew that one would get you. But there's no denying you never had a girlfriend, and Matt said to tell you that the stalker didn't count."

"Matt?" Tyler asked with raised eyebrows. "You've been talking to Matt?"

Eric lifted his shoulders into a lazy shrug. "I thought we were going to watch the game."

Tyler grabbed the remote and flipped on the TV. The game had just started, and not much was going on, yet Eric seemed glued to the screen.

"How are things going at school?"

Eric shrugged again. "Pretty good. I went on a date last night."

"Really? Who is she?"

Eric laughed. "Now you sound like a girl."

"Guilty as charged. Who is she?"

"Someone from band. Now that I have my shit together,

I get to march again. Want to come see the game on Friday night?"

"Yeah," he said, surprised he meant it.

"Maybe you could bring Lanie."

"Eric, Lanie won't be here. She's moving to Atlanta."

"Why?" he asked, his gaze still on the screen.

"Because she took a job there... It's complicated."

"That's not what I heard."

He was starting to smell a rat. Grabbing the remote, he flipped off the game.

"Hey!" Eric protested.

"What did you hear and whom did you hear it from?"

Eric leaned over, trying to snatch the remote from Tyler's hands. "Now you *really* sound like a girl."

Tyler held the remote out of reach. "I'll turn it back on if you talk."

"Fine. Matt. And Kevin."

"*Both* of them?" *Traitors.*

"They're worried about you. Why haven't you answered your phone?"

They'd each called him a couple of times that morning, but he'd been with Lanie, and he hadn't felt like talking. "I needed a break."

"So you figured you'd hang out with me?"

"Yeah."

Eric looked surprised, then grinned. "Now, turn on the game."

Laughing, Tyler obeyed.

They settled in and watched two quarters, but when it turned into a slaughter, Eric said, "I'm hungry. Let's go get something to eat."

"It's two thirty, and we just had a pizza an hour ago."

"So?"

So, indeed.

Tyler drove them to the Plaza. After they parked in a garage, they walked a couple of blocks to Brio.

"That's it, huh?" Eric asked, flicking his hand toward the tarp covering Lanie's store.

He saw no reason to hide it. "Yeah, that's it."

"So she told you she her job was the time management thing, but she was really opening a designer clothes store?"

"Yeah, that's the bottom line, I guess."

"And your law firm was trying stop her store from opening."

Tyler's eyes narrowed. He knew what the boy was up to, but he saw no reason not to go along. The fact that it ate at his soul was penance. "Yes."

"Lanie must hate your guts."

"She doesn't hate me. She said she knew I had no idea it was her."

"So if you don't hate her, and she doesn't hate you, what's the problem? Why are you breaking up?"

"Sometimes things are complicated, Eric."

"I call bullshit."

"Language."

Eric stopped on the sidewalk. "You want me to tell you more about my date last night?"

Tyler was getting whiplash. He pointed across the street. "How about we have this conversation at the restaurant? I thought you were hungry."

Eric grinned. "Good idea."

After they were seated in a booth and had placed their orders, Tyler thumped the table with his index finger. "Okay. I ordered you food, now I want to hear about the date."

Eric grinned. "Claire Hoffstetter. She's the one I wrote the poem for."

"Wait. The one who showed it to the entire school?"

"Yeah, only Claire didn't do it."

"Then who did?"

"Her friends, but they weren't her friends. Turned out they were jealous that I wrote a poem for her, so they made fun of it."

"And Claire let you think she did it?"

"She knew I was hurt either way, and she *had* let her friends read it. She thought it was her fault it happened so she deserved the blame. She figured I'd never want to go out with her after all the hell I went through."

Tyler scowled, smelling a setup. "And how'd you find this out?"

Eric held his gaze. "She wanted to date me, so she found the guts to tell me the truth."

The waiter showed up with their appetizer, and as soon as he left, Eric continued talking. "You know what's really pathetic? A sixteen-year-old girl has more guts than you." He took a sip of his drink and grinned.

Fuck you, Eric was on the tip of his tongue, but given Eric's age and the fact that he'd just pointed out that a sixteen-year-old girl was more mature than him, he held back.

"My situation is different than yours," Tyler said. "Sure, we both have the whole misunderstanding issue, but neither one of us was mad at the other. We were just both very upset that I hurt Lanie's store opening."

"But now she's leaving, and you're letting her go."

"I'm not just letting her go. I'm respecting her decision. She's losing her job and she can't find another one here. So she's moving to Atlanta to work with an old friend. She says she doesn't know if or when she'd move back, and we both know I'll be here. So we're ending it when she leaves."

"So?" Eric said, unimpressed "Bill Messing's girlfriend moved to Raytown, so he got a job at Wendy's to be closer to her."

"Adult careers are a whole lot harder to change than teenagers working at fast-food joints."

"You said Lanie can't find a job here, but attorneys are a dime a dozen. You could find a job there."

"Wouldn't it bother you that I just started hanging out with you and then I moved away?"

Eric shrugged. "Yeah, but I don't want you to let her get away, either. It took you over thirty years to find a girlfriend. You'll be really old in another thirty. And maybe I could come visit you."

The food arrived soon after, and Tyler watched in amazement as his brother plowed through his own fettucine, then moved on to to half of Tyler's salmon. But Eric was so busy chowing down, he didn't have time to talk, which gave Tyler plenty of time to think.

It might not be that hard for Tyler to get a job in Atlanta. At the very least, he could put out a few feelers.

"So..." Tyler said as Eric shoveled in the last of his broccoli. "Let's say I wanted to tell Lanie that I'm considering moving with her. What do you suggest?" He felt like an idiot, but so far, the kid's advice had been sound. Why not listen to him?

"You need a grand gesture."

"A grand gesture?" Tyler asked. "You mean like *Say Anything*?"

"What?"

"You know, the eighties movie with the boom box."

"What's a boom box?"

Tyler groaned. "Never mind. I get it. A grand gesture. Like what?"

"How big are you willing to go?"

It only took a second to come up with the answer. "Big."

Eric's eyes widened with excitement. "Dude, you could get a hot-air balloon. Or do one of those flash mob things."

Tyler shook his head. "No. I already know what I need to do. Are you finished? I fed you and so now I own you for the next hour or so while we go shopping."

"Shopping? You're not going to buy her clothes, are you? Because Tim Merriman bought Delany Nichols a pair of shorts and it did *not* go well. *Epic* mistake. Just sayin'. You should get her a puppy. Girls love those. David Hammerstein bought his girlfriend an Australian shepherd, and she couldn't stop crying." Then he added, "From happiness." He shrugged. "Girls are weird."

"No clothes or puppies. What I have in mind is much better."

Eric gave him a dubious look. "Nothing beats a puppy."

Tyler hoped this was one instance when his brother was wrong.

Chapter Thirty-Five

Sleep didn't come easily for Lanie Sunday night. On Sunday afternoon, she'd gotten a call saying that her legal team might have found a solution to the injunction. The attorneys planned to be at the courthouse first thing Monday morning, and hoped they'd be able to overturn it before the store opening.

Stephanie had been excited when Lanie told her the news, and the two of them called their employees and told them all to come in at nine thirty...just in case. Then Lanie suggested they take the offensive and try to get the media on their side. Stephanie usually sent out press releases, but after the injunction, they hadn't sent them. Lanie had Stephanie type one up and e-mail it to the local newspapers and TV stations, informing them of a surprise opening if all went well. And if didn't, they'd take their story to the media and hope the public outcry over losing a Margo Benson Boutique would put pressure on the store blocking their opening.

At least they hoped it'd work that way.

The hardest part was that she couldn't tell Tyler. He might not be on the case any longer, but he was still tied to the law firm. With any luck at all, she'd open the store, get her promotion, then stay in Kansas City and build a life with Tyler.

But Lanie was so worried she'd clue Tyler in that she told him she was spending the night at her own apartment on Sunday night. Alone. He'd sounded so hurt, she almost told him the truth, but she told herself to stay strong; the end result would be worth it.

On Monday morning, Lanie was at the store an hour and a half early. Weeks before, they'd hired a security team to help with the crowds, and even though they wouldn't know until close to ten if the judge had reversed the injunction, they were going to keep going as though they were opening. The local television stations had run segments about the "secret opening," and now people were already lining up out front. The last thing Lanie needed was for things to get out of hand, so she made sure the security team was up to speed on how to handle the crowds if they opened, and came up with an alternate plan in case they didn't. Once she was assured they were prepared, she went inside and paced the floor, checking everything.

All she could do was wait.

When the employees showed up at nine thirty, she and Stephanie made sure that everyone knew their places... and then they waited.

At ten, they hadn't gotten a call from the attorneys yet, and Lanie and Stephanie peered out the window, wondering how long to wait until they told the crowd that the Margo Benson Boutique hadn't been allowed to open.

"I'm calling corporate," Lanie said ten minutes later. "Maybe they can tell us what's going on." She called the legal department, but the assistant still hadn't heard anything.

When people began to chant—*"We want Margo! We want Margo!"*—Lanie made the executive decision to address the crowd. She and Stephanie came up with a plan, then ducked through the tarp and faced the crowd. The people lining the sidewalk cheered, and Lanie started to address them, but her phone rang in her pocket. She pulled it out to see if it was one of the attorneys, but saw Aiden's name instead. She silenced the call and dropped it into her pocket. He was probably calling to see if the store had opened. She'd call him back later.

The crowd was bigger than she'd expected, especially since there had been very little publicity. People filled the sidewalk from one end of the block to the other and had spilled out onto the street.

"Thank you all for coming for our grand opening!" Lanie shouted as she waved.

Stephanie beamed next to her.

The crowd continued to chant, but Lanie lifted both hands. "I'm sure you all are eager to find out what's behind this tarp. Am I right?"

The crowd whooped and cheered.

"I'm Lanie and this is Stephanie, and we've spent the last five months preparing for this day." Stephanie moved to one edge of the tarp, which had been prepared to be removed, while Lanie moved to the other. "And now, what you've all been waiting for—" They tugged the edge, and the fabric fell, revealing the sign as she announced, "Welcome to Margo Benson Boutique, Kansas City!"

And that's when she saw him.

Tyler was wearing a dark suit, which she'd learned over

the last month meant he was either going to court or meeting
with an important client.

Had he just come from court? Was he back on the case?
No. He wouldn't do that to her—do that to *them*.

But why was he here? Had he shown up out of curiosity?
Was he here for support? She couldn't deny that seeing him
now took her breath away. His gaze was glued to hers, but
his deadpan expression gave nothing away.

Stephanie caught her attention. Lanie still had a job to do.

"Now, we would love for you to come inside and check
us out, but there's a not-so-small problem."

The crowd let out a groan, but Lanie held up her hands
to settle them down. "Stephanie and I are ready for you. The
fifteen employees we have inside are excited to meet you
and show you around, but the Jackson County court system
has decided to keep us closed for a while."

The crowd released sounds of restlessness.

The phone rang in Lanie's pocket again. "Stephanie is going to tell you a little bit about what's happening."

Stephanie gave her a questioning glance, and Lanie
pulled out her phone and gestured toward it. Steph's eyes
widened in understanding and she turned toward the crowd
of people. "We'd like to make it clear that everything about
the store is up to code. The store is perfectly safe. But one
store in the area—"

Lanie moved close to the front door, and checked caller
ID. Aiden again.

The fact that he'd called twice in such a short period was
a warning of some kind, so Lanie called him back.

"Aiden, what's up?"

"Is this a bad time?"

She laughed. "I'm just standing in front of two or three
hundred people. What's up?"

"You opened?" he asked in surprise.

"Nope. We just decided to go ahead and use the publicity to get public support for the store."

"Good thinking."

"That's why you're about to pay me the big bucks," she said with a laugh.

"Lanie, that's part of why I'm calling."

Oh, shit. "Are you going to fire me before I even start?"

"No, nothing like that, but I *do* have something important to discuss. Call me back when you're free."

"Should I be worried?"

"Not at all. I think you'll like what I have to say. Go do your press. We'll talk later."

She hung up and checked her phone to make sure she hadn't missed a call from their attorneys. Was the fact that it was taking longer than expected a good thing or a bad?

Stephanie was continuing her speech, telling them how Montgomery Enterprises wanted to become active in the local community, and playing up the store as a do-gooder underdog. She definitely knew how to engage the crowd.

But Tyler was still in the same place, and Lanie wondered if she should say something to him or ignore him unless he tried to attract her attention.

Stephanie beamed at the crowd. "We'd love to chat with media now and answer any questions you might have."

Stephanie started to head toward the camera crews to answer questions, but she noticed Tyler in the crowd and hurried over to Lanie.

"Why do you think he's here?" Stephanie whispered.

"I don't know."

"He's not doing anything lawyerly, so he's probably here to see you."

He looked so serious, he was making her nervous.

"You up to doing these interviews?" Steph asked.

"Not yet. Let me talk to Tyler first."

"Okay."

Her stomach cramped as she moved to the edge of the crowd, keeping her gaze on him as he moved toward her.

"What are you doing here?" Lanie asked.

"I was worried about you."

She offered him a smile. "Tyler, I'm okay. Really. I need to go talk to some reporters now."

He grinned. "I love watching you work." He lowered his mouth to her ear. "You're sexy as hell, Lanie Rogers."

She flushed as she walked over to the reporters and started taking questions as the crowd continued to grow.

"How long have you been dealing with your unhappy neighbor, and why do you think they want to stop you from opening?" a reporter asked.

Lanie gave her a gracious smile. "I understand why another store might feel threatened, but I want to assure them, as well as the community, that Margo Benson plans to blend into the community and improve the lives of women through both fashion and community service. With that in mind, I'd like to announce that Montgomery Enterprises is donating fifty thousand dollars to the Rose Brooks Center, an emergency shelter for women and children threatened with domestic violence."

The crowd behind her cheered, and Lanie shot a smile toward them.

Several more reporters asked questions, and Stephanie and Lanie took turns answering.

Then Tyler stood at the edge of the crowd with his hand raised. "I have a question."

Stephanie gave Lanie a quizzical look.

What was he up to? "Okay."

"What do you think about grand gestures?" he called out.

She shook her head in confusion. "What?"

Suddenly a marching band started playing.

Stephanie's eyes flew open, and she leaned into Lanie's ear. "I didn't arrange that."

The tune of the song became recognizable as the band rounded the corner of the side street—Bruno Mars's "Marry You."

Lanie's mouth parted in shock.

"Lanie," Tyler said as he closed the distance between them and lowered his voice. "I love you."

She shook her head. "Tyler..."

The band was now marching in front of the store, and Lanie saw Eric standing in the front, playing a saxophone.

"What's going on, Tyler?" she asked louder.

"I know you're leaving, but I'm more determined than ever to make this work. I don't want to lose you." He pulled a ring box out of his pocket, then bent down on one knee as he grabbed her left hand.

She gasped.

"Lanie, I love you. Marry me."

She had always considered marriage a trap until she'd seen Britt and Randy. Randy made her cousin happy and they brought out the best in each other, not the worst like her parents had. Marriage had never been part of her life plan, but she loved Tyler more than she thought it was possible to love someone, and she didn't want to live without him.

Lanie's silence must have worried him. "It can be a long engagement," he said. "Or short. Whichever you want. As long as you say you want to be with me, I'll wait. We can wait years."

Lanie shook her head, trying to get the words past the lump in her throat.

"No?" he asked, his voice tight as he climbed to his feet.

She nodded, still unable to speak.

"Yes, you don't want marry me?"

"Yes!" she forced out. "I want to marry you. I want you." Then she laughed as she brushed a tear from her cheek. "But you're doing it all wrong."

"You don't like the marching band?" he asked with a grin. "That was Eric's idea."

Lanie gave the boy a quick wave, and he beamed.

She turned back to Tyler. "No. I love the band. It's the ring. Most men *show* their fiancée the ring."

His grin spread as he opened the box, revealing the emerald-cut diamond, surrounded by tiny stones.

She put her hand on her chest, trying to catch her breath.

"If you don't like it, we can exchange it."

"No. It's perfect."

He grabbed her left hand and slipped the ring onto her finger, then he glanced over his shoulder at his brother. "She said yes!"

Eric waved his saxophone in response as the crowd broke into cheers.

Butterflies swarmed through Lanie's stomach as Tyler swept her into his arms and kissed her.

But all the excitement didn't change the fact that she was moving to Atlanta. "Tyler, the distance thing. It's never going to work."

"I know," he said. "Which is why I'm going to quit my job and look for a job in Atlanta."

"What?" She shook her head. "No. Your job—you're almost a partner. You've worked hard to get there. You can't give it up. And Eric—you two are just now getting to know one another. You can't move away from him."

"Eric's already given his blessing. We worked it out yesterday. I'm going to fly him to see us once a month. And we're going to FaceTime a couple of times a week."

"But it's not the same."

"Lanie," he said, holding her hand. "Nothing about our living options is ideal, but we're making the best of it. If I have to choose between my job and you, you win."

"Tyler." She couldn't let him do this.

A woman moved through the crowd toward Lanie while the marching band still played on the street behind them. "Ms. Rogers? I'm Dinah Pettier, with Dinah's Fashions. My own store is halfway down the street. I was the one who filed the lawsuit."

The reporters picked up on Dinah's entrance and started shouting questions, but Dinah turned to Lanie. "But my former attorney"—she tilted her head toward Tyler and grinned—"pointed out that I'd end up spending a lot of money I'll never get back. I saw your store as competition, but he suggested that we can work together to increase sales. He even has an event planner who's willing to help set up a joint fashion show to raise money for the Rose Brooks Center."

Lanie stared at her, realizing what she'd implied. "*Wait*. Does that mean you're dropping your case?"

Dinah offered Lanie her hand. "Welcome to the neighborhood."

Stephanie's eyes lit up. "So can we open the doors?"

Lanie was pretty sure legal would want to give the go-ahead, but it was her last day, and she was more interested in making the crowd happy.

She took a step back and shouted, "Margo Benson Boutique, Kansas City, is now open!"

The security guards took over their duty of herding the crowd inside, and Lanie turned back to Tyler. "I don't have to quit now. The store's open!"

His eyes widened in understanding. "You get your promotion."

Why didn't that make her feel better?

But Tyler seemed to notice. "Aiden's job will make you happier. You should take it."

"I don't want you to leave everything you love, Tyler."

"What if you could have what you wanted?" a voice asked behind her.

Lanie spun around. "Aiden. What are you doing here?"

"When I realized you were here, I decided to come by and talk to you in person. I didn't fly home yesterday. I had some business to take care of. Which is why I called earlier. I'm looking at expanding my business and setting up two locations. One in Atlanta and one in Kansas City. I'm still gathering funds for the Kansas City location, so I won't be able to open it for a while, so I need you in Atlanta until I can find someone to fill your spot. But surely you and Tyler can make it work for six months to a year."

Lanie gasped. "Bonus."

"What?" Aiden asked.

"I opened the store. I get a bonus. Fifty thousand dollars."

Aiden stared at her.

"Plus, I have savings," Lanie said, and lifted her chin. "I don't want to be your employee, Aiden. I want to be your business partner."

"Wow. I was *not* expecting that."

"Are you open to it?" she asked.

"I think it's a great idea. But I still need to replace you in Atlanta."

Lanie held up a finger. "Hold that thought." She ran over to Steph, grabbed her arm, and started dragging her toward Aiden. "Come here."

"What are you doing?" Steph asked.

"You can thank me later." Lanie stopped in front of Aiden. "Meet my replacement. Stephanie knows everything I know and practically ran this entire store opening herself."

Aiden grinned. "So she comes highly recommended?"

"Very. Hire her, and you won't regret it. I don't know how I'll live without her. You better snatch her up before I do."

Stephanie laughed. "Oh, I'm being fought over. Every girl's dream."

"Stephanie," Aiden said with a grin, "it sounds like we need to chat. And Lanie, after your excitement dies down, let's sit down and iron out the details. I should be able to have a contract within a couple of days."

Lanie nodded her agreement, but she knew she was going to agree. This was like a dream job come true. She turned to Tyler and gave him a breath-stealing hug.

"I have a confession," Tyler said, turning serious.

"Okay…" she said, worried all over again.

"I said I'd wait years to marry you, but I don't want to. I don't want to wait. I want to get married soon. The sooner I marry you, the better. I want our life together to start right now."

She leaned into him and kissed him. "I like the sound of that."

Epilogue

~

Three months later

Lanie shivered. "I can't believe I'm doing this."

Alarm filled Britt's eyes. She wore a ruby red bridesmaid's dress that matched the red roses in Lanie's bouquet. "Getting married?"

"No, standing outside in falling snow in a strapless wedding dress without a coat."

Holly walked over to the waiting area next to the glass chapel in the botanical garden. "I can still get you one."

"No. I'm still worried it will wrinkle my dress. Isn't it about time to go in anyway?"

Holly smiled. "I just cued them to start the music."

Lanie's eyes sought her wedding planner's gaze, suddenly panicked. "Tyler's in there?"

"Not only is he in there, but he's anxiously watching the door. We'll need to be careful he doesn't see you through the glass chapel walls before you start walking down the aisle."

Lanie smiled, so full of happiness she thought she would burst.

"Who knew he'd be so old-fashioned about seeing you in your dress before you walk down the aisle?" Britt asked. "Especially after all our photo sessions before my wedding."

"I'm not surprised," Steph said, holding her bouquet of white roses to the side as she brushed snowflakes off her red dress. "Turns out Tyler Norris is a romantic at heart. He had to be, after a proposal like that."

Holly glanced up at the wooden doors to the chapel. "It's time."

The group walked over to the doors, then stood to the side. Steph and Britt kissed Lanie's cheek before walking down the aisle.

Holly positioned Lanie behind the wooden door while they waited for the music to change. "Still no regrets you didn't have your dad walk you down the aisle?" she asked.

"No. It would have felt weirder if he did. We're working on getting closer, and I'm happy focusing on that." Besides, she'd been independent most of her life. It seemed more fitting to give herself away. She offered her friend a smile. "Thank you for getting the wedding together so quickly. It's beautiful."

Holly grinned. "Well, honestly, Kevin might have withheld sex if I hadn't agreed to help plan his best friend's wedding." Then she grinned. "Okay, he would have lasted three days tops, but it would have been a miserable three days."

Lanie laughed.

"But I would have done it anyway," Holly said. "And it helped that you set the date practically the same day he proposed. Three months is more than I got for that big socialite wedding last summer. I planned *it* in three weeks."

"The one you and Kevin were married in?"

Holly blushed. "Sometimes things are just meant to be." The music changed, and Holly reached for the door. "It's time. Don't be nervous."

"I'm not," Lanie said, surprised she meant it. All her anxiety had fled. She knew without a doubt this was the best decision of her life.

"Okay," Holly whispered as she stepped backward and opened the door. "Go."

The door opened, revealing the chapel, decorated in red and white flowers. Lanie was surprised at how many people had shown up for a wedding a few days before Christmas. Aiden was in the crowd, as well as Kevin's sister Megan and her husband—her mother was waiting at the reception with Megan's baby. Lanie's parents were there too, but she didn't look for any of them. Her eyes were glued on the man waiting for her at the altar with his little brother and his two best friends at his side.

Adoration and awe washed over Tyler's face, and he looked speechless as she walked toward him.

Their relationship had been a whirlwind, and she knew some people thought they were moving too fast—her parents leading the charge—but sometimes you just knew when something was perfect.

Her life couldn't be any more perfect.

Matt Osborne is the last remaining member of the Bachelor Brotherhood, and he's determined to hold the fort. That is, until he finds himself face to face with his college sweetheart—and her son. Sexy sparks are reignited...and Matt is about to learn the hard way that love *always* finds a way back in.

A preview of *Always You* follows.

Chapter One

⌒

Standing at the edge of a grass soccer field, Matt stared into the sea of parents' faces and resisted the urge to groan. Obviously, word had spread after last season that Coach Matt was relatively good-looking, somewhat successful, loved kids and, most important, was single.

Maybe he should rethink his decision to coach his five-year-old nephew's soccer team. But when he looked down into Ethan's adoring face, he knew he'd never quit. He'd swim through shark-infested waters for the kid— what were a few single moms? Well, more like half a dozen...Just his luck that half his team from last season had aged up.

"This is just the five- and six-year-old peewee division," Matt said, continuing with his introduction while the kids fidgeted behind him, "and we don't even keep official score. The goal is to learn the rules and have fun. Any questions?"

A redheaded woman with a toddler at her feet shot her hand into the air. "Is it true that you're single?"

Matt forced a laugh and rubbed the back of his neck. "Any questions about *soccer*?"

A few of the women giggled, and some of the others looked downright sheepish. He noticed there was one lone man in the group. He stood at the back and seemed to be ogling the women's asses. Matt planned to keep an eye on the creeper.

A brunette lifted her hand, and Matt relaxed. Phyllis's daughter, Becca, was a friend of Ethan's and had been on his team last year. Phyllis, thank God, was very happily married. "I'd be more than happy to coordinate the snack schedule, Matt."

"Thanks." He held her gaze, trying to convey how much he meant it.

Her grin told him she knew exactly what she was doing.

He spun around to face nine excited faces. "Okay. Who's ready to play soccer?"

"We are!" the children shouted, jumping up and down with excitement.

Nine faces. There were supposed to be ten. He pulled the folded printout of the team roster from his back pocket and studied the list. Sure enough, he was missing one. He started calling out the names he didn't recognize, trying to figure out which kid was missing.

"Trevor Millhouse. Billy Houser." Both kids raised their hands. "Toby Robins." No answer.

He scanned the group. "Toby Robins?"

Ethan's hand shot into the air. "He was at school today, Uncle Matt. He said he was coming. He's never played soccer before, and he's scared."

Matt squatted in front of his nephew. "Scared enough to miss his first practice?" He might have to call the boy's mother and ask to talk to him. Maybe he and Ethan could meet them for a one-on-one practice to help him work through his fears.

"Nah," Ethan said, as though Matt had said the most ridiculous thing in the world. "I told him that you'd teach him *everything*." The boy beamed up at him with a grin, showing his missing front tooth, and Matt's heart melted. Matt was thirty-four years old and still single, but he'd always wanted a family—something he wasn't about to shout from the rooftops in front of his current audience. When his sister's husband had pulled the deadbeat-dad card last fall, he'd been more than willing to step up.

"Then maybe Toby's just running late," Matt said. "We'll get started and catch him up to speed when he gets here."

Ethan nodded. "I'll help him."

He rubbed the boy's head. "I'm sure you will."

Matt lined up the kids and passed out a miniature soccer ball to each of them, keeping one for himself. He rested his sole on the top of the ball. "Now, the important thing to remember is that you can't touch the ball with your hands. If you touch it with your hands, you lose it to the other team. But," he said with an exaggerated grin, "you can touch it with any other part of your body." He scooped up the ball with his toe and tossed it into the air, bouncing it from his knee to the top of his head, back to his knee, and then down to the top of his foot before letting it fall to the ground.

The kids released excited *ooh*s and *ahh*s. Matt tried to ignore the appreciative murmurs from the women behind him.

"You can't do that now," Matt said to the kids, "but if you keep practicing, you can learn how. Some soccer players have even made goals with the tops of their heads." He tossed the ball up with his foot again and then bounced it off his head, this time aiming it toward the goal behind the kids.

"Your uncle's so cool..." Becca said to Ethan, with awe in her voice.

Ethan's grin stretched from ear to ear. "I know."

"Okay," Matt said as he jogged over to pick up the ball. But one of the mothers, Miranda Houser, had already run over to pick it up, and tossed it to him.

"Here you go, Coach Matt," she said with a grin.

"Thanks," he said, catching it with his hands.

"You're out!" one of the boys shouted. "You touched the ball with your hands."

"Good job, George," Matt said to his team. "You were listening."

He gave Miranda one last glance before heading back to the kids. Miranda was a single mom too, and her daughter had been on his team last fall. She'd never hinted at an interest in him before, but maybe the sudden competition had encouraged her. He wondered if he should give her serious consideration. She was cute and she didn't come across as desperate. A definite plus. She was an involved mother of three kids and worked for a local insurance agency. Compared to the women he'd dated since college, she had her shit together, but there was no denying that something was missing. Matt had no idea what *it* was, and unfortunately, only one woman had ever made him feel it. And that had ended badly. Tear-your-heart-into-pieces and drown-your-sorrows-with-beer-on-the-couch-in-your-underpants kind of badly.

In fact, a lot of his relationships had ended badly. The last of his long string of crazy ex-girlfriends had turned out to be a wanted bank robber, something he'd only discovered when the two of them were ambushed by police officers while naked and in the middle of sex. It was like something out of a B-movie, only it had actually happened to him.

Last June, he and his two best friends, who'd also had bad luck with women, had agreed to take a moratorium from dating, forming the Bachelor Brotherhood. Kevin and Tyler had not only caved, but were now both happily married.

Fuckers. Could there even be a brotherhood of one? It had been a long time since he'd been on a date—more than a year.

No, he decided, returning to the question of Miranda. She had kids, and he wouldn't screw with their emotions. There was no point in going out with her. The last thing he wanted to do was hurt her... or anyone.

Maybe he was destined to spend the rest of his life alone.

"Coach Matt!" redheaded Trevor shouted.

Matt shrugged off his melancholy. This was not the time to examine his catastrophe of a love life. No, that type of self-analysis went down much better with a beer or two.

"Look at me, Coach," Remy, one of the new boys, called out. "I can kick the ball just like you!" Then the ball at his feet flew through the air and slammed into the nose of one of the new mothers.

"Oh, shit," Matt muttered as the woman screamed.

"Coach Matt said a bad word!" a girl shouted.

The injured mother covered her face with her hands, then looked at the blood covering her fingers and started to wail.

He dashed for his bag and grabbed a clean hand towel and a bottle of water before running over to the still-screaming woman.

The other mothers had circled her, offering sympathy and telling her to lean her head back and pinch her nose. She'd reached up to cover her face again, he noticed. Matt pushed between them as he glanced at Phyllis and mouthed, *Do you know her name?*

"Amy," she whispered in his ear.

"Okay, Amy," Matt said, guiding her to someone's folding chair. "Let's have you sit down, and I'll take a look."

She quieted and sat down, watching Matt with rounded eyes. "I think my nose is broken." Her words were muffled by her hands.

He offered her a reassuring smile. "I suspect it's fine. Kids this age don't have enough power to cause that much damage." He pulled her hands down and examined her face. A slow trickle was dripping from her left nostril, but just as he suspected, her nose didn't look broken. He grabbed her hand and guided it up to pinch her nose. "Just give it a bit of pressure and it will let up in a minute."

She did as he instructed, the fear in her eyes fading.

Her face and hands were still covered in blood, so he opened the water bottle and poured some onto the clean towel.

As he gently washed the blood off her chin, the look in her eyes changed again.

The women around him began to murmur among themselves.

Oh, shit. He'd treated her like he would have any kid on his team, but he could see how the women might misconstrue his intentions. There was a wedding band on her left hand, but he wasn't sure whether he should find that reassuring.

Shit.

He tossed the towel to her as he got to his feet.

"You should be fine," he said, then hurried over to the kids, who were watching with open mouths and wide eyes.

"I want to learn to kick a ball like that," one of the boys said. "I want to give my brother a bloody nose."

"Not me," one of the girls said with a lot of attitude,

putting her hands on her hips. "I want to hit Mitchell Blevins in the balls!"

Matt lifted his hands. "Okay! We don't kick the ball to hurt anyone. We only kick the ball to make a goal."

"But that's not what Uncle Kevin said last week at your house," Ethan said, tilting his head back to look at him. "He said he was going to kick Uncle Tyler in his balls, and he wasn't even playing soccer."

He was going to kill his best friend. "Then Uncle Kevin needs a time-out, and I'll ask Aunt Holly to give him one." Although it wouldn't be the kind of time-out Ethan knew about—and he wasn't likely to find out until he was in a serious relationship, hopefully twenty years from now.

"Your uncle has balls?" Becca asked. "You're so lucky. My uncles only have cell phones."

"Not those kind of balls," the feisty girl who wanted to kick Mitchell Blevins in his private parts said, in a condescending tone. "Those balls." Then she pointed to the crotch of the boy next to her.

What the hell was happening?

Matt grabbed the girl's arm and pushed it down. "No more talk about balls."

One of the little girls started to cry. "I wanted to learn how to kick a ball hard enough to give someone a bloody nose."

"But Uncle Matt," Ethan asked insistently, "how can we play soccer without balls?"

Matt shot an exasperated look at Phyllis, but she was too busy laughing to offer help.

"Everybody listen up!" Matt shouted, and the children gave him their attention. "There are lots of different kinds of balls, but we're just going to talk about soccer balls today. Okay?"

The kids nodded, looking eager to please him, probably so they too could learn self-defense with a soccer ball.

"Oh!" Becca said in excitement. "I get it now. Boys have golf balls."

Matt leaned back his head and groaned.

"There he is!" Ethan shouted. "There's Toby!" He took off running toward the street where the parents had parked their cars.

"Ethan!" Matt shouted. "Come back!" He liked to think Ethan was smart enough not to run into the street, but he'd learned over the last six months that five-year-olds sometimes did stupid things for no good reason.

The boy ignored him, but Matt felt better when he saw a small boy running toward his nephew. The woman chasing him looked like she'd come straight from work. Her skirt hugged her curves, the effect accentuated because she was bending forward. Her high heels kept sinking into the soft ground, and her shoulder-length, golden blonde hair kept falling into her face.

"Toby!" she called after him. "Wait for me!"

Thankfully, Ethan had changed directions. He was running back toward Matt, with Toby on his heels.

Ethan stopped in front of Matt, panting with excitement. "He's here, Uncle Matt! He's here!"

Ethan's excitement was infectious, and after glancing back at the other kids—they were happily kicking their soccer balls in a dozen different directions—Matt grinned at the boy standing behind his nephew. He was a cute kid, with dark blond hair and bright blue eyes. Matt noticed his pale complexion and made a mental note to make sure he was slathered with sunscreen when they played their soccer games under the midday sun.

"Hi, Toby. I'm Matt. Glad to have you on the team." Matt held out a hand to shake with the boy.

Toby giggled as he shook his hand.

Matt glanced up at the woman making her way toward them. Something about her felt . . . familiar. But maybe it was the stirring he felt down deep. How long had it been since he'd felt like this? Not even with Sylvia, the bank robber.

"Is that your mom?" he asked the boy, trying not to sound too interested.

"Yeah," Toby said with a scowl. "She was late. *Again.*"

Was that a British accent? Ethan had mentioned that Toby "talked funny," but Matt had figured the kid probably had a lisp. Ethan had one too, after his front tooth fell out at Matt's house the weekend before.

"That's okay. You haven't missed much."

"I don't know how to play football," the boy said with a frown.

Ethan chortled. "I told you it's not *football*. It's *soccer.* Uncle Matt says I'm too little to play football, isn't that right, Uncle Matt? But he played in high school, and I'm gonna play too, when I'm big like him."

Toby's frown increased, and Matt wanted to put him at ease. "Ethan says you're new. Where did you live before?"

"London."

England? Had his parents been transferred to Kansas City and found a home in the suburbs?

Matt squatted in front of him, balancing on the balls of his feet. "Well, there you go," he said with a grin. "We call it soccer here, but you call it football in the UK."

The woman was closer now. She was pulling her heels out of the ground like she was doing leg-lifts, and while she was looking down, her head tilted away from him, he couldn't help noticing that her legs were sexy as hell. *Focus.*

"Toby," she said, "I told you to wait. We don't know if it's your team or not."

Her voice sounded familiar too. That stirring feeling inside him turned a bit uneasy. Surely he was just hearing things...

"Mum," Toby groaned, "Ethan's on my team! I had to hurry or I was going to miss practice." His worried gaze met Matt's. "I don't know how to play."

"Don't worry." Matt patted Toby's shoulder as he tried to get a good look at the woman's face. He smiled at the boy. "We're all learning the basics right now. Ethan, get Toby a ball and we'll get star—"

A ball walloped Matt on the back of his head with enough force to make him lose his balance. Before he could right himself, he fell forward. Ethan and Toby backed out of his way as he landed in the damp grass, his hands breaking his fall.

"Coach Matt!" the kids shouted.

"You killed him!" one of the girls cried out.

Another girl screamed.

Matt tried to sit up, but another ball hit the back of his head with enough force to make his teeth rattle.

"Remy! Stop that!" one of the mothers shouted. "Quit kicking balls at your coach!"

"It's just like Angry Birds!" the boy said as another ball sailed over Matt's head.

"If you don't stop," Becca snarled, "I'm gonna kick *your* balls."

Remy screamed.

Matt rolled onto his back, wondering how practice had gotten so out of control. Maybe he should just call it and start again on Thursday night.

The kids huddled around him, looking down with curious glances.

"Uncle Matt?" Ethan asked, sounding worried. "Are you still gonna teach Toby how to play soccer?"

Matt closed his eyes and groaned, and when he opened them, Toby's mother was leaning over him. Her hair had fallen into her face again, but she tucked it behind her ear. While it promptly fell back, he had seen her uncovered face for a few brief seconds. Sucking in a breath, he told himself again that he was imagining things. But he knew better. He'd been wrong to think these kids didn't have enough force to do serious damage.

He must have a traumatic head injury that included hallucinations, because he was staring up into the face of the woman who had broken his heart so many years ago.

ABOUT THE AUTHOR

Denise Grover Swank is a *New York Times* and *USA Today* bestselling author who was born in Kansas City, Missouri, and lived in the area until she was nineteen. Then she became a nomadic gypsy, living in five cities, four states, and ten houses over the course of ten years before she moved back to her roots. She speaks English and a smattering of Spanish and Chinese, which she learned through an intensive Nick Jr. immersion period. Her hobbies include witty (in her own mind) Facebook comments and dancing in her kitchen with her children (quite badly, if you believe her offspring). Hidden talents include the gift of justification and the ability to drink massive amounts of caffeine and still fall asleep within two minutes. Her lack of the sense of smell allows her to perform many unspeakable tasks. She has six children and hasn't lost her sanity. Or so she leads you to believe.

You can learn more at:
  DeniseGroverSwank.com
  Twitter @DeniseMSwank
  Facebook.com/DeniseGroverSwank

Sign up for Denise's newsletter to get information on
new releases and free reads!
http://DeniseGroverSwank.com/mailing-list/

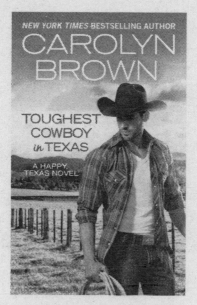

TOUGHEST COWBOY IN TEXAS
By Carolyn Brown

New York Times bestselling author Carolyn Brown welcomes you to Happy, Texas! Last time Lila Harris was home, she was actively earning her reputation as the resident wild child. Back for the summer, she's a little older and wiser...But something about this town has her itching to get a little reckless and rowdy, especially when she sees her old partner-in-crime, Brody Dawson. Their chemistry is just as hot as ever. But he's still the town's golden boy—and she's still the wrong kind of girl.

Fall in Love with Forever Romance

UNTIL YOU
By Denise Grover Swank

Tyler has always been a little too popular with women for his own good. Ever since he and his buddies vowed to remain bachelors, Tyler figured he was safe from temptation. Lanie and her gorgeous brown eyes are about to prove him so, *so* wrong. Don't miss the next book in the bestselling Bachelor Brotherhood series from Denise Grover Swank!

Fall in Love with Forever Romance

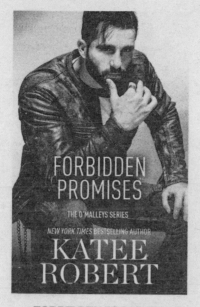

FORBIDDEN PROMISES
By Katee Robert

New York Times and *USA Today* bestselling author Katee Robert
continues her smoking-hot O'Malleys series. Sloan O'Malley has left
her entire world behind and is finally living a life without fear. But
there's nothing safe about her intensely sexy next-door neighbor. Jude
MacNamara has only ever cared about revenge, but something about
Sloan temps him...until claiming her puts them both in the crosshairs
of a danger they never saw coming.

Fall in Love with Forever Romance

MAYBE THIS LOVE
By Jennifer Snow

Hockey player Ben Westmore has some serious skills—on and off the ice—and he's not above indulging in the many perks of NHL stardom. When a night in Vegas ends in disaster, he realizes two things: 1) it's time to lie low for a while, and 2) he needs a lawyer—fast. But the gorgeous woman who walks into his office immediately tests *all* his good intentions. Jennifer Snow's Colorado Ice series is perfect for fans of Lori Wilde and Debbie Mason!